Get up! Get up!

Jill tried, but her numbed limbs wouldn't obey. They seemed detached as fatigue captured every muscle and sapped her will. She was about to give in to a lethargic warmth creeping through her when an anxious voice jarred her as firm hands dragged her from the snowbank.

What happened?"

His hot breath bathed her face, and as he brushed away the snow from her eyelashes, she recognized him under the brim of his Western hat. His name moved thickly on her frozen lips. "Hal."

His anxious face bent over her. "Are you all right?"

She tried to answer, but her chattering teeth wouldn't let the words out. Tears of relief crystallized on her lashes.

"Never mind. You're okay now. I'll get you to the ranch on horseback." He lifted her up in his arms and placed her on his horse.

When he swung up in front of her and ordered her to hold on tight, she did as she was told, resting her cheek against the warmth of his back. She closed her eyes and gave herself up to a relieved bliss that blotted out all thought but a thankful prayer that he'd found her in time.

Dear Reader,

In the Colorado mountains, snow comes in on a gust of wind, reaching blizzard conditions in a matter of minutes. Here, the Rampart Mountain Rescue Team is never lonely. But this year there's even more activity than usual for the team, as not only Mother Nature but mystery is swirling in their midst.

Get snowbound with the ROCKY MTN. RESCUE trilogy by three of your favorite Intrigue authors. For thrills, chills and adventure, ROCKY MTN. RESCUE is the place to be.

If you've missed any of the books in this trilogy, you can order #449, *Forget Me Not* by Cassie Miles or #454, *Watch Over Me* by Carly Bishop, by contacting Harlequin Reader Service. In the U.S.: 3010 Walden Ave., P.O. Box 1325, Buffalo, NY 14269. In Canada: P.O. Box 609, Fort Erie, Ontario L2A 5X3.

We hope you enjoy all the books in the ROCKY MTN. RESCUE trilogy, where an icy blizzard rages…and heated passions burn!

Regards,

Debra Matteucci
Senior Editor & Editorial Coordinator
Harlequin Books
300 East 42nd Street
New York, NY 10017

Follow Me Home
Leona Karr

Harlequin Books

TORONTO • NEW YORK • LONDON
AMSTERDAM • PARIS • SYDNEY • HAMBURG
STOCKHOLM • ATHENS • TOKYO • MILAN
MADRID • WARSAW • BUDAPEST • AUCKLAND

Love to a dear cousin, Pat Nelson,
a loyal fan in Emmett, Idaho.

ISBN 0-373-22459-1

FOLLOW ME HOME

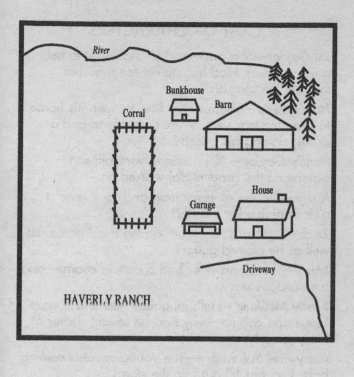

River

Bunkhouse

Corral

Barn

House

Garage

Driveway

HAVERLY RANCH

CAST OF CHARACTERS

Jill Gaylor—She answered a rescue call to help a pregnant teen. Had her stalker followed her through the blizzard?

Hal Haverly—The rancher had to open his home to stranded travelers. Were a murderer and a stalker among his guests?

Randy Gaylor—Jill's fourteen-year-old son worshiped the ground Hal walked on.

Kirby—Did the ex-navy man and cook have a special recipe for trouble?

Zack—Did Hal's ranch hand play mind games as well as he played guitar?

Larry—The blond skier had a certain charm—and a suspicious story.

Scotty McClure—Hal's neighbor had a fishing lodge and cabins—why had he sought shelter at Hal's ranch?

Gary and Sue Miller—The young couple's coming baby brought Jill out into the storm.

The dead man—His stalled car blocked the road to Hal's ranch.

Chapter One

Northern winds swept down the high peaks of the Colorado Rocky Mountains, and heavy winter clouds masked a feeble afternoon sun. Jill Gaylor glanced uneasily out the window as a thickening snowfall coated the valley below. *Bummer,* she thought, using her son's favorite word. The weather forecasters were predicting up to three feet of the white stuff in the mountains. No doubt skiers at the resort about twenty miles away were dancing on the slopes, but one person's pleasure is another's headache, she thought with a sigh. The switchboard at Rampart Mountain Rescue had been lit up like a Christmas tree all day, and she'd taken dozens of emergency calls.

"We're in for a good one, all right." Zeb Tucker frowned as he ambled over to her desk. He shook his gray head. "Gonna be socked in by morning."

"I know," Jill Gaylor agreed with an anxious edge to her voice. Her boss had donated space to Rampart's Mountain Rescue office in the Slade's Adventures building where she worked, and she'd offered to help out whenever an extra volunteer was needed. Her office was just across the hall from this small room, so she was able to man the phone when emergencies like this January blizzard arose. For the last hour she'd been telling the sheriff's office, personnel and everybody else that every available Mountain Rescue volunteer was already out on an emergency call. She doubted very much that any of the dozen volunteers would be returning soon in the worsening weather. Already the small mountain town's narrow main street was obscured by whipping snow and darkening shadows, and only a few blurred lights dotted the enveloping gloom.

"I'm sorry, all of our volunteers are out," she kept repeating. "I'll give you some other numbers to try. Yes, I understand. Leave your name, and if there are any changes, I'll let you know." She looked at the long list of people needing help and knew that the list would only grow longer as the hours went by. This was her first Colorado blizzard and a far cry from the mild climate of Southern California, where she'd lived nearly all of her life. She didn't know what to expect. She'd been told that the weather forecasters were often fooled when it came to predicting weather in Colorado, because the Rocky Mountains could stall or change the direction of a storm front, but her hopes that they'd gotten this blizzard prediction wrong had faded.

"Want me to take over the phone for a spell?" Zeb asked.

She smiled at the spry man in his seventies. Thank heavens for his company. Zeb had lived his life in Rampart, hung around the Mountain Rescue office, doing odd jobs, shooting the breeze with all the volunteers and telling everyone about the days when Rampart was just a collection of listing cabins on the side of a mountain. "Thanks, Zeb, but I need something to do."

He snorted. "As if you don't keep yourself running in two directions at once."

"I like to keep busy."

"You keep yerself too durn busy, I'm a-thinkin'," Zeb said with blunt frankness. "It's time you put all that California rat race behind you. How long you been in Rampart? Five…six months?"

She nodded. Had it really been that long? She still felt like a newcomer. And a little unsure of herself. Even though she'd been a widow for eight years, handling the full responsibility for herself and her fourteen-year-old son was not easy. Funny how life can take a sudden turn when you least expect it.

Last summer, she'd made the decision to quit her office job at a small West Coast commuter airline company and move to Colorado. She had met Jack Slade during one of his trips to California and, while chatting with him, had learned that his company, Slade's Adventures, transported skiers and hikers by helicopters into the high mountains of Colorado. Apparently impressed with the efficient way Jill handled the small airport's office, he'd mentioned that he was looking for someone with her background to manage his office in the small mountain town of Rampart. When he asked her if she'd be interested in making a move, she felt as if her stalled life had suddenly been given a green light.

Colorado? She'd been in the Rockies on vacation a couple of times. Clear air, mountain valleys, white-crested rivers and jagged peaks. Sheer delight! She'd been surprised by how quickly the decision to accept his offer was made. The move had been a heaven-sent answer to her growing worries about raising her fourteen-year-old-son, Randy, in an unhealthy urban environment. She thought she'd left all the ugliness of a crime-ridden city behind. But she'd been wrong. Terribly wrong.

She stared unseeing out the snow-splattered window,

and her stomach tightened. Up until a month ago, she'd been convinced that coming to Colorado was the best decision she'd ever made. Now she wasn't sure.

"You should be settled in good by now," Zeb insisted when Jill fell silent.

"I know." She answered, without any conviction in her voice.

"What's the matter, gal? Don't seem likely that just the storm's putting lines around those pretty topaz eyes of yours."

Jill let her fingers press the side of one of her temples, closing her eyes for a second without answering.

Zeb leaned over the desk, his spiky gray eyebrows knitted in a frown. "Still getting them heavy-breathing phone calls?"

She shivered. "Yes."

"Just some damn fool playing games."

"It's not just the calls, any more." She straightened and her light brown eyes darkened. "Someone's been leaving stuff on my doorstep."

"What kind of stuff?" The lines in his weathered face deepened.

"Last week it was a copy of Stephen King's, *Nightmares and Dreamscapes*. The week before that, a filmy pink scarf. Both wrapped in plain brown paper. No address." She swallowed. "That means they were hand delivered."

"Well, now, I don't see nothing to get excited about if someone throws a couple of presents in your direction. No cause to think the phone calls and gifts are tied up somehow."

Jill's hand trembled as she reached into her jeans pocket and drew out a white envelope. "This was in my mailbox this morning."

Zeb's gnarled fingers worked at the flap, and she watched his face grow stern as he pulled out a snapshot. He looked at it in disbelief. "What the—?"

Jill swallowed the thickening lump in her throat. Someone had pasted her head from another photo on a nude woman reclining on a red couch in a sexy pose. In the cutout of Jill's face, she was smiling. Her brunette hair fell over her shoulder in its usual long braid, and her shining eyes looked ahead as if she were greeting someone. When had it been taken? And where? She shivered. Someone had been close enough to take a picture of her and she hadn't even known it.

"Some damn weirdo trying to be funny," Zeb said with disdain.

"Look on the back."

Zeb turned the photo over and squinted at the printing on the back. "Next time, wear the pretty scarf."

Jill said in a shaky breath, "It's the caller. I know it is." She was furious that some nut was destroying her longed-for sense of peace. Coming to Colorado had been her attempt to exchange the perils of city life for solid values of a small mountain town. Now she found herself harassed by someone as unbalanced as the nutcases who usually migrated towards a metropolis.

"Time to turn this crap over to the sheriff," Zeb growled as he handed back the photo. "Have him trace the calls. He'll find the gutless swine. And then we ought to string the yellow-bellied coward up on the nearest tree." Zeb clamped his jaw shut as if he were just the man to do it.

At that moment, Jill's teenage son wandered into the office. Sending Zeb a warning look not to say anything about the upsetting picture, she quickly stuffed the envelope back in her pocket. Randy didn't need to know about the sexual harassment.

"What's happening?" Randy asked, then bit into a candy bar he'd just purchased from the vending machine in the hall. As usual, a hank of his auburn hair hung over one eye.

"Everything's quiet at the moment," she told him. "Get your hair out of your face."

He gave it a swipe. "Cripes, the kids in L.A. would never believe a storm like this." His eyes popped with excitement as he peered out the window. "Wait till I tell them we got snowbound for a month."

"A month!" Zeb shook his head. "You better watch what you're saying, boy. I spent one winter holed up a drafty old cabin. Nothing but the lonely sound of wind piling snow as high as the roof rafters. Why, I could tell you stories you wouldn't believe."

Randy winked at his mother. She knew he'd deliberately set the old man up for one of his tales. A wash of affection for her son swept over her. Randy was fourteen years old, and his most recent growing spurt was evident in his gangling arms and legs. He had a crooked smile that was a lethal weapon when it came to getting what he wanted from his mother. He was going to be a girl killer in another year or two, she thought with mixed feelings.

"Sounds like a pretty exciting time to me," Randy said when Zeb had wound down. Then he turned to his mother. "Are we gonna bed down here for the night, Mom?"

"Looks like it. I'll have to stay by the phone."

The small mountain house that she'd purchased wasn't far from the office and offered a panoramic view of the valley and river below. In good weather, she loved hiking down to the office, but in weather like this, the twisting hillside road challenged her secondhand Jeep. Since some emergencies kept the volunteers on call for extended periods, a special room in the building was equipped with a small kitchen and sleeping accommodations. She could tell from Randy's flashing eyes that he was viewing this whole thing as an exciting adventure.

She smiled at him as he again brushed back the wayward shock of reddish brown hair that had fallen over one eye. Just like his father, thought Jill. Sometimes her heart caught in pain seeing so much of her late husband in her son, even though eight years had passed since they'd lost him to a fatal heart attack.

The jangling ring of the telephone instantly brushed aside her personal thoughts. "Rampart Mountain Rescue," she answered in a brisk, efficient tone. "Jill Gaylor, speaking."

"Hal Haverly here. I've got a problem."

"Yes, Mr. Haverly."

Randy perked up at the name and asked eagerly, "Is that Hal?"

Jill held up a silencing hand. Randy knew the Colorado rancher because he'd been at the Haverly ranch numerous times and come home with ecstatic accounts of learning to ride like a real cowboy. Jill was careful not to say anything derogatory about Hal Haverly in front of her son, but the few times she'd met the rancher, he'd been rather cool and distant. She had decided that he must be a different person when he was working with the 4-H kids. "What kind of a problem, Mr. Haverly?"

"A young couple got stranded in their car near the ranch road. They were driving one of those dinky cars that ought to be outlawed. Anyway, I brought them to the ranch house, but you'll have to send someone out here as soon as you can.''

''I understand your concern but—''

''The young woman is pregnant. Very pregnant!'' he emphasized. ''She says the baby isn't due for three more weeks, but she doesn't look too good to me.''

Oh, no, thought Jill.

''You can understand my concern.'' He gave a nervous laugh. ''I really need someone to help me out.''

He sounded scared. *And probably with good reason.* She could picture his deeply tanned face, strong masculine features, and longish, sun-bleached hair drifting out from the edges of his western hat. Unmarried and somewhere in his early thirties, he'd been polite when Randy had introduced them. The rancher had pointedly eyed her with arresting blue eyes that had brought a foolish warmth to her cheeks. Then he'd completely ignored her as he worked with the kids, helping them to mount horses for rides around a small corral. Obviously the kids were his sole interest, and that was fine with Jill.

''Maybe the woman's just tired. After she's rested, she'll probably be fine.''

''I certainly hope you're right. In any case, there are three bachelors here at the ranch and none of us know anything about comforting a mother-to-be, let alone assisting her if something should...uh...start happening.''

''Have you called the sheriff's office for medical assistance?'' she asked evenly.

''Doc Evanston is already out on a call. Don't know when he'll be back. They told me to check with your rescue outfit.''

''I'm sorry, Mr. Haverly, but I don't have anyone to send.''

"The young woman's no more than seventeen, and scared out of her wits. And her husband isn't dry behind the ears yet himself. I need somebody to be here with her." His persuasive tone certainly would have convinced her if she'd had any choice about sending someone.

"I really am sorry, Mr. Haverly, but all of our rescue volunteers are out. Even Mr. Slade is bringing in some stranded skiers, and I haven't heard anything from him. I don't have anyone to send."

"There must be somebody," he insisted. "What about you, Mrs. Gaylor? You'd do fine."

"Me?" she stammered. The request took her so much by surprise, she was both irritated and amused. "I just answer the phone. I don't go out on calls."

"You know where the ranch is," he said as if he hadn't heard her. "You've picked up Randy here several times."

"Yes, but—"

"The roads are still open. If you take it easy, that old Jeep of yours ought to make it to the ranch all right."

"You don't understand. I'm only a dispatcher. I don't go out on calls," she repeated with less conviction. "I really don't have the training."

"Training? All you have to do is provide some womanly support until the storm passes over."

"I would like to help but—"

"Good," he said before she could finish.

"I didn't say I'd come."

"But you will, won't you? And you'd better leave right away. The roads are blowing over and you'll want to get here before dark. Thanks a million." He hung up before she could say a word.

Fuming, Jill stared at the phone. She'd never been

treated in such a high-handed manner. Who did he think he was? And why did he get under her skin so readily? What was there about the man that threw her off balance.

She'd been asking herself that question every time she saw him riding his cream-colored dappled horse or swinging down from the saddle with masculine ease. For some paradoxical reason, she resented it when he ignored her while she was waiting for Randy, but she was equally furious when he noticed her in some casual way that left her confused. She wasn't used to being completely dismissed by members of the opposite sex. Her usual challenge was keeping male admirers at arm's length.

"What did he say to get your dander up?" Zeb asked, looking at the high color in her cheeks.

Randy frowned. "What did Hal want, Mom?"

She took a deep breath to settle her indignation. "There's a couple stranded at the ranch. The young woman's expecting a baby and needs somebody with her." Then she repeated Haverly's request—no, insistence—that she come and stay with the pregnant woman until the storm blew over.

"Are ya going?" Zeb asked.

"No, of course not. I'm needed here."

Zeb raised a bushy eyebrow and didn't answer. Randy opened his mouth to say something, then shut it as if he'd had second thoughts.

Jill squirmed under their scrutiny. "Well, why are you two looking at me like that?" she demanded curtly.

Neither of them answered.

"Zeb?" She made the older man look at her. "You don't think I ought to go, do you?"

He shrugged. "Guess you ought to be making up your own mind."

In spite of herself, Jill began to consider what would be involved. No dangerous rescue or anything like that. Even though she'd spent several rigorous weekends participating in new volunteer training, she wasn't anywhere near ready to assume full responsibility as a rescue volunteer. Maybe assisting in a limited situation wasn't all that much beyond her. At the very least, she'd have the satisfaction of doing something besides just telephone referrals. Her mind raced on, leveling objections like pins in a bowling alley. Both Zeb and Randy were capable of handling the phones. Plenty of times they'd both relieved her when she had to take care of other matters. Certainly keeping a frightened mother-to-be company—which was all it would probably entail given she was three weeks away from her due date—until the storm lifted wasn't any great challenge. After all, being a mother herself, she could ease the young woman's fears.

"Ya really want to go, don't ya?" Zeb asked as if he'd read her thoughts.

"Well, maybe I should," she hedged. Despite her resistance to Hal Haverly's smooth manipulation, she wanted to help out if she could. She would have hated to be in the young woman's shoes, expecting a baby, stranded at a ranch with a bunch of men. Jill remembered her own apprehension as her delivery date drew nearer. The young woman's anxiety had to be even worse. Every kick of the baby was a possible alarm clock. The sense of total isolation. Yes, the mother-to-be needed someone to allay her fears as much as possible. Jill took a deep breath, "Yes, I think I ought to go."

"I'll go with you," Randy volunteered eagerly.

"No," she firmly told her son.

"Bummer," he muttered under his breath.

"You can be more help here. Someone has to refer all the calls to the sheriff's office. And if any of our volunteers come in, have them check with the sheriff or highway patrol for their next assignment."

Randy visibly puffed up. "Sure, Mom, we'll handle things. Don't worry. Piece of cake. I've done it before."

Zeb put his hand on the boy's shoulder. "Looks like we're going to have a tale of our own to tell about this here storm."

Jill gave Zeb a grateful look. He was making an adventure out of what was sure to be tedious labor, and she knew Randy would be in good hands while she was gone.

"Don't be worrying about us. We'll be just fine. You'd better get a leg on 'fore the storm gets any worse."

"I'll handle the phone," Randy said with exaggerated importance. "I've done it plenty of times."

"There's food in the office fridge, and you can bed down in the back room until I get back," she told them.

The exterior of Slade's Adventures' headquarters looked like a rustic mountain lodge, but the interior of the two-story, log-sided structure was as modern as the satellite dish affixed to the roof. Behind the offices, rooms set aside for rescue volunteers included a sleeping room with bunks, a small kitchen and a storage room. Each volunteer had his own locker for personal belongings, and all of the regular volunteers made sure they had the proper clothing and gear before they went out on a call.

Hurrying down the hall to the lockers, Jill quickly stuffed a backpack with extra clothing—a pair of flannel pajamas with a short matching robe, a cardigan sweater, a pair of faded jeans—plus a few personal items that she always kept ready for marathon stretches while handling the telephone. She decided she wouldn't need any outdoor equipment, nor much of anything else, but she did add a small first-aid kit to her gear. She slipped a knitted sweater over her high-necked pullover and tucked her stretch pants into fur-lined boots. Randy had given her a pretty plaid woolen scarf for Christmas, and her new blue quilted down jacket had a hood that tied under her chin. After she'd zippered the jacket and slipped her hands into snug leather gloves, she felt like a bulky Eskimo.

Zeb came in the back room, nodded his approval and then said, "Mr. Slade just radioed in."

Her boss had taken a small group of skiers up to a peak in the Never Summer Range at the first light of dawn. "He's coming in then?"

"Cutting it close," Zeb said. "With the storm settling in like this."

"They'll make it in okay, won't they?"

"Slade can handle the rescue with the best of them."

She nodded, knowing it was true. "Well, I guess I'm ready." Nervous excitement added to the warmth radiating through her body as they returned to the office.

"You be careful, now. Take it slow," Zeb lectured. "Don't be spinning your wheels with too much gas. And if you have to brake, tap the pedal, don't slam it down all at once."

"Don't worry, I'll be fine. I'll remember everything you've told me." The old man had given her the same lecture about driving on icy, snow-covered mountain roads every time there was a snowflake in the air. Even on clear days, he viewed her driving with suspicion. She knew he'd never believe she'd left her city driving behind.

She hugged her son and gave him some last-minute instructions, which she was sure Randy only half heard, but he was a good kid and she knew what a help he'd been in the office before. "Love ya," she said, much to his chagrin.

Looking at his precious face, she entertained second thoughts about leaving. She'd moved them to a small town, thinking it was safer than the big city they'd come from, but bad things happened in Rampart, too. She couldn't believe the ordeal that another rescue volunteer, Grant Richardson, and his wife, Susan, had gone through with the recent kidnapping of their small son. Would Randy be safe with just an elderly man looking after him?

"I'll be fine, Mom," Randy said as she hesitated.

"Don't you worry none. I'll see to it this young fellow is fine as rain," Zeb assured her.

She hugged Randy once more and started to repeat all the instructions but caught herself. She knew that they exchanged amused looks behind her back as she left the office.

Her car was parked in an attached garage behind the building. When she'd bought the five-year-old Jeep, the eager seller had assured her that it performed well on icy roads, but she hadn't yet put the four-wheeler to any real test. Driving back and forth to work was all the mileage she'd put on it. Putting on chains and driving over mountain passes and slipping and skidding on narrow roads was not her idea of recreation. She'd thoroughly enjoyed the Colorado summer and fall weather, but the verdict on winter was still out.

Jill's gloved hands were rigid on the steering wheel as she drove out of Rampart on a snow-packed two-lane road that ran through a mountain valley, cupped on both sides by vaulting rock cliffs and thick drifts of evergreens.

She left the outskirts of the mountain town behind. Leaning tensely forward, she reduced her speed. The distance between Rampart and the Haverly Ranch had taken less than thirty minutes when she'd driven there before, but that had been early September. She'd enjoyed the drive and the fall colors of flaming red oak and golden aspen. Now there was no color anywhere, just a pristine white that sucked her car into a whirling cauldron of snow.

With every passing minute, the wind quickened, sending snow whipping across the road and obscuring her vision. Nothing in her experience in sunny California had prepared her for this alien world of assaulting wind and snow. Trees and rocks on both sides of the road were already masked by layers of thickening white, and she could barely make out the edges of the pavement as she fought against the mesmorizing effect of snow swirling into the feeble radius of her headlights.

Turn around. Go back. She might have heeded the inner voice if there'd been any opportunity to turn the Jeep around, but the road was narrowing with every mile. She couldn't tell where the pavement ended and the dirt shoulder began.

Was hers the only car on the road? There was no sign of lights ahead or behind her. Maybe worsening conditions had already closed the roads from the nearby ski resorts, where most of the through traffic originated. She looked at her odometer, trying to judge how close she was to the dirt road that turned off to the Haverly Ranch, hoping she wouldn't miss the cattle guard and the rock pillars on either side of the entrance and drive by the turnoff without seeing it. Nothing looked the same in the whiteout and her rapidly moving windshield wipers couldn't keep the glass cleared for more than a few seconds.

No wonder she didn't see the parked car in the road.

Like a black wall, it suddenly rose in front of her headlights without warning. Frantically she braked, but too late. The impact sent both of the vehicles sliding on the slick, snow-packed highway.

As her Jeep turned sideways, its back wheels went off the road, then lost traction with the pavement and sank at a pitched angle into a mounting snowdrift. For a terrifying moment, she sat stunned in the tipped vehicle. Then blessed relief swept over her. She wasn't hurt, not even jarred.

Thank heavens she'd been driving slowly. As the windshield wipers fought the accumulating snow, she peered out at the car she'd hit. From what she could tell it was a dark sedan that had spun sideways onto the shoulder of the road when she hit it. She half expected the driver to get out to see who had rammed into him, but no one appeared. Had the car been abandoned? Had someone left it in the middle of the road, or were they stranded inside the vehicle the way she was? She was positive the car's taillights had not been on or she would have seen them before she hit.

All right, don't panic.

Swallowing hard, she forced herself to analyze the situation. The Jeep's engine was still running. Even though the back of the Jeep was lower than the front end, she reasoned that if she shifted into the lowest gear, and the back wheels had any traction at all, she might be able to drive up onto the road again. She wondered what kind of advice Zeb would give her in this situation.

Easy. Easy. Don't gun it. Cautiously, she pressed on

the accelerator. To her horror, instead of the vehicle moving forward, the opposite happened.

"Oh, no!" she gasped as the momentum of the spinning wheels jarred the Jeep and it slid even farther down into a snow-filled culvert.

She fought paralyzing panic. What should she do? The wheels had no traction at all. Now, almost half of the vehicle was buried in the snow. She remembered something about the danger of a blocked exhaust pipe sending lethal gas fumes into a car, so she quickly turned off the engine.

She sat there with her gloved hands stiffly clutching the steering wheel, not believing the horrible reality. She worried that if she didn't get out of the Jeep right away, the blowing snow would soon pack the front doors too tightly for her to open them.

Should she stay in the car? Let herself be buried inside? At any minute the Jeep might slip farther down the embankment. She knew then she'd never be able to climb back up to the road.

Peering through a thin coating of snow collecting on the windshield, she could still see a vague outline of the dark sedan. At least it had stayed on the gravel shoulder and was close enough to offer safer shelter than her nearly buried vehicle. The terrifying vision of being trapped in the Jeep drove her to a quick decision.

She grabbed her backpack on the seat beside her. Making sure her hood was tight around her face, she shoved the car door open and braced herself against the onslaught of driving wind and snow. Her lined hood gave her face some protection. But still her eyelashes were instantly heavy with clinging snowflakes. Since the back end of the car was lower than the front, she had to fight her way up the snowy bank to the edge of the pavement.

As she trudged forward across the road, she brushed at her face, keeping her focus on the dark car. When she reached it, she saw that the windows of the late-model Buick were covered by snow, making it impossible to see inside. The car must have been stalled for some time, she reasoned as she stumbled around to the driver's side and cleared the window of snow.

She peered inside.

The driver, a man, was sitting there, but he didn't turn to look at her.

"Hello. Hello." She pounded on the window. On some detached level, she noticed the young man's bad complexion and sideburns.

Still no response. Was he deaf? Or was something else wrong with him? Had the impact of her Jeep hitting his car knocked him out? This possibility made her try the door. It was unlocked.

She jerked it open. "Are you hurt?"

No reaction.

She touched his husky shoulder. His body was stiff and rigid, as if he'd frozen to death. She knew then that he was dead. As her gaze fell from his face to his chest, she put her hand to her mouth and screamed. Blood stained his clothes from a gaping wound that looked like a bullet hole.

All rational thought left her. She panicked. Some sensible inner voice told her to get in the car with the dead man. She'd have shelter there…but she couldn't do it. As if the horror before her eyes threatened to reach out and engulf her, she slammed the door shut.

The Jeep. Go back to the Jeep.

Stumbling in the deep snow and gulping painfully

cold air into her lungs, she lurched away from the Buick. The road was fast disappearing in a moving wave of whiteness. Brushing away clinging snow from her face, she peered through the enveloping snowfall.

Where was the Jeep?

She'd lost all sense of direction. Stumbling forward, she couldn't even see where she'd come across the road to the sedan. Now she didn't know if she was going toward the buried Jeep or away from it. With rising panic, she realized that she was completely disoriented.

Then, above the whisper of sweeping snow, she heard a sound like a motor. Another car! Someone was coming. She began waving her arms even though she couldn't see anything. After several long, anxious moments, she realized that her ears had been playing tricks on her. Only the hushed sound of sweeping snow filled the suspended silence. She'd been hallucinating.

Her clothes were layered with snow. Every step was labored. She couldn't see where she was going. The thickening flakes swirled around her, blinding her in near zero visibility. She had no choice but to go back and get in the dead man's car. There was no room for squeamishness. Every decision she made now was a matter of survival.

She squinted through veils of snowflakes, dancing and swirling around her in a mad frenzy, and brushed at her face and snow-laden eyelashes.

But where was the dark sedan?

Slowly she turned around, searching, straining to see something, anything that would give her some bearings. Every inch of her body was growing heavier with the passing minutes as the light fluffy snow began to weigh her down and sap her energy.

Keep moving!

She stumbled in one direction and then another, walking like a blind man with her hands in front of her. She knew that the snowfall was so thick that she might walk smack into the sedan before seeing it.

When her gloved hands brushed against something solid, she gave a silent gasp of joy. Then her relief faded. The surface was not metal but rough. Rounded. Like a post. One of her gloves snagged on barbed wire.

She tried to move away from the fence, but after a few wavering steps, her path was blocked again, this time by a pile of waist-high boulders. As she tried to move around then, the ground suddenly dropped out from under her feet.

She cried out as she fell. Not a harsh fall. A gentle, sinking downward, into the betraying soft warmth of an enveloping snowbank.

Get up! Get up!

She tried, but her numbed limbs wouldn't obey. They seemed detached as fatigue captured every muscle and sapped her will. Some remote part of her mind noted the absence of urgency. Her inner commanding voice grew silent. A strange contentment flowed into her body. She was about to give in to a lethargic warmth creeping through her, when she was rudely jerked out of the enveloping cocoon.

An anxious voice jarred her as firm hands dragged her from the snowbank. "My God, what happened?"

His hot breath bathed her face and as he brushed away the snow from her eyelashes, she recognized him under the brim of his western hat. His name moved thickly on her frozen lips. "Haverly."

His anxious face bent over her. "Are you all right? Where's your Jeep?"

She tried to answer, but her chattering teeth wouldn't

let the words out. Tears of relief crystallized on her lashes.

"Never mind. You're okay now. I'll get you to the ranch on horseback." He lifted her up in his arms and carried her to a horse that was stamping and snorting clouds out of his nostrils.

Under ordinary circumstances, Jill would have been terrified of the beast, but she didn't even murmur when he placed her on the horse behind the saddle. When he swung up, locking her arms around his waist and ordering her to hold on tight, she did as she was told.

As they made their way through a thick drift of trees, cascades of snow tumbled down upon them from outstretched branches of ponderosa pines. Jill rested her cheek against the warmth of his back and tightened her arms around his protective strength as her body rose and fell with the strong rhythm of the horse. She closed her eyes and gave herself up to a relieved bliss that blotted out all thought but a thankful prayer that he'd found her in time.

At first he had cursed the storm, but now he saw how it could be turned to his advantage. The danger and challenge only heightened the sweetness of the conquest. He couldn't have planned things better. Now he could be with her and she'd never suspect. Let the storm come. He smiled. Everything was falling into place. If she only knew....

Chapter Two

Hal felt her arms tighten around his waist in rhythm with the rise and fall of the horse's gait. She was like a child holding on for dear life, and he wondered if she'd ever been on a horse before. He put one hand over her tightly clasped hands, holding them firmly and guiding the reins with the other one. Her body, pressed against his back, gave warmth to his own chilled flesh. When he'd lifted her out of the snow, his heart had nearly burst with fright because she'd felt so small and fragile in his arms. He was shaken by the near tragedy. What if he hadn't found her in time?

"We're almost there," he called over his shoulder. He thought she gave a strangled reply but he wasn't sure. A razor of cold air numbed his face, and he sank his chin lower in the collar of his sheepskin coat. Snow fell in showers upon them as he slowly urged the horse across a narrow clearing between the ranch house and a thick stand of trees bordering his mountain pasture.

Though visibility was down to almost zero, Hal relied on both his own and his horse's instincts to get them back to the ranch. Brr. The temperature must be dropping like a lead weight. Sheets of snow whipped across the ground, swirling in a blinding pattern. This kind of storm was death to man and beast—and women who didn't know how to drive on slick roads, he grimly added to himself. He never would have insisted that she come if he'd known the storm was accelerating faster than any storm he'd ever seen before. He was still stunned by so narrowly averting a tragedy. After he'd hung up the phone, he'd begun to have second thoughts.

As the minutes passed, his worry increased. Even if she had been driving at a snail's pace, she should have reached the ranch sooner. Then he chided himself for worrying. The woman had told him she wasn't going to come. Most likely, she'd never even started out, but a nagging uncertainty hadn't let him rest. Finally, he'd called the rescue office and his worst fear had been confirmed when Zeb told him that she'd been gone almost an hour.

Saddling up his horse and going after her had been pure gut instinct. And it had paid off. Her car must have stalled and she'd decided to hike to the ranch. If she hadn't made it to the entrance posts, he never would have stumbled upon her. She should have stayed in the car. Even as he silently fumed, a rising sense of guilt nagged at him. *You're the one who insisted that she come. It's your fault she was in the storm in the first place.*

"Well, I'm damn glad she's here," he muttered, knowing himself for a coward when it came to pregnant women. He could handle a mare birthing a foal or a brand-new calf slipping out into the world, but he sure as hell didn't know what to do with a frightened seventeen-year-old girl ready to have her first baby. He just prayed the storm cleared before the stork made a landing in his guest bedroom.

The rock exterior of the house was a dark, barely visible shadow against the white landscape. A cluster of outbuildings—a peak-roofed barn, garage, and bunkhouse—were being obliterated in cushions of rounded snow. Thank goodness for real horsepower. The battery in his four-wheel-drive had refused to turn over. He'd put off buying a new battery one storm too long. He'd have to call into town and have one sent out.

As his experienced eyes swept across the rocky pasture, he could just make out a herd of cattle humped against the storm, he silently swore. *Damn fool cattle.* Instead of facing into the wind as horses had the good sense to do, his steers instinctively turned away from the blowing snow, which allowed the wind to lift up hairs and form spikes of ice all over their hides. He knew he'd lose several head to the storm, a loss he couldn't afford. Not now. Not when someone was determined to sabotage his efforts. Anger and frustration rippled through him and he clenched his hands, whitening the knuckles of his strong fingers.

He reined in the horse near the back door of the house, and swung easily out of the saddle. Then he reached up and lifted Jill down with the ease of handling a child. ''We're here.''

A thankful prayer hovered on her stiff lips. Although she'd come to the ranch several times to get Randy after a 4-H horseback-riding event, she had never been inside the sprawling stone ranch house. Braced against the wind, with his arm around her shoulders, she let him propel her forward to an outside door leading to an enclosed porch.

At that moment, a tall, snow-covered man, wearing a stocking cap and navy coat, came around the corner of the house. His arms were loaded with split logs. ''Thought we'd better be laying in more wood. Got a doozy of a storm settling in," the man said through a scarf tied around his face. As he followed Hal and Jill inside the enclosed porch, he eyed her and asked, "Is she the rescue gal, boss?"

"The same," Hal answered.

The touch of irony in his tone wasn't lost on Jill. Both of them knew that he was the one who had done the rescuing. Her pride bristled that Hal Haverly probably would not let her forget it.

"Where'd you find her?"

Hal ignored the question. "Take Mrs. Gaylor inside, Kirby. See if you can get her thawed out while I take care of the horse."

"Sure thing." The muffled man nodded and held the kitchen door open for Jill. Hal went back outside, disappearing in mountain waves of snow as he led the horse toward the barn.

Jill felt a blessed warmth rush at her as they entered a spacious, homey kitchen. Leaning up against the closed door, she tried to catch her breath, shivering and shaking snow from her clothing onto the waxed tile floor. She brushed at snow-laden lashes and blinked to focus on the room, which promised all the comforts of heaven to her chilled body.

A wagon-wheel chandelier hung over a large kitchen table flanked with high-backed wooden chairs that were an antique dealer's dream. Pots and pans hung in an orderly array over spotless counters, and a large six-burner stove with an oven the size of a car trunk dominated one red brick wall near a wide-hearthed fireplace. The room was like an oasis, quiet and serene, removed from nature's fury outside and filled with tantalizing aromas of fresh bread and strong coffee.

"Got hung up in the storm, did you?" the man asked

as he dumped his wood in a box by the fireplace and tossed off his stocking cap and jacket. "Hal thought as much when you didn't show up. I knew he'd bring you in. I'm Kirby. Ranch hand, chief cook and bottle-washer around here."

He didn't look like a cook, Jill thought. Too thin. All sharp angles in his face and very little fat on his rangy build. Hard to guess his age. Forty, maybe. There was a trace of gray in his dull brown hair. His eyes were his best feature, a clear hazel that relieved the unattractive sparseness of his bony features.

"Here, let me help you off with your wet things." Deftly he lifted off the backpack, unzipped her jacket and slipped it off her shoulders. "Come on over by the fire and dry out."

Her frozen limbs seemed slightly detached from the rest of her body, and she wavered unsteadily as they crossed the kitchen to a well-worn brown leather chair placed in front of the fireplace. Gratefully she sank down into the hearth-side chair. A snapping fire glowed red as it flung sparks in the air and sent pine-scented heat radiating into the room. Never in her life had her whole body felt so strange, and emotionally she was still reeling from the terrifying experience of nearly freezing to death.

"What happened? Your car stall?"

She shook her head. Without explaining, she leaned back into the soft cushion of the chair and closed her eyes, wondering if she would ever forget the near-tragedy of the last hour. The horror of what had happened came back like a scene playing in her mind's eye. She wished her teeth would stop chattering and her body would stop quivering with the bone-deep chill. *Get hold of yourself. You're safe now.*

"Here, drink this. A bit of brandy will get your blood flowing again." He handed her a half-filled glass and watched as she cupped her numb fingers around it.

After several sips of the fiery liquid, she handed the glass back and croaked, "Enough."

He set the glass aside. "Better get them boots off." She glimpsed a large tattoo of an anchor on his arm as he bent down in front of her and slipped off her boots. Her feet felt stiff and wooden, and she didn't protest when he took each foot in turn, massaging them with his long bony fingers.

Her chilled flesh began to revive under his touch, and a prickling warmth returned to her lower limbs.

"Feeling better?"

"Yes, thank you." She noticed then that the sharp angles in his rather homely face had softened as he stroked her feet. An expression in his hazel eyes bordered on the sensuous. She was suddenly uncomfortable. She pulled back the foot in his hands. "That's enough. They're warm now."

A smile flickered at the corner of Kirby's lean mouth as he stood up. "You're Randy's mom. I've seen you when you've come to pick the boy up."

"Oh, do you help with the 4-H kids?" Jill didn't remember seeing him. If the cook had been around, he'd stayed in the background and never spoken to her.

"Sometimes. Mostly I just fix something for them to eat. You know, hot dogs and the like. They work up an appetite when they're riding around the place."

"Randy loves coming here."

"I told him he had the prettiest mom in these parts." Kirby smiled. "I was hoping for a chance to meet you. Who says things don't work out? Here you are. Right in my own kitchen. Reckon we can get to know each other real well now.''

She didn't like the flirtatious edge to his manner, but she decided to ignore the suggestive overtone of his friendliness. "I could use some coffee, if you have any made."

"Always have a pot on the stove. You want me to add some more brandy to it?"

"No. Just black, thank you." Her shivering began to subside, but her outdoor adventure had taken a lot more out of her than she was willing to admit.

"Here you go." Kirby handed her a steaming cup of strong coffee.

She thanked him and wrapped her fingers around the warming mug. Sipping the hot liquid, she felt color returning to her face. The brandy, coffee and heat from the fire were doing their work. She almost felt human again. Even now, she couldn't really comprehend that she'd survived such a horrible nightmare and was now safe. Who would have believed that a man on a horse would rescue her? Something right out of Old West folklore.

She wondered what the attractive Hal Haverly would have to say when he came back to the house. No doubt he thought her an utter idiot. She'd made about every mistake in the book. No, it wasn't her fault, she mentally corrected herself. It was that darn sedan stalled in the middle of the road. Then the horror came back. The dead man. The blood. At the memory, her stomach took a sickening plunge.

HAL FINISHED RUBBING DOWN his Appaloosa quarter horse and put him in a stall with plenty of hay. "Good job, Red,'' he said, patting the horse he'd named after the reddish spots on his tan hide.

Walking down the long line of stalls, he checked on the rest of his stable, eight horses in all. He stopped to stroke the neck of one of his favorite mares. ''How you doing, Calico?'' He leaned against the stall gate, watching Calico's new foal sway on long legs as the filly tugged on her mother for dinner. A man could make a fool of himself over such a pair, he thought with pride. The Appaloosa foal was perfect. Absolutely beautiful. He wished his father and grandfather were alive to see how he'd carried on the ranch and improved the breeding of these dappled horses.

He was proud of his heritage. His grandfather had settled in northern Colorado in the late 1800s. He'd bred Appaloosa horses and run cattle. Even though the demand for strong cowboy ponies had lessened with the years, Hal's father had kept the ranch going, and now it was his turn. The Haverly ranch was one of the few in Colorado preserving this colorful western strain of horses. As far as Hal was concerned, their beautiful coat patterns, striped hooves in black and white, and wispy manes and tails couldn't be matched for unique beauty. The market for this hardy, agile, quick-moving steed was growing again and, until recently, the future had been looking prosperous for him and the ranch.

His smile faded and his mouth hardened as his thoughts veered in a different direction. The ranch was his heritage, and he'd be damned if anyone was going to take it from him. *Don't think about that now.* He turned away from the mare's stall, knowing that the horses would be all right until morning. He'd have to make it back to the barn tomorrow to feed and water them. Blizzard or not, he and his ranch hands, Zack and Kirby, would have to keep up their daily chores.

Knotting several lengths of rope together, he hooked one end on a nail outside the barn door, then trailed the rest of the rope after him as he fought his way through the biting snow to the house. When he reached the back door, he secured the end of the rope to an iron dinner chime hanging just outside. With luck, the rope guide would keep him and Zack from losing their direction in the storm as they made their way from the house to the barn.

When Hal came into the kitchen, he swept off his cowboy hat and sent it sailing to the top peg of an antler coatrack. As he slipped off his rancher's coat, he saw Jill sitting in his favorite chair in front of the fire, and his gut reaction was not a simple one. Not even one that made sense.

A golden glow touched her face and burnished her deep brown hair with a softness that tempted a man's fingers. Cushioned in his favorite chair, her trim figure irresistibly drew his eyes, with her supple legs, shapely in damp stretch pants, and a knit sweater molding her full breasts. There was no reason that the sight of her sitting there should startle him. And yet he felt off balance. Even threatened. For a brief moment her face wavered, and in a trick of memory, another pair of lovely eyes looked at him from the past, provoking and possessive. Once his life had held the promise of a woman sharing his hearth, but those dreams had been destroyed with a mockery he'd never forget.

He quickly reined in his memories and walked over to her with a inquiring smile. "How are you doing? Better?"

Jill had seen the startled look in his eyes when he

came in, as if he was surprised to see her there. "Much better," she said, returning his smile.

"Good. Where's Kirby?"

"He went upstairs. I was just about to go up myself and meet the young couple."

"I owe you a big thank-you for coming," he said as he stood in front of the fireplace with his back to the warming flames.

Jill's eyes slid up to his face, hoping he hadn't noticed the assessing flicker of her eyes over his well-developed physique. He wore a dark blue wool shirt and tan-colored western pants that rode low on his hips and smoothly molded his thighs and legs. The times she'd been at the ranch with Randy, she'd watched those long legs swing easily over a saddle and had marveled at the way his body rose and fell in rhythm with a horse's gait. Even at a distance he was physically impressive; close up, he was almost devastating. "No thanks necessary, Mr. Haverly," she said evenly.

"Hal," he corrected as he met the steady gaze of her eyes. Yes, they were the color of warm brandy, he decided and was irritated with himself for noticing.

"Mine's Jill," she offered in return.

"I know. Randy told me. He brags a lot about his mother." Then he sobered. "I really didn't know the storm was settling so fast until...until you didn't show up and I got worried. I'm sorry, I insisted you come. I thought you could handle winter driving. What happened?"

Jill forced herself to speak in an even, clear voice. "I was almost here. Then I hit a car. A dark sedan that wasn't moving. I didn't see it until too late and I rammed into the back of it."

"There was another car?"

She nodded. "Right in the middle of the road."

"With someone in it?"

She moistened her lips. "Yes, a man."

"And we left him out there? Why didn't you tell me earlier? For heaven's sake—"

"You don't understand."

"I sure as hell don't," he swore before he could catch himself.

Her chin came up. "I'll explain if you'll just give me a chance."

"Then do it!" He caught himself. Wrong tone. There was enough stubbornness in the lift of her chin to warn him that she wasn't anyone he could order around. He'd have to handle her gently, like a maverick colt. For a moment, he wondered how much spirit she had in that delicious-looking body of hers. And about the challenge of taming it. Then he clamped down on these ridiculous wanderings and said evenly, "Go ahead. I'm listening."

"When I couldn't get my Jeep back on the road, I thought I'd be better off in the other car that was still on the pavement across the road. But when I got to the sedan...when...when I got there..." She stammered and swallowed hard. "There was a man...sitting in the front seat."

"And?" he prodded, when her voice faltered.

"He was dead."

He stared at her. "Dead?" Then he shook his head. "Poor guy. Doesn't take long to freeze to death with temperatures plunging this low."

"That's what I thought at first. He was sitting there all stiff and rigid." She moistened her dry lips. "But he didn't freeze to death."

"Then what?"

"There was blood. And an ugly wound. I think he'd been shot."

"Shot? You're sure about that?"

"I'm not certain. But it looked that way to me. Anyway I panicked. I started back to the Jeep and got disoriented, but I kept moving until I ran into that pile of rocks, and then, by some miracle, you found me."

"What did the man look like?"

"Dark hair, bad complexion. Kinda stocky. About twenty-five, I'd guess." She searched his face. "You know anyone like that?"

He shook his head. "Doesn't ring a bell, but that's not surprising. The whole valley is overrun with strangers. The blasted ski resorts are spreading out all over the place. Rampart's becoming one of those tourist-infested towns. Never used to be anything more for Sheriff Perkins to do than to round up livestock that broke through a fence."

"We'd better call him. Tell him about the sedan."

Hal nodded. "Yes, I'll let him know. But I suspect that Perkins has higher priorities right now than bringing in a corpse."

She sighed, agreeing as she remembered all the emergency calls she'd referred to his office.

He started across the kitchen toward a wall phone, but before he reached it, the telephone rang as if on cue. "Haverly Ranch," Hal answered briskly, and then his tone softened. "Oh, hi, Randy. Yeah, your ma's here. Safe and sound. Just a minute." He held the receiver out to her. "Your son's checking up on you."

Jill instantly felt guilty. "I should have called him as soon as my teeth stopped chattering." She took the receiver from Hal and said brightly, "Hi, honey. Yes, I made it just fine," she fibbed. "How you doing? Any more emergency calls?"

Leaning up against the wall with her head lowered, she listened to his excitement about referring several calls to the proper authorities. Thankfulness and love sluiced through her just hearing his almost-manly voice. "Good job, honey. Now you stay inside! Don't leave the building for any reason. I'll be back as soon as I can."

"Sure, Mom. Zeb says I'm taking up the slack even better than he could."

"I'm not quite sure what that means, but keep it up." There was a bubbling excitement to Randy's chatter, and she was relieved that her son was regarding the situation as high adventure. "Bye now. I love you." She smiled as he mumbled a whispered "Love you" back as if he didn't want Zeb to hear him saying such mushy things.

She hung up and turned around. Hal had left the room, and when she heard a door closing a short distance down the hall, she wondered if there was a nearby bathroom. Anyway, it was time to go upstairs. She was slipping on her boots when the phone rang again. As she hurried over to it, her first thought was that Randy had thought of something else he wanted to tell her, but when she picked up the receiver and said, "Hello," there was a moment's silence.

A man's puzzled voice asked, "Did I get the wrong number?"

"I don't know? Whom were you calling?"

"Is this the ranch?"

"Yes. Did you want to speak to Mr. Haverly? He's out of the room but if you'll wait a moment, I'll—"

"I just wanted to know if he's got electricity. I'm his neighbor, Scotty McClure, at the fishing lodge. My wires went down. I don't have a backup generator the way he does.''

"The lights are still on here, Mr. McClure.''

"Well, thank you very much. I'd be interested to know who Hal has answering his phone, Miss—?''

"Jill Gaylor. I'm a volunteer with Rampart Search and Rescue.''

"Is there a problem? Someone in trouble?'' he asked anxiously.

Before she could explain about the stranded couple, Hal came into the kitchen. "Just a moment, Mr. McClure. Here he is.'' She handed him the receiver. "Your neighbor.''

"What's up, Scotty? No, we haven't lost our power.'' Then he turned and looked at Jill as he said, "Yeah. I'm running a rescue mission here.'' He laughed at something the other man said and then quickly filled his neighbor in on the situation.

As he talked, Jill noticed that hair the color of sun-ripened wheat curled damply on the nape of his neck, and as he shifted his weight, solid buttocks swelled the fabric of his tight, western pants. She looked away quickly, not wanting him to know that she was the least bit aware of anything about him. She remembered his distant politeness when she'd picked up Randy, and she was determined to return the same while she was under his roof.

"Sure, we could use some extra grub. Thanks, Scotty.'' He hung up.

His neighbor must be a good friend, she thought. There had been a lightness in Hal's voice as he'd chatted with him. "Your boy all right?'' he asked Jill, obviously concerned.

"Fine. He's in good hands. Zeb will keep Randy under his thumb until I get back."

"Good kid, and smart too. He has a natural way with horses. But I guess you know that."

She shook her head. "He's never been around animals before. We've always lived in the city. I want to thank you for spending time with the 4-H kids."

"I get as much out of it as they do," he answered rather briskly. He didn't like mothers gushing over him, and tried to keep his distance from them, even when it came to an attractive gal like Randy's mother.

At that moment, the sound of stomping on the back porch told him that Zack had finished his chores. The kitchen door flew open and the ranch hand came in, briskly flailing his arms and sending snow flying in every direction. "Brrr. It's like the North Pole out there."

"Did you manage to get that feed out to the pasture all right?" Hal quickly asked the young cowhand. Zack had only been with him a couple of months. Keeping steady help on the ranch was almost impossible, especially with the ski resorts so close and needing lots of strong, young workers. Few unattached men wanted to put in hours of hard physical labor on a ranch when they could live on the fringes of the resorts and spend their time skiing. Hal suspected Zack had kicked around quite a bit. He was twenty-nine, kind of a loner, but he had the gift of gab when he wanted to use it, telling jokes with the best of them. Hal recognized a drifter when he saw one, so he had little hope that the ranch hand would stick around until spring.

"Dumped a half-dozen bales over the fence." Zack said, shedding his knee-length jacket and cowboy hat. He was stocky, medium height, with dark hair lying longish on his neck, giving him the look of a country-western singer. "But the water tank's frozen over. Drifts are already five feet in some places. Wouldn't be surprised if we get snowed in for a week."

"A week?" Jill echoed. "Surely the storm will let up...by morning?"

Zack gave her a slow, frank appraisal from head to toe. Then he grinned. "Hi. You're the gal from the rescue patrol, right?"

She nodded.

"I'm Zack."

"Glad to meet you, Zack," she answered, a little unnerved by the cowboy's broad, admiring smile.

"The boss said you were coming." Zack cocked his head. "But I have to admit that I didn't expect you to be so darn good-looking. Great to have a pretty gal around the place for a change, isn't it, boss?"

Hal laughed and nodded. "I admit it gets pretty monotonous looking at the likes of you and Kirby."

Jill was suddenly uncomfortable with this turn of conversation. "Where will I find the young couple and what are their names?"

"Sue and Gary Miller. Top of the stairs," Hal answered. "First bedroom to your right. Front of the house." Then he added, "You can take the bedroom across the hall from the Millers."

"What about Kirby and me, boss?" Zack asked. "We'll have to be staying at the house. Too dangerous trying to find our way to the bunkhouse in this blizzard."

"You can have the other two upstairs bedrooms."

"Suits me," said Zack with a bold wink at Jill. "Kinda cozy, all around."

Jill ignored the wink and quickly left the kitchen. Lovely. What could be better? A handsome host triggering her hormones, his cook wanting to massage her feet, and his lusty cowhand trying to make time with her. Great. Just great.

She went along the hall to the front of house, where a staircase led to the upper floor on one side, and a pair of double doors on the other side opened into a large living room dominated by a huge stone fireplace. Through the doorway, she glimpsed Indian rugs scattered on the hardwood floor and comfortable-looking western-style furniture. Walls of knotty pine logs rose in varnished layers to a high ceiling. In spite of the homey furnishings, the room had a deserted air about it. She wondered if Hal Haverly ever sat in front of the huge fireplace or let his hired help make use of the spacious room.

As she climbed the stairs, she decided that the house must have been standing for a long time, probably built for a family. She'd heard that the Haverly Ranch was the oldest spread in the valley, and one of the last to hold out against land developers who were buying up everything in sight.

She was halfway up the stairs when she met the beanpole cook coming down. Much to her surprise and annoyance, Kirby stopped on the step above her, deliberately blocking her way. "Got thawed out, did you?"

Because of his tall rangy build, Jill had to bend her head slightly backward to look up into his lean face. "Yes, I feel almost human again."

"Brandy'll do that."

She didn't know what more to say. When he didn't move out of the way, she stepped to one side so she could go by him. She was instantly uncomfortable when he deliberately crowded her so that his body brushed against hers as they passed. Controlling an urge to give him a scathing glare, she went on up the stairs.

An arched window on the landing might have given a view of the nearby mountains if the glass hadn't been caked with snow, but as she passed the window, she was glad that she couldn't see outside. The wailing, raging wind and the sound of biting snow hitting the house was enough. Would she ever forget the terror she'd felt stumbling blindly in the storm? Would it always be with her, the memory of how helpless she had felt, facing the near-certainty of freezing to death? She'd never understood such tragedies before, but now she realized just how quickly a person could become disoriented and surrender to the elements. She would never treat the challenges of threatening weather so casually again.

The upper hall was carpeted and lighted by a series of brass fixtures on the wall. A murmur of voices floated out of a front bedroom a few steps down the hall, so she knocked lightly on the open door and stuck her head in. "Hello, may I come in?"

A young man with curly blond hair and a freckled face sat on the side of a bed, holding his pregnant wife's hand. Both of them looked relieved when she said, "I'm Jill Gaylor. I'll be keeping you company until the storm's over."

He quickly stood up and held out a hand. "I'm Gary. This is my wife, Sue."

They were just kids, both of them. Sue was a pretty blond girl of about seventeen, who should have been going to football games and hanging out in shopping malls instead of having a baby, thought Jill. Her husband, Gary, wore glasses and a Kansas City Chiefs sweatshirt that hung loose and baggy on his slight frame.

The young man's harried expression eased slightly as he shook hands with Jill. "Mr. Haverly said someone was coming to be with Sue. She's not due for three more weeks," he assured Jill. "So we'll be with her parents in Hartford, Kansas, when the baby comes."

Jill nodded. "How you doing, Sue?"

"All right. Just tired," she said with a wan smile.

"A little break in your trip will do you good," Jill assured her.

"We had to call my folks and tell them we were held up," Sue said, as if Jill needed to know that they were responsible people.

"Aren't you cutting it close, traveling at this late date?" Jill could not help but ask. Didn't they know that first babies don't stick to a timetable? "Maybe you should have waited."

"Couldn't," Gary said shortly. "I lost my job. We had to give up our apartment. I was working as a bank teller in Provo, Utah, when the bank was taken over. Most of the personnel were let go. Sue's folks said to come and stay with them until we got things sorted out."

"We came this way to check out a new bank branch opening in Steamboat Springs, Colorado," Sue explained. "We gambled on the weather staying good."

"We'd have made it to Hartford in a couple more days if we hadn't hit this blasted storm. Anyway, the Steamboat interview went good. I think I'll have a job in about six weeks. We'll move back then."

"We like Colorado." Sue smiled at her husband. "Don't we, honey?"

He nodded. "It's a great place to bring up a kid. All this open space. Clean air. Are you from here?" he asked Jill.

"No, California." Both of them looked at her as if she had said Hollywood. The next thing they would ask was if she knew any movie stars, so she said quickly,

"But Colorado's my home now. Are both of you originally from Kansas?"

"Yes." From Sue's excited chatter, Jill could tell she was eager to get back home to her parents and the small town where she'd grown up. "Both our grandparents, Gary's and mine, are still living," Sue told her. "They were all at our wedding. The church was filled with flowers. And that's where our baby will be christened." Her eyes glowed with such happiness that Jill breathed a silent prayer that the good Lord would do his part to make her dream come true.

Both Gary and Sue were interested in hearing about the Mountain Search and Rescue volunteers. As she talked, Jill wondered what challenges the rest of the members were facing. There would be plenty to share when they got together again. "I've only answered the phone, until today," she admitted.

"I guess everything is quiet and peaceful in a place like Rampart."

Jill thought about the nagging worry she'd been living with for the last month. She'd made up her mind to report the disturbing phone calls and weird gifts. She probably should have done it earlier, but she hated to put herself in the public eye. Rampart was a small town, and no doubt the gossip grapevine was hale and hearty. Foolishly, she'd kept hoping that the person would tire of the game, but the suggestive photograph had banished that hope. She had no choice but to go to the sheriff. Maybe just reporting the harassment would put an end to it.

"We could be on our way tomorrow." Gary smiled at his wife as he said this, but the worried frown on her forehead remained.

"Traveling is hard on anyone," Jill said. "It's good

that you can rest up before you take off again.'' Then, trying to guide the conversation into a lighter vein, Jill asked them if they had names picked out for their baby, and for a few minutes the storm outside was forgotten.

"I remember how excited I was when I was carrying my son.'' Jill chatted about her own pregnancy in a bright, uplifting way and was rewarded by a lessening of tension in Sue's face. When the young woman closed her eyes sleepily, Jill nodded to Gary and they quietly left the room.

"When do you think we can get back on the road?'' he asked anxiously once they were in the hall. "I haven't heard the forecast.''

"Neither have I. If it stops snowing tonight, the roads could be cleared by late tomorrow. Until then, you might as well relax.'' She gave him a reassuring smile. "This layover might be a blessing, give your wife a chance to rest up for the last part of your trip. Try to relax. Get some rest yourself.''

"I don't feel much like resting. Too keyed up.''

Jill had no idea if there were any current magazines or books in the house. She'd only brought one paperback with her, and she doubted the historical romance would be this young man's choice of reading matter. "Why don't you look around and see if you can find something to read,'' she suggested.

"I like *Sports Illustrated.*'' He grinned. "Especially the swimsuit issue.''

Jill doubted that Hal Haverly subscribed to anything as cosmopolitan as that, but who knew? She was ready to admit he was an enigma. Gary thanked her again for coming and she urged him to relax. "It's going to be all right. Better get some rest yourself. You've still got a long drive ahead of you.''

He nodded and disappeared back into their bedroom. Jill decided to go down to the kitchen and get the backpack that she had dumped by the back door. She let her hand trail down the polished oak banister as she went downstairs. Just as she reached the bottom step, she heard a fierce banging on the front door and a muffled voice shouting, "Open up! Open up!"

As quickly as she could, she crossed the front foyer and jerked open the door. When a snow-covered skier clutching skis and poles bolted in, she pulled back in surprise. She couldn't see anything but the man's eyes through the holes in his ski mask.

"Brrr!" He dropped his skis and poles on the floor, slipped off a backpack, and pulled off the knit face covering. She stared in disbelief at the tall young man with a blond ponytail and an earring in his left ear.

"Thanks, honey. That's some storm out there."

"What on earth?" she gasped aloud. "The ski resorts are miles from here. How did you...?"

He laughed at her bewildered expression. "Ever heard of cross-country skiing?"

"In this weather?"

"Wasn't like this when I started out yesterday. Spent last night in a ski hut on Silver Mountain, but I knew I'd better find my way down before I got stranded without food and wood to keep warm."

"You've been out in this storm all day?" She had no idea where Silver Mountain was, but she couldn't imagine anyone skiing anywhere in such blinding snow.

As if he read her mind, he said, "The visibility was worse than I expected. Luckily I knew this ranch house was somewhere close. And here I am." He quickly jerked off a glove and held out his hand. "Larry

Crowder. I hope you don't mind me spending a night under your roof.''

Before she could answer, she heard footsteps behind her and turned as Hal reached them. His blue eyes widened in astonishment as his gaze fell on the tumbled skis, poles and the young man.

''I heard him pounding on the door,'' Jill explained quickly.

Larry stepped forward. ''It's the storm, sir. Your wife let me in.''

''She's not my wife,'' Hal corrected smoothly, as if that was the first thing to get straight. ''What in the world are you doing out in this storm?''

The skier explained the reason he'd shown up at the rancher's door. ''I went farther than I had planned and couldn't get back. Had to spend the night on Silver Mountain.''

The guy must really be a skiing addict, Jill thought. And pretty stupid to ignore the weather forecasts. Hal must have felt the same way, for he echoed, ''Silver Mountain? That could be suicide in this storm.''

''I know that now. Bad timing on my part, for sure. But if I can spend the night, I'm sure I'll be able to ski out of here tomorrow.''

''Not likely,'' Hal said flatly. ''Day after tomorrow, maybe. At least that's what the forecasters are saying.''

''Oh, no,'' Jill said anxiously. ''Are they really predicting the storm will last that long?''

''Well, they're wrong often enough,'' the skier offered helpfully.

Hal silently hoped to heaven this was one of the those times. He couldn't imagine having his life totally disrupted for God knew how long with all these extra people. ''Well, shed those wet things and come on into the den. I was just having a drink with a neighbor of mine, and I imagine you could use a warmer-upper."

"Yes, thank you, sir."

Hal hesitated a moment. "What about you, Jill?" The use of her first name threw her for a minute. "Would you care to join us in the den? All male company, I'm afraid."

From his tone, she didn't know if he was warning or challenging her, but in either case, she wasn't about to let him dictate what she should or should not do. The young mother was sleeping, and there wasn't anything she could do upstairs at the moment.

"That sounds inviting." She was perfectly capable of handling herself with the opposite sex. Even though he might prefer her to fade into the background, she was stubborn enough to say, "I believe I'll join you for a few minutes."

She was convinced a brief smile tugged at his lips, but it was so fleeting that a second later she wasn't sure. He led the way to an open door just beyond the foot of the stairs. The den was a man's room, all right, Jill saw with one quick glance. Mounted stuffed animal trophies and photographs of fishing and hunting parties decorated the log walls. Hunting guns filled two gun cases, and she was surprised to see a high glassed-in bookcase behind a large desk that dominated one side of the room. There ought to be something on those shelves that would provide Gary and Sue with a little reading material, she thought.

Zack sat on a couch facing the fire with a can of beer in his hand. He didn't get up, but a sandy-haired man sitting beside him quickly rose to his feet as Hal made the introductions.

"My neighbor, Scotty McClure. He owns the fishing

lodge and cabins on the next property and is known to all the anglers in these parts as 'You-Should-Have-Seen-The-One-That-Got-Away' McClure.''

The Scotsman laughed good-naturedly but Jill thought the fisherman's smile was a little forced. Apparently Scotty took his fishing exploits seriously. "And this is Jill Gaylor who spoke with you earlier."

"Pleased to meet you in person," he said as he shook her hand. "Was worth battling the blizzard to drive over here and join the party. Power lines at my place went down. Good thing I got myself over here or I'd be freezing my butt off."

He was somewhere in his middle thirties, she guessed. The outdoor type, rather large-boned but carrying his weight well. "You gave me a start when you answered the phone," he admitted. "Couldn't believe Hal had a woman under his roof. Might have known it would take a Colorado blizzard to get a pretty lass inside his doors. Not that any gal would put up with his cantankerous disposition for long."

Hal took the ribbing in good sport, as if he was used to his neighbor's teasing. Jill sensed an affectionate bond between them. Apparently Hal related well to kids like Randy and fishing buddies like Scotty. Had he ever allowed a woman in his life? she wondered. She suspected that his deep resonant voice and easy confident manner would probably have a devastating effect upon any woman he decided was worthy of his attention.

Forcing her attention away from her host, she realized with a start that Zack had risen to his feet and was glaring at the skier as if the young man's blond ponytail and earring made him some kind of alien. Even before the men spoke two words to each other, Jill could feel a spark of animosity between them. Great, she thought, that's all she needed, snowbound with two aggressive males acting like charging bulls.

Jill eased down into a comfortable chair, and when Hal asked what she'd like to drink, she glanced at the small, built-in bar. "Scotch and water would be nice." She didn't know whether he was surprised by her choice—a man's drink, after all. And not very Californian. Had he expected her to request a banana daiquiri? She felt him studying her as he prepared her drink and poured himself a shot of whiskey. A betraying warmth eased into her cheeks and she was annoyed at herself for allowing his attention to make her blush.

As he handed her the glass, his eyes met hers with the hint of a teasing smile. "I hope it's strong enough."

Keeping her eyes locked with his, she raised the drink, and took a sip. She pretended to weigh the taste for a second, then smiled. "Perfect."

A resonant chuckle came from deep in his chest as he turned away. When he took a seat across the room from her, she was strangely disappointed. In spite of herself, she was intrigued by this man and admitted that she'd like to know him better, much better.

None of the men made an effort to include her in the conversation, and the rise and fall of male voices was rather pleasant and a change from her solitary widowhood. She sipped her drink and relaxed.

A few minutes later, she was startled out of a pleasant reverie when Kirby stuck his head in the door. "Come and get it. Grub's on."

Jill stood up, set down her empty glass on the bar and turned to Hal. "I'll take a tray upstairs and eat with Sue and Gary."

"No, not tonight. The fellows would never forgive me if I let you slip off by yourself," Hal said, his persuasive smile doing all sorts of things to his dark blue eyes. "Please eat with the rest of us."

"All right," she agreed, not wanting to make an issue of it. In a way, she was pleased that he was insisting on her company.

She expected that they would eat in the kitchen, but Hal led the way to a spacious dining room adjoining the large front room. Jill was astounded to see that a long table had been spread with a lovely white cloth and matching dishes and glassware. An overhead chandelier made of tiny stained-glass pieces sent colored light twinkling on the elegant table below.

Her astonishment must have registered on her face because there was a satisfied gleam in her host's eye. "When my mother and father were alive, they always set a fine table, and we never had evening meals in the kitchen."

With surprising deftness, he seated Jill at the head of the table, himself at the foot, and the other men, including the cook, took their places at the long table.

Even though a fire had been built in the fireplace, there were signs that the dining room was usually shut off from the rest of the house. Jill could tell that the dinner preparations had been hasty, and she wondered why the rancher had bothered with the extra effort.

"Chow time," Zack said when everyone was seated. He flushed at Hal's scowl. The cowboy looked self-conscious as he handled the fragile serving dishes circling the table. Next to him, the skier paid little attention to anyone else as he loaded his plate and made no pretense about hiding a ravenous appetite.

Kirby might not look like a cook, she decided, but if the perfectly cooked trout, buttered potatoes, lightly seasoned, and a green bean casserole were an example of his culinary skills, he certainly knew how to prepare a delicious meal. When she complimented him, the Adam's apple in his long neck bobbed up and down, and the smile he gave her made his lean face seem almost boyish.

Scotty, sitting at her right, proudly informed her that he had supplied the rainbow trout. With only a smile as encouragement, he launched into fishing stories that had the other men groaning and shaking their heads in skeptical disbelief.

Jill felt Hal's eyes on her during the meal and wondered what he was thinking. Several times she was startled when a deep laugh came from his chest. Tiny smile lines appeared around his eyes, and his mouth was suddenly relaxed and terribly appealing. When he radiated warmth and acceptance, and when his smile included her, she was drawn to him in a way she would never have thought possible. In those moments, she realized she was seeing the man that her son held in such affection.

Their eyes caught once for only a brief moment, but with startling impact. Quickly she lowered her gaze. It's the storm, she told herself. Nothing more. The disturbing effect he was having on her was the result of frayed nerves and a bone-deep weariness. She didn't linger after she had finished her apple cobbler, but quickly excused herself from the table.

"Just ask if you need anything," Hal said, rising to his feet at her departure.

"I will, thank you."

None of the other men rose from their chairs, and a fresh wave of male conversation followed her out the door. All her things, backpack and wraps, had disappeared from the kitchen and she assumed someone had taken them up to her room.

She ran upstairs and went immediately to check on the Millers, glad to see that Kirby had brought up trays with the same delicious meal he'd prepared for everyone else.

"Well, I think I'll turn in," she said a few minutes later, when there seemed to be nothing she could do for the expectant mother. Physically and emotionally drained by the events of the day, she was ready to find a bed and climb into it. "You be sure to call me if you need me. Have a good night."

Outside, old man winter was still raging, but inside the stone house there was reassuring warmth and comfort. She crossed the hall to the bedroom Hal had said would be hers and was delighted with what she saw. The cozy room was just what she would have imagined for a homey ranch house. Wallpaper in a floral print and blue drapes harmonized with simple maple furniture and a large brass bed covered with a thick multicolored quilt.

She was glad to see her backpack lying on the bed and her wraps hung in the closet. As she started to unzip the backpack, she noticed something lying on the floor beside the bed. Reaching down and picking it up, she turned it over in her hand with disbelief.

A bookmark.

The same one that she was using to mark her place in the paperback she'd brought with her. She was certain that she'd packed the book at the bottom of her backpack. How had the bookmark gotten on the floor unless…unless someone had been looking through her things.

A cold chill ran up her back.

He'd watched her walk out of the dining room and smiled to himself. Things were going even better than he had imagined. He loved being close to her, breathing the same air and enjoying the tantalizing way she moved. He loved touching her things. He couldn't believe that she could look straight into his face without knowing how much he desired her. Her indifference mocked him. Belittled the love he felt for her. How could she be so blind to the torment that had plagued his nights and days? But the time would come when she would know. And soon.

Chapter Three

Jill sat on the edge of the bed and fought back a swell of uneasiness mingled with rage. She'd always valued her privacy. Just the idea of someone stealthily going through her possessions infuriated her. Maybe she was jumping to conclusions, but even as she tried to find another reason for the bookmark being on the floor, she failed to come up with any other explanation than the disturbing and obvious one—that someone had been going through her things. But why, for heaven's sake? Were they after money? If so, they'd overlooked the wallet she had placed in a small zippered pocket. But maybe there hadn't been time for a thorough search. Nothing seemed to be missing, but she couldn't be sure. She'd only brought some clothes and the bare essentials. And she'd packed in such a hurry that she wasn't quite certain what she'd stuffed into the bag. If the bookmark hadn't been on the floor, she wouldn't even have been aware that someone had gone through her belongings.

All of the men, including Hal, had easy access to her bedroom as they came and went up and down the stairs. With the arrival of the skier and the Scotsman, and the storm deepening with every hour, sleeping arrangements had been changed to give the two unexpected guests the

remaining bedrooms, while Kirby and Zack were going
to bed down on couches in the den. Any one of them,
including Gary Miller, could have spent a few minutes
in her room at any time during the day or evening, as
they'd all left the gathering periodically—to use the rest-
room she'd assumed.

Feeling uneasy, she made certain her door was locked.
Then she wearily climbed into the wide brass bed and
burrowed down into the warmth of blankets and thick
quilt. Although exhausted from the physical and emotional demands of the day, she couldn't relax. A mounting wind wailed under the eaves of the house, and the
peppering of iced snow against the windows brought
back the terrifying experience of struggling through the
blinding snow. She relived the horrifying moments of
opening the car door and seeing the dead man covered
in his own blood. Hal had said he didn't recall a car of
the kind she'd described, but there had been a flicker in
his eyes that made her wonder. Had he called the sheriff?
She'd forgotten to ask.

Jill's wandering thoughts settled on her unwilling
host. She felt a flicker of sympathy for him. Obviously,
the storm had completely disrupted his life, and having
a houseful of uninvited guests would stretch anyone's
patience and hospitality.

All through dinner she'd felt his eyes flickering over
her. What was going through his mind? Perhaps he was
remembering other gatherings in the family dining room.
Was he seeing his mother seated at the end of the table,
enjoying her pretty floral dishes, smiling and making
conversation with her guests? She wondered what kind
of son Hal Haverly had been to his mother, and, more
importantly, what kind of mother had she been to him.

Then she chided herself for letting Hal Haverly dominate her thoughts.

It had been a long time since a man had captured her attention on any level. She wondered if she was immune for life to ever falling in love again. At heart, she was a sharing person, finding joy in giving and receiving, and at times she was damn lonely. Even though she was blessed by having Randy to love and care for, she knew that he had a life of his own to live. She'd met plenty of men in the workplace, enjoyed male company on occasion and even dated a few special guys for extended periods. But none of them had tapped that deep reservoir of emotion that she'd once known. Had she deliberately erected barriers around herself? Was she afraid of letting herself fall in love again?

She flounced over in bed and impatiently fluffed the soft feather pillow. Why on earth was she asking herself such questions at this particular moment? She knew the answer and was disgusted with herself. For some stupid reason, the rancher had gotten under her skin. She wondered what it would be like to receive the full force of his smile. Tonight at dinner, had there been a kind of magnetic pull as their eyes caught, or had it been her imagination? Maybe he had just been acting as a hospitable host, laughing and smiling, and she was guilty of fantasizing.

Well, no matter, she told herself, turning over on her side. She deliberately switched her thoughts away from Hal Haverly and settled them on the frightened young girl across the hall. Just having another woman around had eased Sue's anxiety and lessened the worried frown on her husband's face. Yes, she'd made the right decision in coming, Jill thought with satisfaction. The young couple needed support and reassurance. As soon as the roads cleared tomorrow, they'd be on their way again with a tale to tell about being snowed in at a Colorado ranch. *And as soon as they leave, I'll get back to Randy and take him home,* she thought as she curled up with her cheek against the soft pillow. Her son would be proud of his mom. This time, when the other rescue volunteers returned, she'd have her own story to tell. Her whirling thoughts settled down and she slipped away into a refreshing sleep.

THE NEXT MORNING she awoke when a fierce assault of wind and snow seemed to rock the house to its very foundation. For a moment, on the edge of sleep, disoriented by the strange ceiling above her head and the unfamiliar bed, her thoughts were muddled. Then she remembered. And as she lay there, listening, her chest tightened. The storm was still raging. In fact, it sounded worse than when she'd gone to bed. She had convinced herself that the brunt of the storm would pass over during the night, but all hope for the Millers to be on their way quickly faded.

The bedroom's chilly air prickled her skin as she threw back the covers. Thankful for her warm flannel pajamas and matching robe, she grabbed a change of clothes and a few toiletries. Cautiously opening the door, she peered out and was relieved that no men were in sight. The Millers' door was still closed, but the other two doors at each end of the hall were open and the rooms appeared to be empty. Hal and the other two men must already be downstairs. She quickly made her way to the bathroom just down the hall.

Earlier, Jill had decided that the master bedroom must have a bathroom of its own, because no masculine personal items were evident in this bathroom. Several towels and a couple of bars of soap had been set out for use by the stranded guests but, otherwise, the bathroom was as impersonal as a hotel's. No sign that it was in daily use. Bathroom fixtures in a delicate blue matched modern ceramic tile and a bright linoleum in a morning-glory pattern.

Jill locked the door, adjusted the flow of water from the bathtub shower, and ignored the tingling of her skin as she quickly stripped. She breathed heartfelt thanks for the stream of hot water, which filled the room with steam as she showered.

After briskly rubbing herself with one of the large, sweet-smelling towels, she dressed in a pink turtleneck sweater and blue jeans. Never one to spend a lot of time on toiletries, she brushed damp bangs onto her forehead and French braided the rest of her dark brown hair in a long plait over one shoulder. This simple hairstyle was flattering, and she was glad that she had decided several years ago to give up beauty-shop haircuts and perms. After a quick touch of pale gloss lipstick and a dusting of face powder to dull the shine on her slightly pug nose, she was ready to face the day.

The Millers' door was still closed when she was ready to go downstairs. She heard men's voices as she went down the hall to the kitchen and found Larry, Scotty and the cook sitting at the table talking, eating, laughing and drinking coffee. The conversation broke off abruptly when she came in, and from the expressions on their faces, she suspected someone had been telling an off-color joke.

"Good morning." She sent a smile around the table, determined not to let them make her feel like an intruder. All of them hastened to return her greeting.

"Morning."

"Sleep well?"

"Ready for breakfast?"

As her gaze passed around the table, they all seemed perfectly at ease with her, but had one of them been in her room going through her things. Which one?

"Have a chair," Kirby invited, getting up.

"Thanks, but I want to use the telephone first and check up on my son."

The cook shook his head. "Phone's out."

Jill's voice was slightly unsteady as her stomach muscles tightened. "Are you sure?"

"Deader than a doornail." Kirby thoughtfully massaged his narrow chin. "Wouldn't be surprised if it's out for quite a spell."

"You worried about your boy?" Scotty asked. "Isn't someone looking after him?"

"Yes. He's in good hands. But I don't like the idea of being completely cut off from him," she said as the reality of being snowbound hit her with unexpected force. Even though she knew that Zeb could be trusted with Randy's safety, she needed reassurance that all was well with her son. Until that moment, she had not felt completely trapped. She chafed at the sudden helplessness that poured over her. Being totally isolated in this ranch house with strange men and with no way to contact her son or anyone else suddenly brought home the reality of the storm's total isolation.

"Might as well sit down and have some breakfast," Kirby said briskly, holding out a chair for her next to Larry. "Won't be much grub left once these fellows get through loading up their plates."

Jill wasn't hungry, but she sat down at the table. Her appetite had been curbed by tight stomach muscles. She knew without looking outside that the house and everything else was still being buried in the blizzard.

"Guess we're all damn lucky we made it here," Larry said as he leaned back in his chair.

Jill's nod was forced.

"I'm surprised the electricity hasn't gone out," Scotty said. "Wind must have been heavier down at my place."

"Radio says the whole area is socked in," Kirby offered. "Not a chance of getting the roads cleared for at least another twenty-four hours."

"I was hoping I could ski out later today," Larry said. "But I guess I'll have to stick around till the storm lifts." He grinned at Jill. "Might as well enjoy ourselves. Don't you agree, Jill?"

His suggestive tone irked her. Larry's tanned face was a sharp contrast to the weather outside, and Jill wondered if the skier spent time on a tanning machine. With his blond hair and blue eyes, all the man needed was a heavy Scandinavian accent to pass for a Nordic athlete. There was an air of conceit about him that she didn't like.

"I thought you skiers were crazy enough to get out in any kind of weather." Scotty's tone was one of slight distaste as he goaded Larry.

Larry didn't seem to notice or chose to ignore it. "Takes a blizzard like this to keep us indoors, that's for sure. Of course, there are benefits to getting snowbound." Once more he leveled his blue eyes on Jill. "You know something? I didn't realize it until this morning but I've seen you around the heliport office. You work for Slade's Adventures, don't you?"

She nodded.

"I thought so," he said with satisfaction.

Jill didn't remember him, but then she stayed pretty much in her office, avoiding the traffic of vacationers coming and going on flights into the high mountain country.

"Sometimes I drive the resort shuttle to pick up skiers when they arrive. I guess you never noticed me," Larry said tipping his chair back and smiling at her.

"No, but the place gets pretty busy and crowded with skiers arriving and leaving all the time."

"Yeah, I know. Who would have thought we'd be thrown together like this? I'm glad I'm here." He winked at her. "You might need someone to protect you from all these good old boys."

Kirby snorted as he brought Jill some coffee. "Look who's talking? A ski bum with an earring." The tattoo on the cook's arm moved with a flexed muscle. "You couldn't protect a baby chick in a henhouse, sonny boy."

Larry let his tipped chair slam to the floor and jerked to his feet. "Wanna bet?"

"Hey, hold it, fellows." Scotty glared at both of them. "If Jill needs any protection, I'll take care of it." The freckles on his ruddy face stood out like pox.

Jill wanted to laugh. Was this some kind of mountain he-man acting out? She wasn't even flattered to be the center of this ridiculous display of machismo. If there hadn't been a charged undercurrent in the room, she would have made fun of the whole exchange, but she sensed that the men were dead serious. She decided the best way to handle this clash of aggressive male hormones was to dismiss it. "It's too early in the morning for heroics," she said with a wave of her hand. "What's for breakfast, Kirby?" she asked the cook with false lightness. "Are those fresh biscuits?"

Kirby nodded, but he didn't take his eyes from Larry until the skier sat back down. Then the cook turned back to the stove and lifted some biscuits from a pan onto a plate.

"Hal will have all our necks in a sling if we start any rough stuff," Scotty cautioned.

"Where is Hal?" Jill asked, wishing that their host would make his presence known before muscle-flexing houseguests and hired men started shoving each other around.

"Out at the barn. He and Zack are looking after the horses. Not much else they can do in this weather. The rest of the livestock will have to survive on their own. He lost all his spring calves a while back. Just got sick and died." Scotty shook his head. "Tough break."

"Hard enough to make a place like this pay when things are going good," Kirby agreed, setting a plate of sausage and biscuits in front of Jill. "Keeps the three of us hustling, taking care of the stock and the house."

She started to protest that she didn't eat sausage or bacon, but she didn't want to antagonize Kirby, so she buttered a biscuit and nibbled on a link sausage.

Scotty leaned back in his chair. "Plenty of speculators offering good money for land round here."

"I wonder how long Hal will hold out." Kirby frowned. "I've been here nearly six years. Kinda gotten used to the place."

"You could probably get a job at one of the resorts," Larry said. "They're always advertising for a greasy fry cook."

Before Kirby could react to the deliberate insult, Scotty cut in. "I been thinking about selling out myself, but there's nothing I'd rather be doing than fishing and shooting the breeze with the folks who rent my cabins."

The Scotsman chuckled deeply. "I tried working and decided loafing was better."

"Sounds good to me," Larry agreed wistfully.

"What do you do for a living, Larry?" Scotty asked bluntly.

"A little of this and that," the blond skier answered. "Keeping my eyes open for a bonanza. All of this valley is going to be condos one day, just like Aspen and Vail," he said with conviction. "Greatest ski country in the world. Do you ski, Jill?"

"No, I haven't tried it yet."

"That will never do. How about a private lesson or two?" Larry leaned toward her. "I bet I could have you on the slopes in record time. What about it? Is it a date? They tell me I'm a great teacher." His eyes narrowed suggestively.

"Well, my son has been talking about learning to ski," Jill answered evenly, ignoring the obvious come-on. "Maybe we could arrange a lesson or two for Randy."

Kirby laughed openly. "Way to go, Jill. Guess she got you on that one, big boy."

Scotty joined in the ribbing. "I'm sure teaching your son was exactly what Larry had in mind."

To his credit, the skier tried to act amused but didn't quite make it. Obviously, Larry resented being rebuffed, thought Jill. Thank heavens, there was little likelihood of their paths crossing again. A conceited ski bum was not on her list of people she cared to have in her life.

"Are you as good at playing pool as you are at ski-ing?" Scotty challenged Larry. "Or would you like a few lessons from the master?"

"I can hold my own with a master," Larry answered

crisply. "If the master has a few bucks to make the game interesting."

"A Scotsman is always ready to accept honest winnings," Scotty replied, easing to his feet. "Come along, let's give Hal's pool table a warm-up. How about you, Jill? Want to play or watch?"

"Neither, thanks," she answered quickly. "I'll be busy with the Millers this morning, as soon as they're up and about."

The two men left the room. She had just finished her second biscuit, and Kirby was refilling her coffee cup when Gary came into the kitchen.

"How are you and Sue this morning?" Jill asked him. She thought the young man looked less tired than the evening before, but there were still worry lines in his forehead.

"The storm kept us awake till after midnight." He searched her face. "Do you think it's ever going to let up? We're not going to get out of here today, are we?"

"Doesn't look that way."

He groaned. "Sue's going to have a fit. She's already up and about, getting our things together. She's planning on getting dressed and coming downstairs shortly."

"That's good news. After breakfast we'll try to find something to pass away the time," Jill said. Time was going to be heavy on all their hands. Maybe they could take a tour of the house and enjoy some of its rustic charm. Of course, Hal might regard such interest as snooping. Jill wondered if she should tell him that someone had gone through her backpack. No, she decided. Maybe Hal had checked her out himself. Because she was from California, he might have been worried that she was a city girl who couldn't go anywhere without a stash of drugs. Or he could have told Kirby to check out her belongings. Somehow she didn't think the cook would do it of his own volition, but someone had.

A few minutes later Kirby left the kitchen to join the pool players in the den and Gary took breakfast trays upstairs, leaving Jill sitting alone in the kitchen. She was still thinking about her backpack, and the possibility that Hal had been the one who searched it, when Hal himself came in from outdoors. Her suspicious thoughts made her quickly give her attention to her coffee.

As HAL DISCARDED his coat and hat, he felt a sudden joy at seeing her sitting there in a pink sweater that hugged her breasts and slender waist. The whole kitchen seemed to take on a glow with her presence. Her brown hair glistened with a clean freshness that made him want to bury his nose in its softness. She'd been in his thoughts since dinner last night, and he'd found himself wanting to hurry his chores so he could get back to the house. When she deliberately turned her eyes away from him and stared at her coffee cup, he felt like someone had doused him with cold water.

He hardly knew what to say, so he settled on a brief, "Good morning."

"Morning," she replied, keeping her eyes lowered as she sipped her coffee.

He slid into a chair opposite her. Beating around the bush wasn't his style. "What's wrong, Jill? If there's something not to your liking, come out with it. Is it your room? Your bed?"

Her head came up. "My bedroom is lovely. The bed was wonderful. It's not that."

"Then what? There was less of a chill in the barn," he said with a wry smile. "Did I do or say something?" He watched uncertainty flicker across her face, and then her eyes steadily met his as if she had decided to be upfront about whatever was bothering her.

"All right." She drew a deep breath. "Someone went through my backpack. I don't know why, but someone was snooping through my things. They didn't take anything. My wallet was in a zippered compartment, and none of my money was gone. Nor anything else that I can tell."

"Then how do you know?"

As she told him about the bookmark, an uneasy trembling was evident in her voice. "The marker must have fallen to the floor when the book was taken out. I wouldn't have known about the search if the bookmark hadn't been beside the bed. I don't know who or why. I'm just telling you that I know someone went through my things."

"I see." Now he understood her cold reception. "And you think it could have been me."

"It could have been anyone in the house," she said evenly. "But I admit I was thinking that you might be checking me out."

He leaned back in his chair, not knowing whether to be insulted or amused. "And why would I search your backpack?"

"I don't know. I don't know why anyone would."

"Neither do I. I'm sorry it happened. I don't have any idea who did it, but I'll try to find out." *Who in the devil was fooling around in her room?* He had no way of knowing. Kirby and Zack had slept in the den. Scotty and the young skier had shared an upstairs bedroom next to his, and the Millers were in the room across from Jill. Counting himself, there were six men in the house and two women. How in the hell could he know who was snooping around?

"If nothing was taken, I guess there's no harm done," he said reassuringly. She nodded, but something in her manner told him the incident had disturbed her deeply, even scared her. He was surprised. She didn't seem like the kind of woman to be easily frightened. "Keep your door locked when you're in your room," he told her. "I'll be around to keep an eye on you."

"You may have to stand in line," she said with a grateful smile. "I've already had several offers this morning."

"It figures," he answered, returning her smile as he got up and poured himself coffee. A pretty gal in the house with four single men. He'd bet there were compliments flying all over the place. Leaning back against one of the counters, he sipped his drink in companionable silence.

Jill was uncomfortably aware of his forceful presence as she glanced up at him. His clean-shaven face had a healthy glow from his time outside and, once again, his light-colored hair was slightly curly from dampness. He wore a faded pair of Wrangler jeans and a bright plaid shirt. Avoiding his candid blue eyes, she asked about the storm.

"The temperature's still dropping. If this deep freeze lasts much longer, I'll be lucky to save half the stock." He frowned. "Don't know how I'll make up for the loss. Not much of a profit margin as it is."

"I'm sorry. It doesn't seem fair. I can understand why you wouldn't want to sell the ranch."

"Sell it?" His eyes darkened. "Who's been talking to you?"

"Someone just mentioned that land investors were interested in buying the property." She didn't know what else to say and felt like an idiot for having mentioned something that she knew absolutely nothing about. As he remained silent, lost in thought, she was aware of an underlying sadness about him that she had missed before. Tiny lines etched around his eyes deepened and made her wonder what personal battles he'd fought.

He turned around to the coffeepot and filled his cup again. "This storm is still kicking up. No telling how long we're going to be cooped up like this. What about the Millers? Have you seen them this morning?"

She nodded. "Gary says Sue is feeling fine. I think getting out of her room would be good for her. You have a lot of interesting things in the house. Would you mind if we looked around?"

"I don't mind. Even if the weather breaks, I don't think they should be in a hurry to leave. Nor should any of the rest of you. Better stay put. Traveling when the roads are ice-packed is pure stupidity."

She was surprised by his generosity. Obviously he was a man who valued his privacy. She would have bet that he was ready to send them all on their way at the earliest opportunity. "It's a blessing you were able to rescue the Millers when you did."

"Darn lucky. The storm hadn't even settled in and they were slipping all over the road. If they'd been driving decent wheels, they might have beaten the storm to the Kansas border. Those tiny foreign cars—" He broke off as a loud shout vibrated through the house and they heard someone yell, "Yahoo!"

Hal's head jerked up. "What's going on?"

Jill laughed. "Scotty and Larry are in the den playing pool. Sounds as if somebody made a good shot."

Hal's eyebrows lifted. "I hope they're not betting. Scotty's the worst kind of a hustler."

"Uh-oh," Jill said, remembering the way the Scotsman had challenged the skier. "I think it's too late."

"I'd better see if I can keep the lid on."

Scotty waved his pool cue in greeting as they came in. Larry was staring at the table as if trying to decide on the best shot, while Kirby leaned up against the bar, grinning.

"What you doing, Scotty?" Hal demanded. "Fleecing the poor guy?"

"Just teaching him a little strategy, that's all. You know, the same way I gave you a few lessons." Scotty's eyes were bright and his face flushed.

Hal mentally groaned. He liked Scotty, but there was a competitive streak in his neighbor that made winning any contest almost a religion. He knew that the Scotsman encouraged all-night poker parties when his cabins were full of vacationers. He often bragged about getting double the rent after a game or two. Once a gambler, always a gambler, thought Hal. "Watch it, Larry. You'll leave here without your skis if you don't watch out."

"I can take care of myself," Larry snapped back, but there was a hard look in his eyes that made Jill uneasy.

"No rough stuff, fellows," Hal warned. "Let's keep everything friendly-like."

Jill decided it was time for her to leave. She slipped out the door and was surprised when Hal caught up and walked down the hall and up the stairs with her.

"Sorry about that little scene," he apologized. "Tempers get short when boredom sets in. Men need ways to let off steam. I'd rather handle a bunch of mustangs. At least you have some idea what horses are going to do."

"Have you and Scotty been friends for a long time?"

"Four or five years. He bought a run-down fishing lodge on a few acres of wooded property and has built some nice cabins for rent. A dyed-in-the-wool fisherman.''

"Does he have a family?''

Hal shook his head. "Lost a wife and kid in some kind of tragedy. Doesn't talk much about it.''

For some reason his tone made her think about the dead man in the car. "Did you call the sheriff's office before the phones went out?''

"I tried but couldn't get through.''

"The sheriff should be out looking for whoever shot him.''

"Who'd be out on the highway shooting people in weather like this?''

She'd been asking herself the same question. "What do you think happened?''

"My guess is, the guy turned coward because he thought he was going to freeze to death. Some people are like that. They'll throw in the towel without a fight.''

Jill frowned. She hadn't seen a gun, but then she hadn't been looking for one. One glance at the dead man had been enough to send her fleeing from the car.

As they reached the top of the stairs, Kirby came out of the Millers' bedroom, carrying an empty breakfast tray and soiled towels. He growled something about the damn place turning into a Holiday Inn.

"Just pretend you're back in the Navy, Kirby,'' Hal chided with a grin.

Jill was more sympathetic. She knew that cooking and cleaning for three bachelors was a lot different than keeping up with five additional, unexpected guests. "I'd be glad to help, Kirby. Just make me a list and I'll give you a hand.''

"Well, now, that's mighty nice, Jill.'' His mouth softened as he looked at her. "I'd be a fool to turn down an offer like that."

"Forget it, Kirby," Hal told him with a friendly slap on his shoulder. "She's not here to play house with you. You recruit Scotty and that Larry fellow if you need some extra hands. And Zack's going to need help shoveling paths as soon as the wind settles."

"Don't be thinking I'm going to do Zack's work and mine, too!" he spat, his Adam's apple bobbing angrily in his thin neck. "He can darn well help out with dishes and mopping floors. And if Jill wants to help me, she can!"

"Back off, Kirby," Hal told him with a smile that didn't reach his eyes.

"Why? So the boss has a free hand?"

Hal's jaw tightened. "Careful, Kirby. Don't be shooting your mouth off."

The cook shrugged his narrow shoulders. "I only call 'em like I see 'em."

"Then you'd better make sure your vision's twenty-twenty."

Kirby gave a short laugh that had no mirth in it. "Right, boss." He pushed past them without another look at Jill.

"Kirby has had his problems," Hal said quickly by way of explanation. "He's proud of being a Navy man, but I think he's carrying some scars, and I don't mean physical ones. He hasn't been successful with women, I know that, and given the accepted reputation of sailors, he must have some pretty deep ego problems. But he's a good cook and he's been with me longer than most of the fly-by-night guys I've had around here."

She remembered how Kirby had massaged her icy feet

and the uncomfortable feeling that his expression had triggered. "He seems kind of lonely."

"Don't be thinking Kirby's some kind of wounded bird you can fix with a pretty smile and a soft hand," he warned Jill. "Keep your distance or all hell might break loose."

"Don't worry. I have no intention of creating an incident of any kind." Men! Was there something about a blizzard that raised their testosterone level? Jill wondered, remembering the scene at breakfast.

Sue Miller was sitting on the edge of her bed in a bathrobe, her fair hair brushed and her eyes clear and bright. With the resilience of youth, she had bounced back from the tired, frightened young woman of yesterday. Her young husband stood by her, looking rejuvenated himself.

"No need to ask you how you're feeling, Sue," Jill said with a laugh. "You look super."

"I feel super." She gave Hal a broad smile. "I can't thank you enough, Mr. Haverly, for all you've done for us. Gary and I won't forget your kindness." She patted her fat tummy. "And neither will Junior or Susie. I guess we'll be on our way later today."

"Have you looked outside?" Hal waved toward the windows, which were framed by heavy green drapes. "The wind has lessened, but there's still enough snow flying around out there to make for zero visibility."

"But Gary said the weatherman reported that the storm was moving slowly out of the region."

"That doesn't mean a darn thing. There's enough punch left in the storm to keep us socked in for another twenty-four hours, at least. And after that, it'll take time to dig out. If you're thinking of leaving before tomorrow or the day after, forget it."

At Sue's crestfallen face, Jill said quickly, "Now that you're feeling well enough to move around, the time will pass more quickly."

"You don't have to eat here in your room," Hal told them. "We just thought trays would work better when you were tired."

"Frankly, I'd appreciate another woman's company downstairs," Jill said. *Would I ever!* "And I know you'd enjoy seeing more of this lovely old house. I bet Hal can tell you some wonderful stories about this place."

Sue was all in favor. "Oh, we'd love to hear them, wouldn't we, Gary?"

"Sure thing."

Hal's eyes twinkled. "You might find a few interesting characters in the Haverly genealogy."

"Like Bat Masterson or Buffalo Bill?" Gary asked eagerly. His boyish face was flushed and animated.

"Sorry." Hal laughed. "None as colorful as that. At least none that we brag about. It was my grandfather that came West when he was a young man looking for adventure. He never intended to settle down in Colorado, but the Rocky Mountains got in his blood. I guess he passed the addiction down to my father and me. Anyway, if you like looking at fine horse pictures, I've got plenty of them," he said, rather sheepishly.

He'd never admitted it, but Jill suspected he was delighted to have a chance to show off his love of horses. No wonder Randy had been caught up in his spell, Jill thought. The way enthusiasm radiated from him, Hal Haverly could make a horse-lover out of anyone.

After he'd gone, Jill suggested that Sue move to one of the easy chairs while she changed the bedding. "Be back in a minute," Jill told her and went down the hall looking for a linen closet. She was about to give up when she checked the hall bathroom and found a cupboard that held an odd assortment of towels, pillowcases and sheets. None of the linens were new, and Jill suspected that Hal hadn't replenished the supply for a long time. When she peeked in a box at the back of a shelf, she was surprised to find several pairs of lovely embroidered pillowcases that appeared never to have been used.

She was debating whether she should make use of them when Scotty walked by the open door, then stopped and poked his head in. "Looking for something?" he asked.

"Clean bedding," she said quickly.

"Did you find some?"

"Yes." Impulsively, she held out the fancy pillowcases so he could see them. "I was trying to decide whether I should take these or not. They don't look used. Someone put a lot of work into them."

"Probably Hal's mom or Carrie."

"Carrie?"

"Hal's first and only love."

First and only love. The casual words hit Jill with a charge she hadn't expected. Well, there was the answer to one of her questions. There had been a woman in his life. "Oh?" Jill responded in a questioning way, hoping Scotty would be forthcoming with more information to satisfy her blatant curiosity.

"A childhood sweetheart. Guess everybody knew from the time they were in grade school that they were going to get married."

"And did they?"

"Nope." Scotty smiled as if enjoying her obvious curiosity.

"What happened?"

"It didn't work out. From what I gather, Carrie went off to the big city and never came back. Made a true woman-scorner out of Hal, she did. A few nice gals have tried to change his mind, but without any luck. Once burned, forever wary, as the saying goes."

"Well, that partly explains his guarded attitude," Jill said thoughtfully.

Scotty eyed Jill for a long moment. "You haven't got a chance in hell of hooking up with him, you know."

Jill's indignation instantly flared. "What makes you think I'm the least bit interested in 'hooking up with him,' as you put it?"

"Whoa! Don't get your dander up. I just thought a widow with a boy to raise would be more than interested in an eligible, good-looking man like Hal."

"For your information, I've done very well looking out for myself and my son for eight years, and I intend to continue to do so. On my own," she added with emphasis.

"I admire you for that," Scotty said in a patronizing tone that made her even more furious. She couldn't help but wonder if Mr. Hal Haverly had the same misconception—that she was on the prowl for a male provider.

She hastily put the fancy pillowcases back in the box, took out some sheets and worn pillowcases, shut the linen-closet door and brushed by Scotty with a curt, "Excuse me."

With energy fueled by inward seething, she made up the Millers' bed and straightened up the room. Scotty's warning about trying to "hook up" with the rancher made her sizzle. Why was it that a widow was fair game for every snide remark about being on the hunt for another man? That kind of pioneer necessity had gone out with the covered wagon. Women weren't helpless chattels anymore. They could fend for themselves and their children. Scotty's crude warning not to consider Hal a prospective husband was like a lighted flare against a bundle of firecrackers. Men! Who needed them? As far as she was concerned, the sexist attitude of all the men in the house left plenty to be desired.

Sue said she'd like to go downstairs after she took a nap, and Jill agreed. "Good idea. I think I'll do the same. I'll be across the hall when you're ready."

Jill stretched out on the bed, but her thoughts were too busy for napping. *His one and only love.* The phrase kept repeating itself despite her efforts to put it aside as unimportant. Hal Haverly's past was no concern of hers. None at all. Interesting, though. He'd been in love and planned to marry his long-standing sweetheart. He must have been deeply wounded when this Carrie decided to desert the ranch and him.

Jill felt a pang of compassion for him. She knew how hard it was to turn away from dreams of a future that was never going to happen. From what Scotty had said, more than one woman had tried to change his mind about remaining single. He obviously had chosen a solitary life. Maybe he was afraid to let any female get that close to him again. She wondered what the woman who had stolen his heart forever had been like.

About three o'clock, Gary tapped at her door. "Sue's up and dressed, ready to go."

"Good."

"Are you sure it's all right for us to look around?" Sue asked anxiously as they prepared to go downstairs. "I don't think Mr Haverly likes the idea of all us being here. He seems rather—"

"Distant?" Jill finished with a faint smile.

"Well, kinda," she admitted.

"How can you say that?" Gary said indignantly. "Look at what the man's done for us. Brought us in from the storm. Given us a guest room and everything we need."

"I think it's so sad." Sue sighed. "Him living here all alone. A good-looking man like that."

Gary laughed. "My wife is an incurable romantic."

"I just want everyone to be as happy as I am."

Gary leaned down and kissed her. "Come on, sweetheart, let's get some exercise." He put his arm around his wife as she got clumsily to her feet.

The three of them walked slowly down the stairs. When they reached the front hall, Jill heard Hal's voice above the thud of pool balls in the den. She wondered if he was trying to keep Larry from losing to Scotty by taking him on himself.

"Shall we take a peek at the living room?" she asked, not above using the opportunity to satisfy her own curiosity. A glimpse through the doorway invited a closer look at Indian rugs and western paintings, and she wondered if the room's furnishings would reveal any hidden facets of their host's character.

Even though there was a chill in the large room and all the windows were coated with snow, there was the promise of warmth from huge logs laid in a stone fireplace dominating one wall. Jill could imagine a roaring fire sending dancing light on golden knotty pine walls and reaching upward to the high, peaked ceiling. Furniture that was clearly old and very valuable included deep cushioned chairs, game tables, high-backed sofas and several breakfronts filled with exquisite earthenware pottery. Some pieces looked old and others quite contemporary.

Jill was intrigued by a collection of arrowheads

mounted in a shadow frame and, next to them, a pair of silver spurs hanging on the wall. She wondered if the spurs had belonged to his father or grandfather. An old long-necked bottle holding a bouquet of golden wheat had been placed on a small table next to a delicate porcelain candy dish. A variety of large and small pictures, mostly watercolor mountain scenes, were signed M. Haverly. Jill would have bet "M" was Hal's mother. The past and the present mingled in a harmonious way she'd never seen before.

Sue's interest was fleeting and when Gary suggested they move on to the kitchen, his wife readily agreed. Jill told them to go ahead. "I'll catch up with you."

She wanted to stay a moment, walk quietly around the room, and enjoy the ambience of this house that had been built to last, to survive man and nature, and to enrich the lives of those who lived under its roof. This sense of belonging to a place and other people was foreign to her. The loving couple who had adopted her as an infant had been city people, and even as a child her life had been spent in modern, efficient dwellings, crisp and economical. After she married, home became a series of apartments, some nicely furnished, offering the amenities of a swimming pool and exercise room, but everything about them had been transitory, like the tenants who lived there.

As Jill stood in the center of the room, she felt the solid permanence of the house, and she was jealous of a sense of belonging that she'd never felt. Her adoptive parents couldn't have been more loving, but she'd missed having the kind of family roots that were so apparent in this house. She wondered if Hal knew how lucky he was and how rich he was in all the things that mattered.

She carefully made her way around the room and was admiring a colorful kachina doll when she heard approaching footsteps. She turned around as Zack came into the room.

"Oh, hello," she said, trying not to sound disappointed. On some vague level, she'd wanted it to be Hal. There was some nebulous desire to share this moment with him.

The ranch hand wore a studded denim vest over a western shirt and jeans, and a huge silver buckle accented his waist. He was bare-headed, and his rather long dark hair hung on his neck and drifted forward on his cheeks. The sun had put creases around his eyes, and his complexion was ruddy from wind and weather.

"Whatcha doing?" There was a slight swagger to his walk as he came over to her.

"Just looking around."

"Not much to see. But I reckon you're pretty bored, shut up like this." He hooked a thumb over his belt. "You must be plenty busy at that place where you work. People coming and going all the time. Is that fellow, Slade, an easy man to work for? Better than your job at that airport in California?"

Jill wasn't about to discuss her boss or her job. "How'd you know I worked at an airport?"

"Rampart's a small town. Especially where a pretty gal is concerned. Word gets around with the buzz of a bumblebee. I didn't know you were one of them mountain rescue people."

"When there's an emergency, I act as a kind of dispatcher."

"Some of the guys in the local bar were talking about it. Sounds a heap more exciting than hanging around this place all the time. I just might sign up as a volunteer.

Whatcha think?'' His dark eyebrows rose questioningly. He stood so close to her that she fought a sensation of being trapped by his sturdy hips and broad chest.

"We can always use another dedicated volunteer," she said, moving slightly away. "But there's a lot of training and time involved. It's like another job."

"Reckon, I could handle that. Been punching cows all my life. Same old thing, day in and day out. Gets durn old after a while. A man needs excitement in his life. I'm thinkin' a woman does, too. You know what I mean?"

She forced a laugh. "I've had enough excitement in my life. The duller the better."

"Don't seem likely, not a gal like you," he argued. "Not by a long shot. Just the way you move and talk tells me you like adventure. I even wrote a song about you last night."

She was too surprised to say anything. Why would this good-looking cowboy be writing songs to a widow with an adolescent son? Even though their ages were probably not that far apart, she felt years older. Her disbelief must have shown in her expression.

"Yep. Got all the lyrics, but still working on the chords. I'll play my guitar and sing it for you when I'm finished. Maybe tonight. Would you like to hear it?"

What could she say? "That…that would be nice," she stammered. "But I may be busy. I have to stay close to the Millers. Now, if you'll excuse me, I need to catch up with them and make sure that Sue doesn't overdo."

"That gal's too durn young to be having a baby," he said flatly as they walked across the large room "My ma had eight kids. I was the oldest. I had to grow up fast, you know what I mean? Ma just didn't have time for all of us. Can't ever remember having her to myself.

Your son is lucky. Real lucky. I seen the way you love him when you came to the ranch after him those few times.''

A wistful edge to his words made her ask, ''Is your mother still alive?''

He shook his head. ''Nope, that's why I left. I figured it was time. Drifting around is kinda lonely sometimes. But I've made up my mind. Going to get something for myself. I figure it's about time, you know what I mean?''

The intensity of the question as he searched her face made her uneasy. ''I'm not sure. I guess it depends upon what you want.''

''And whether you have the guts to go after it,'' he added bluntly.

With relief, she left him in the den with Larry, Kirby, and Scotty, who were getting up a poker game. Then she joined Sue and Gary in the kitchen. Hal was with the young couple, and Jill was surprised to see that the three of them were looking through some photo albums that Hal had spread out on the table.

He leaned over Gary's shoulder, pointing to particular photographs. ''Appaloosa horses. Great mounts for western riding. Turn a calf on a dime. And beautiful, don't you think? All those different-colored markings.''

Jill smiled to herself as he talked about the spotted horses. There was so much pride in Hal's voice, you'd have thought the rancher was showing off his kids.

Sue motioned to a chair beside her. ''Come join us, Jill,'' she invited, handing Jill one of the photo albums.

As Jill flipped through it, she chided herself for deliberately hoping to find a picture of a young woman that might be Carrie. Her curiosity was disappointed. All the albums were horses, men and scenery. If there were any photo albums of a personal nature, Hal had not offered them for viewing.

When Sue and Gary left the kitchen to go back upstairs, Hal drew Jill aside. "I think there are some baby things still stored in the attic. A cradle and such. Do you think the Millers would take it amiss if I offered some of the things to them?"

"Not at all. I think they'd be delighted."

"Shall we take a look? See what we can find?"

His eager invitation surprised her. She laughed and said, "Sure."

"We'll take the back stairs." He motioned to a closed door at one end of the kitchen. He grabbed her hand in a boyish fashion as they mounted a narrow staircase that led past the second floor and upward to the attic level. A dim wall light sent their shadows upward, and in the narrow confines of the staircase, she was terribly aware of his firm, muscular stride.

"Sorry about the dust," he apologized. "I forgot that these steps haven't been swept for a long time. My brothers and I used to use this stairway all the time, especially when we played hide-and-seek." He laughed at the memory. "The attic was a favorite place of ours. We'd disappear for hours up here, pretending it was everything from a cave to a castle. We had a good time, all three of us ornery as the devil. I'm afraid we gave my mother plenty of gray hairs."

Her soft warm body brushing against his in the stairway triggered a closeness she hadn't felt for a long time. She could tell he felt at ease talking about his family, which was puzzling, since he hadn't struck her as the type of man to open up to anyone.

As he talked, Jill envied his childhood memories. As an adopted only child, she'd missed out on sibling fun, and the wonderful mad pace of family living. "You have two brothers? Where are they?"

"One's a dentist in St. Louis, and the other has a small business in Idaho."

"You're the only one who stayed on the ranch."

"Yes," he said shortly and didn't elaborate. "Stay here," he ordered when they paused to open the door to the attic. "I'll turn on a light."

Two windows, one at each end of the long room, were caked with snow, and she couldn't see anything but light and dark shadows until he pulled a chain on a light hanging from an open rafter. As bright light flooded the attic, she gasped at the amount of boxes and stacks of everything imaginable reaching from wall to wall. Jill was overwhelmed by the accumulation, which must have spanned more than one lifetime. She'd never seen anything like it, and could have spent hours rummaging through all kinds of things that undoubtedly qualified as antiques.

"Kind of a mess," he granted as he looked around. "I think I remember seeing the cradle back there." He motioned toward one end of the room. "Come on, let's see what we can find." Once again he took her hand as he led the way through a maze of furniture, boxes, barrels, trunks and chests.

"There it is." Hal pushed a couple of boxes out of the way, reached back in a corner and brought out the biggest cradle she'd ever seen. She was positive that even a one-year-old could have slept comfortably in it. Beautifully crafted and mounted on a platform, the bed swung easily as Hal gave it a slight push. "What do you think?"

"I think it's beautiful."

"My dad made it. Big enough for twins, he always

told mom." Hal chuckled. "There were twins in his family way back, and I think he always kept hoping."

"Are you sure you want to give it away?"

Even in the dim light, she saw the shadow that crossed his face. "It's not doing anybody any good up here. No use holding on to it."

Jill wanted to argue that there might come a time when he would regret having given it away, but she held her tongue. It was his life. He had the right to live it the way he wanted, but it was a shame, a darn shame. She'd never seen anyone better with kids.

He picked up the cradle, and she started to follow him as he carried it back to the attic door, but some paintings piled on a chest caught her eye. They were in a style similar to the ones in the living room. As he set down the cradle and came back to her side, she asked, "Is M. Haverly your mother?"

"Yes. Maribelle Haverly. Mom loved to draw and paint. I can remember her sitting out in the meadow, spending hours drawing some fool bird," he said with obvious affection. "She made the whole family go on nature walks all over these hills. I think she painted every Rocky Mountain wildflower that ever bloomed." His voice softened. "It's been a long time since I thought about those family outings."

"You were blessed to have a mother, father and brothers to share your youth."

He nodded. "I guess I didn't realize it at the time."

"Some of us weren't so lucky," she said in a strained voice, and he was startled by a sudden swelling of tears at the corner of her eyes. As she bent her head to hide her face from him, he saw her breasts rise and fall with quickened breath. "I'm sorry," she said and tried to brush by him, but he stopped her.

"What is it? What did I do or say to make you cry?"

She shook her head. "It's not you."

"Then what?" He asked anxiously as he gently brushed a tear from her cheek.

"Bad memories of growing up alone, I guess."

"Want to tell me about it?"

The sincere invitation in his voice changed a ready "no" into "Yes, I think I would."

They sat down on a nearby trunk and, impulsively, he put a comforting arm around her shoulders. He was surprised how natural it felt sitting close beside her in a dusty old attic, sharing an intimacy that came upon them unaware.

She told him that she'd never had a sense of having a real family while growing up. "When I was born I was put up for adoption. My parents—the couple who adopted me—were good to me but they were older. They didn't know what to do with a lonely little girl who never felt like she belonged. I hated Sundays and holidays because there never was anyone to share the fun. The only home I knew was a small, close apartment with no yard." She let her gaze rove around the cluttered attic. "Nothing like this wonderful house for playing hide-and-seek."

He couldn't imagine living any place where there wasn't a lot of space and a lot of animals. He wondered, too, what it would've been like not knowing who had given birth to you. As she leaned back in the cradle of his arm, he was suddenly aware that if she turned her head and looked up at him, those devastating eyes would sweep away every ounce of willpower. And if she closed her eyes and offered her lips, he was sure he would kiss her.

The intimacy growing between them was charged, and

he didn't know how to handle it. Slipping his arm around her had seemed a natural thing to do in her distress, but offering avuncular comfort was one thing, giving in to a bewildering awareness of sudden desire was another. What could he say to defuse the situation? He was no good at mouthing empty platitudes. He'd never felt adequate when it came to putting his own feelings into words. He was still trying to decide what to do or say when she eased away from his embrace and stood up.

"Did you want to look for some other baby things?" Her voice was still husky, but her eyes were clear and steady as she looked at him.

"Maybe later." He was at once disappointed and relieved that she had put some distance between them.

They made their way to the door where he'd left the impressive cradle. When she looked down at it, a faint smile crossed her lips. "I think we've forgotten something."

"What?"

"There'll never be room in the Millers' car for it."

"I'd completely forgotten they were driving one of those dinky foreign models. I guess you're right. They won't have room to take it," he agreed, and was surprised at the flood of relief that went through him.

THE REST OF THE AFTERNOON passed quickly for Jill. She stayed with Sue and Gary in their room until dinnertime, then they all came downstairs together. Once again, they ate in the dining room. Kirby served a hearty man's stew that had tender vegetables swimming in smooth rich gravy, slices of fresh sourdough bread and rich carrot cake for dessert.

Conversation around the table was free and easy, and Jill thoroughly enjoyed herself. Hal went all out to make everyone comfortable, and when he made a point of talk-ing with her, especially, she felt a little embarrassed about what had happened in the attic. She didn't know what made her give way like that. It must be the storm or this house that was causing her emotions to come to the surface—or maybe it was just getting to know Hal Haverly, the man her son thought the world revolved around. She wasn't sure how their relationship had moved so quickly to one that allowed for sharing per-sonal confidences, but she knew that Randy would be pleased that they'd taken steps towards being friends.

After dinner, she accompanied the Millers back up-stairs. Sue was tired, so Jill bid them an early good-night and went to her room. She could hear men's laughter floating up from downstairs. Hal had invited her to join them for a nightcap, but she had refused. She thought he looked disappointed, but it could have been her imag-ination.

Randy was on her mind as she made ready for bed. She couldn't help but worry. She longed to tell him good-night and give his slender shoulders a warm hug. He'd gotten too big for her to tuck him in the way she'd always used to, but he was still her little boy, and she missed him. A warm fullness eased into the corners of her eyes just thinking about him. As she swiped at the tears, she told herself that by tomorrow, the telephone would probably be back in order.

The latest radio report had said that the storm was moving out. Good news for Colorado, but the forecasters were predicting that Kansas was in line for its share of wind and snow. That meant the Millers could expect to drive right into the storm again as they left Colorado, and Jill felt obligated to stay until Sue was safely on her way to her parents' home.

Sighing, Jill laid down her book and was just reaching for the light when she heard the whisper of footsteps outside her locked door. Gary was supposed to call her if Sue needed her for any reason. She waited, expecting his light knock.

Nothing. Only a brooding silence.

Someone was there. She was sure of it.

The knob turned against the lock, then the soft footsteps moved away, though she couldn't tell in which direction. Maybe Hal was just making certain she had followed his orders to lock her door.

But maybe not.

And if not Hal, who?

He was glad she was keeping her door locked. It infuriated him the way the other men were looking at her. Wanting to claim her inviting body just the way he did. But she was his. He'd known it the first moment he'd seen her. He blessed the storm for bringing her to him. Watching her smile, feeling the warmth of her breath upon his face when he talked to her, and knowing that soon the waiting would be over created an exhilarating torment that he hadn't felt for a long time. He'd been patient. He knew from the moment he saw her that she was going to bring him peace at last. That first day, when he saw the way she smiled at the boy running toward her and held out her arms, his chest had ached with the need to be held close and loved like that. His thoughts sped ahead to the preparations he'd made. Soon...soon...soon.

Chapter Four

About four o'clock in the morning, Jill was awakened by a demanding knock on her door. Sitting up with a jerk, she took a few seconds to get her bearings. Then she heard a muffled voice in the hall calling her name, "Jill! Jill!"

She grabbed her short robe, shoved her feet into her slippers, and bounded across the floor. Quickly she turned the skeleton key in the lock and opened the door.

Gary stood there, his eyes rounded with worry. "It's Sue. She needs you." He grabbed Jill's arm and said loudly enough to wake everyone in the adjoining rooms, "You gotta come right away."

Jill silently groaned. "What's wrong, Gary?"

"She's having contractions."

"How long ago was the first one?" *Please, God, not yet…not yet.*

"About an hour ago. Sue thought it was just a cramp but now she's had another one."

They hurried across the hall and into the Millers' bedroom, where Sue was propped against a couple of pillows.

"Gary says you've had a pain or two?" Jill said as

she took Sue's hand. One look at the young woman's frightened face tightened Jill's own chest.

Sue nodded. "Contractions."

"Are you sure they were contractions and not something else? Just a stomach pain?" Jill asked hopefully.

"I've never felt anything like this before. Pain all around my middle, like giant hands squeezing me in two."

Good description, thought Jill. She brushed back damp hair from Sue's sweaty forehead. "How many have you had, Sue?"

"Just a couple." Her voice trembled. "Do you think I'm going to deliver now?"

"Could just be false labor," Jill said in as much of an upbeat tone as she could manage.

"She can't have the baby now." Gary's voice rose in panic. "Do something."

"Take it easy, Gary," Jill said firmly.

"We have to do something. Call a doctor. Get to a hospital."

"Calm down!" Jill's tone was sharper. This was no time for new-father hysterics.

"How can I? My wife needs help."

"You're not doing her any good flying off in all directions. It's probably a false alarm. Sometimes these things happen when a woman gets close to delivery."

"Really?" That possibility held him for a brief minute. "Are you sure?"

"It's going to be all right." Sue gave her husband a wan smile.

Hal stuck his head in the bedroom door. "Is everything all right?" His hair was mussed from sleep, and he'd thrown on a plaid flannel shirt that was buttoned halfway down to a faded pair of jeans. No shoes, only socks on his feet.

"Sue's having contractions," Gary blurted out.

Hal's eyes narrowed as they took in Sue's ashen face and then fixed on Jill. All she could do was nod and follow him out into the hall.

"What's happening?" he asked in a worried whisper. "Is she going into labor?" The furrows in his forehead deepened, and the lines round his mouth were every bit as tight as Gary's.

"I don't know. She's had a couple of contractions."

He groaned. "The baby's coming now...today?"

"Maybe not," Jill answered evenly, despite building worries and a knot in her own stomach. "I was just telling Gary that sometimes this happens in false labor. Lots of women head for the hospital thinking they're going to have a baby, only to have to go back home and wait for another two weeks."

"Do you think that's what it is?"

Jill decided to be honest. "I haven't a clue. She's close enough to her due date for anything to happen. Maybe the pains will peter out. Maybe not. She could be starting delivery."

"But it could be false labor?" he insisted as if he wasn't willing to even consider any other option.

She nodded. "We should know in a few hours. The contractions will get harder and closer together if this is the real thing. And if she's going into labor..." her voice faltered. "If she's going into labor, I don't know what we're going to do."

Color drained away from his face, then he seemed to catch himself. "I guess there's nothing to do but wait and see. And then we'll just have to deal with the situation as best we can," he said in a firm, assured tone.

She nodded but she had little confidence that her best would be good enough. They both knew she had come to the ranch to be a companion to the pregnant young woman, nothing more. She certainly wasn't qualified to act as midwife or anything close to it. She was only here because Hal had failed to get anyone else to help. Another woman's presence in the house was better than none at all—but not much better, she thought, feeling sickening quivers in the pit of her stomach.

"I'm glad you're here, Jill," he said, his grateful eyes caressing her face. "Damn glad."

"This is more than I can handle," she said quickly. "Just because I've had a baby myself doesn't qualify me to deliver one. There's no way I can deal with this." Her helplessness exploded as fury. "We need medical help! Pure and simple! Don't you understand?"

"Easy, easy," he soothed. He knew that she was scared to death. And the way things were going, so was he. "We'll just have to take things as they come, won't we? As you say, this could be a false alarm."

She swallowed hard, and gave him a forced smile. "Pray that it is." Both of them took a deep breath as they returned to the room.

"She can't have the baby now. It's not time. It's not time." Gary kept saying the same thing over and over as if constant repetition would make it so.

Hal put a steadying hand on the young man's shoulder. "Don't be running to meet trouble before it gets here, Gary. Let's get a weather forecast. Maybe the storm's passed over sooner than predicted. Might start clearing today."

"But what if it doesn't?" Gary asked in a frightened voice.

"Go with Hal, Gary. Better for Sue to rest as much

as possible." *And better for you to keep out of the way,* Jill added mentally. Dealing with an expectant father's uncontrollable anxiety along with everything else was more than she could handle at the moment.

"We'd best make ourselves scarce for a bit." Hal escorted him to the door. "Let's check and see if they've got the phones working."

Sudden hope buoyed Jill. What a blessing that would be. Any communication with somebody knowledgeable would be a godsend. Jill gave Hal a grateful look as he took Gary by the arm. He winked back and gave her a thumbs-up.

Hal knew that Gary was only half listening to his reassuring words as they made their way through the silent house to the kitchen. He went directly to the phone. As he had expected, it was still dead.

Damn, he silently swore and quickly turned on a portable radio. A weather forecaster repeated what he already knew—the worst blizzard in a century had paralyzed Colorado and Wyoming. The bad news was that the storm had curved back on itself and was no longer moving out of the region. There had been little change in the last twenty-four hours, with high winds and snow continuing to fall, shutting down all roads, disrupting telephone service, and halting all travel, including air traffic in and out of the region.

Gary's youthful face was drawn and pale as he sat listlessly at the table and rested his head in his hands. Hal searched for something positive to say but came up short. He'd never been one for spouting empty promises. There was no way to bring in competent medical help for his wife. The deepening fright in Jill's honey-brown eyes was warning enough about what lay ahead. And with the telephone wires down, they were on their own—one woman and five men, none of whom knew a damn thing about delivering a baby! He ran an agitated hand through his uncombed hair just as Kirby and Zack came into the kitchen.

"You looked worried, boss. We've got enough grub to last a week," Kirby assured him. "And a backup generator if the power goes off."

"Doesn't look like we'll be doing chores," Zack said with undisguised pleasure. "No use trying to dig out the drifts until the snow stops falling."

Hal's thoughts momentarily settled on the crisis the storm was creating for him personally. A prolonged snowfall would take its toll on his animals. He knew there was little more he could do. He'd made certain there was feed and water in the barn for the horses. As best he could, he had provided for the livestock in the pastures and corral. He didn't like the helpless feeling that came over him. Buried under snowdrifts, the whole ranch operation was at a standstill. If this blasted storm didn't lift soon, they might be a week digging out.

Raising his head from his hands, Gary said in a choked voice, "My wife's having her baby."

"What?" both Zack and Kirby said together.

"We don't know that," Hal said, giving Gary a reassuring smile. "Let's not jump any creeks until we have to. Jill says that lots of women go through something like this."

"Sue's having pains," Gary insisted. "Contractions."

"Uh-oh!" Zack said, knowingly. "She's in labor, all right. A few of them and wham, off to the hospital. In a few hours, another kid." His mouth hardened with the memory. "That's the way it always went with my mom."

Kirby shrugged. "You couldn't prove it by me. I stay

clear of that kind of stuff, but I always thought women knew how to take care of these things themselves.''

"Not always. Sometimes—'' Zack started to elaborate.

"Why don't you fix us some breakfast, Kirby,'' Hal said smoothly, cutting Zack off. He didn't see any value in idle chatter adding to Gary's anxiety. The young man was already tied up in knots.

When Scotty and Larry joined them a few minutes later, Gary dumped his worries on them. Neither the skier nor the Scotsman had much to say, but everyone seemed on edge and prickly. Hal was aware of the growing tension as a heavy silence settled on his snowbound guests.

When Jill came down into the kitchen a short time later, he didn't need to ask whether Sue's contractions had let up. Her tense expression was answer enough. She had dressed, exchanging her pajamas for a pair of jeans and a multicolored ski sweater, but her long hair was still tangled from the night's sleep, and the anxious lines in her face hadn't eased. He wanted to put his arm around her again, and assure her that everything would be all right. Instead, he had to tell that the phone was still out and repeat what the weatherman had said.

"How's my wife?'' Gary demanded anxiously.

"The contractions are no closer together and no more intense than they were before. And that's a good sign.''

"How close?'' Zack asked.

"About forty-five minutes.''

Zack nodded. "She's in labor, all right. I was telling them about my ma. She dropped babies easy like. Nature takes care of these things,'' he told Jill.

Don't I wish, she thought silently. Just the thought of

being responsible for the delivery of someone else's baby was paralyzing.

Kirby wiped his hands on his apron. "Got some biscuits in the oven, Jill. Hash brown potatoes and bacon in the skillet. And I'm about ready to scramble up a Mexican omelette. Nothing like a good breakfast to set things right."

Jill's nervous stomach instantly rejected the heavy, spicy menu, but she didn't want to hurt Kirby's feelings so she said, "I think Sue could handle tea and toast a little better." Though she knew a woman in labor shouldn't eat anything, she didn't want to alarm Gary by admitting what she knew in her gut to be true—his wife was going to have this baby...soon.

Scotty frowned. "Aren't you going to eat any breakfast? You look as if you've been up all night."

She pushed back a strand of tousled hair. There hadn't been any time to worry about her looks, but suddenly the scrutiny of five men in the kitchen made her acutely aware of her disheveled appearance.

"You kinda look like the morning after, Jill, if you know what I mean." Larry grinned knowingly.

"Like a filly rode hard and put away wet," Zack agreed.

"That's enough, fellows." Hal sent a warning look around the table. "Jill doesn't need your tomfoolery."

"No need to get riled up about a little teasing," Scotty chided Hal. "They'd didn't mean anything by it."

Jill wished that Hal had let the remarks slip by. Undoubtedly, these men had spent many hours in this kitchen, laughing, teasing, and enjoying each other's company. She didn't want to cause any friction between them.

"A cup of coffee and a couple of biscuits will be fine

for me," she quickly told Kirby. "Just put them on the tray with Sue's tea and toast." Then she turned to Gary. "I have to get back upstairs. Will you bring up the tray when it's ready?"

As she left the kitchen, Hal fell into step beside her and walked with her to the foot of the stairs. "Is there anything else you need?"

"Not at the moment." She quelled a nervous quiver trailing up her spine. "But, frankly, I don't know what to do if she goes into hard labor."

"My birthin' experience is limited to the barn. I've pulled a couple of foals when a filly was in trouble and helped several newborn calves into the world, but animals have an instinct about these things. They pretty much do what has to be done." At her fallen expression, he added quickly, "But I think I could follow directions if someone told me what to do." He raised a questioning eyebrow.

"Don't look at me. As I said before, having a baby doesn't qualify me to deliver one. I've never even seen puppies born. And what if Sue gets into trouble?" Her lower lip trembled in spite of her determination to keep it steady. "There must be some way that we can get her medical attention."

"Like digging out twenty-five miles of highway in a blinding blizzard?" He shook his head. "Look, if there was any chance I could reach Dr. Evanston or anybody else and drag them back here, I'd give it a try. But, just now, I can't see any way to get help." He touched her arm. "But things could change. And this could still turn out to be a false alarm." His voice rose hopefully.

"You want the truth? The baby's coming."

"How soon?"

"I don't know. But does a few hours one way or the

other matter? From what you've said, there's no hope of the situation improving fast enough to get medical help. And I don't know what to do. Having life and death in my hands is a little more than I can handle.'' Unbidden tears sprang into her eyes.

He hadn't intended to touch her, but when she lowered her head and her slim shoulders trembled, his arms instinctively went around her. She leaned against him the way she had in the attic, and once more he felt a surge of emotion from her nearness. As her sweet length pressed against his thighs and chest, unbidden desire sent a spiral of heat surging through him. The scent and feel of her utterly seductive femininity overwhelmed him. Unconsciously, he tightened his embrace, and let his hands slip down the inviting curve of her back and waist. As she leaned into him, she raised questioning eyes and he knew that she was experiencing the same unbidden flare of passion.

He reluctantly dropped his arms and she moved back. For a split second, neither of them said anything, then, to hide his own embarrassment, he said as casually as his uneven breath would allow, ''Emergencies have a way of bringing out unexpected feelings.''

''Yes,'' she agreed in a thick voice. His embrace had ignited latent desires that flared under his touch, and she hadn't meant to give way like that. Her own body had betrayed her. For a brief moment in his arms, she'd felt an emotional surrender and a dangerous longing. Her heart was still leaping around and her breath was short. The physical contact had shaken her more deeply than she was willing to admit. But at the moment, she wasn't up to handling any more confusion. There were more important things to think about than her bewildering feelings.

"I'd better get back upstairs." She avoided his eyes, as she turned away and hurried up the stairs. Pausing outside the Millers' bedroom, she took a minute to collect herself. Once the emergency was over, her sensible self would return. Often people behaved irrationally under pressure but once normalcy returned, so did common sense. Having delivered this mental lecture, she felt back in control. Bracing herself, she went into the room and saw with relief that Sue had fallen asleep.

Jill glanced at her watch. Not quite an hour had gone by. If the contractions were settling into a pattern, the next one would come in about ten minutes. Even as the thought passed through Jill's mind, Sue groaned and opened her eyes with a startled expression. "Oh, no."

Jill bent over her. "Another contraction?" she asked anxiously.

Sue shook her head.

Good, Jill thought with relief. The contractions weren't coming closer together. Maybe there was hope after all. "What is it then?"

Sue swallowed hard. "My water broke."

Jill silently groaned. She knew what that meant. All hope of false labor pains was instantly wiped out with this news. She must have blanched, because Sue gave a frightened sob when she saw Jill's expression. "The baby's coming, isn't it?"

Jill met her anxious eyes with as much reassurance as she could and explained what had happened. "You're in labor, all right. Your baby has moved low enough for its head to put enough pressure on the bag of water to break it."

"I'm going to have the baby? Now? Today?"

Jill nodded.

"How soon?"

"All babies come in their own sweet time," Jill said as lightly as she could while praying under breath, *Dear God in heaven, what'll I do now?*

"Well, I guess this is it, then," Sue whispered in a choked voice. "We'll be needing some of the baby things we packed in one of our suitcases. I'm glad Mr. Haverly insisted on bringing everything from our car." She nodded toward some cheap luggage sitting in the corner. "We should have bought more things, but I'd planned to go shopping with Mother. She said she would see to everything when we got home. Mother said she'd be with me when..." Sue's voice suddenly broke. In an instant, she dissolved from a married woman into a young girl crying for her mother.

Jill put her arms around her, searching for some reassuring words, when they heard footsteps in the hall and Gary strode into the room with the breakfast tray. "Here you go, sweetheart, tea and toast."

Sue's eyes spilled over with tears.

"What's the matter?" He froze.

"The baby's coming. My water broke."

Gary's bravado instantly disappeared. "Oh, my God."

Jill reached out and took the tray from him before he dropped it. Stunned, Gary sat down on the edge of the bed and took his wife in his arms. "It's all right, honey. It's all right. Oh, my God!"

Jill turned away from the distraught young couple and walked over to a window. Now that the birth was inevitable, she seemed unable to organize her thoughts. She should be planning ahead. Deciding about what should be done. But her mind had shut down. As she stood there, her eyes narrowed against the brightness outside. Ice crystals created an intricate web on the windowpane and a huge cottonwood tree growing near the house was only darkly visible, its branches a dim tracery against the blowing snow.

Jill shivered and hugged herself, but the chill prickling of her skin had nothing to do with the wintry scene outside. *The baby was coming.* No doubt Sue was dilated enough for the baby's head to be engaged. She remembered her own delivery. She'd awakened in the middle of the night with a soaked bed, and Randy had been born about nine hours later. A quick delivery, they had told her, but the labor had seemed anything but quick, even though she'd been in a Los Angeles hospital with the best of care.

She remembered a flurry of nurses poking her and reading monitors. Her doctor, a young man who always wore outlandish ties, periodically breezed in and out of her room. Once when he had his stethoscope on her rounded tummy, he laughed and told her, "Your little one has the hiccups." How lucky she had been. She'd had all the care in the world and a wonderful healthy son to show for it.

"Jill... Jill..." Gary's strained voice brought her out of her reverie. "Sue's having another contraction."

Jill glanced at her watch. Right on schedule.

"It's a little harder than the other ones." Sue gasped as Gary stepped back from the bed and let Jill take his wife's hand.

When the contraction had eased and Sue was limp with relief, Jill turned to Gary. "Your wife needs her bed changed and a fresh gown. There are linens in the bathroom closet. Will you see to it? I'll be back in a minute." She bounded out the door and ran smack into Hal, who was just about to turn into the room.

"Whoa! I was just coming to check on things."

She pulled him down the hall a few steps, lowered her voice and told him what had happened. "It's coming. The baby's head must be engaged, getting ready for delivery. Even though Sue's a large girl, there's no telling how long a first labor will be. It's possible that we could get somebody here in time for the delivery if we could reach them in the next few hours."

"But we can't. We have no idea when the phone lines will be up again and—" He stopped short, as if a thought had hit him with a sudden jolt.

"What?" she asked anxiously. "What is it? What are you thinking?"

"Scotty!" His face brightened. "I think he has a cellular phone in his pickup. We can use it to call out. Even if help can't get here, someone can tell us what to do."

As he saw an instant glow radiating in her face and her eyes luminous with sudden hope, he impulsively leaned over and kissed her hairline. "We may be okay after all. Hang in there." She smiled at him as if he'd just handed her the biggest bouquet of roses in the world, and he felt ten feet tall.

Hurrying back downstairs, he took the steps two at a time, swung around the newel post and strode into the kitchen, shouting, "Scotty, did you drive your pickup over here?"

The ruddy-faced fisherman had just thrown a couple of logs on the fire and was busy poking at the embers. "Sure did. Why?"

"You still got that cellular phone?"

"Yeah, why?"

Hal remembered how he teased the Scotsman about spending money on something that kept him informed of problems at his resort, when he could have been blissfully ignorant of them while he was away from the place.

Now he was damn grateful. "Where's your truck parked?"

"A few hundred feet down your driveway. I had to abandon it before I made it to the house. It stalled and the snow was piled too high to drive any closer. I hiked the rest of the way."

"Well, grab a shovel. You, too, Zack. We've got some digging to do. The stork's moving in faster than we expected. We'll have to get your phone, Scotty, bring it back to the house and keep in touch with medical help as we need it."

Scotty brushed back a shock of reddish hair. "Can't do it."

"Why not?" he demanded impatiently. "We dig a path out to the pickup. Get the phone. Bring it back to the house—"

Scotty interrupted him. "The phone's power base is the car's battery. I didn't buy the kind you can carry around with you. Sorry. You'll have to transmit from the truck. Too bad. I can see what you were thinking."

Hal's hopes faded for minute-by-minute medical assistance as the delivery progressed, but all was not lost. "All right, we'll have to make the best of it. Maybe we can get the pickup into the garage, so the phone will be more accessible. We can still keep in contact and get the necessary instructions for delivering the baby." He mentally cursed himself for letting the battery on his Bronco go dead. They might have been able to transfer the cellular to his vehicle but now that was out of the question. They would have to use Scotty's truck.

"Have you looked outside, boss?" Zack asked. "Even finding the pickup in this whiteout will be a miracle, let alone trying to move it through a mountain of snowdrifts."

"You won't catch me out in it," Larry said, glaring at Hal as if he were some kind of commander giving orders to a recruit.

"Maybe it looks worse than it is," offered Scotty. "We could give it a try, Hal."

Kirby spat, "Don't be stupid. Folks freeze to death just a few feet from their door in weather like this."

Zack nodded in agreement. "Can't see your nose in front of your face. Better let things be, if you ask me."

Hal fought back a sharp retort born of utter frustration. He knew they spoke the truth, but it galled him to give up without even trying to get to the phone. He knew better than to think he could dig his way to the truck alone. And he couldn't put other lives in danger by forcing them out in the storm.

"I'm willing to give it a try if you are," Scotty offered. "I've got a camper shell on the back. We could hole up there if we can't get back."

Hal hesitated and then shook his head. Even if they made it to the phone, what good would it do just to alert the authorities that they had a woman in labor? No one could get to them. At least not until the storm lifted. Having a cellular phone in the pickup was of little help unless they could get to it easily. During the height of a fierce blizzard, there was little chance of that.

Hal didn't know what to do. He had prided himself on being able to confront problems and solve them by his wits, but he'd never been faced with a situation completely beyond his control. How in heaven's name could he waltz upstairs and tell Jill Gaylor she was on her own?

SUE'S CONTRACTIONS were now coming more frequently and were much more painful. When Hal appeared in the bedroom doorway later in the morning, Jill knew from his sober face that the news wasn't good.

She went out into the hall with him as he explained the situation. She only half listened to him, as her mind was racing a mile a minute, but she knew what he was telling her—no cellular telephone, no minute-by-minute medical assistance, and no help of any kind forthcoming. She moistened her dry lips. "I see."

"You don't have to shoulder this alone, Jill. Just tell me what I can do to help." He lowered his face close to hers, and as his fingers gently smoothed wayward hair from her cheeks, he gave her a wry smile. "You want me to go boil some water?"

She laughed softly. The old cliché suddenly lightened her mood, and the deep intimacy in his eyes gave her the strength she needed. "No, let's let Gary do it. He needs something to keep him busy. And when things start happening, I think he should stay downstairs."

"How soon do you think—"

"Not for hours yet. At least, I don't think so. Things aren't moving very fast." When she thought about what lay ahead, her pulse missed a beat. "I guess I'll know what to do when the time comes."

"Hey, if cabdrivers can deliver babies in a back seat, we ought to be able to do it."

We? The pronoun brought a foolish spurt of relief. The situation had strongly bonded them together in a way she wouldn't have thought possible. Now she wasn't alone, although she couldn't have put the feeling into words, and for the moment, she didn't even try. She simply mumbled an almost inaudible, "Thank you."

His warm breath bathed her face. "No, thank you," he said, his voice betraying thick emotion. "When you need an extra pair of hands, let me know. Until then, I'll stay out of your way. Okay?''

"Okay." She straightened her shoulders, impulsively squeezed his hand, and went back into the room to see how the mother-to-be was doing.

All day long the time between contractions shortened. Jill was relieved that Sue was able to manage some controlled breathing that was part of a natural birth course she'd taken in Utah.

"Good girl," Jill said, encouraging her.

"We took a few classes but never completed the program," Gary admitted. Deep furrows in his forehead and a nervous twitch at the corner of his mouth matched his pale complexion. He kept moving his hands, rubbing them against his pant legs and tugging at his sweatshirt. Some first-time fathers might be an asset in a delivery room but Gary, obviously, wasn't going to be one of them, Jill decided.

Sue continued to give her husband weak smiles of encouragement throughout the day. "No need for you to fret so. My mother always said the women in our family were pioneers. So I guess I'm one, too. I'll have this baby and everything will be just fine. Just fine. Just fine," she kept repeating even when pain brought sweat glistening to her brow.

As the time became nearer for the delivery, Jill prayed that Sue's optimism would prove to be valid. She prepared as best she could with fresh linens, towels and a tray, which held a pair of sterilized scissors and white twine.

By mid-afternoon, Sue's contractions were a minute apart, and Jill knew it was time to get Gary out of the room and ask Hal for help. She sent the agitated father-to-be downstairs with orders to stay there and with a message for Hal. "Tell him it's time to boil water."

When he came into the room a few minutes later, she gave him a grateful smile. His solid presence was needed. "I think *we're* going to have a baby soon."

The marked emphasis on the "we're" did not escape him. He briefly touched her flushed cheek and smiled back. "*We're* ready." The dire test facing them made them a team. He'd never experienced this kind of closeness before. A wonderment stirred within him that had nothing to do with the reality of the moment.

"I'll need you to stay at the head of the bed with Sue until she delivers," Jill said, her voice surprisingly steady. "Then I'll need your help with the baby."

Admiration suffused the smile he gave her. Faced with the inevitable, somehow she'd found a wellspring of strength and confidence. Impulsively, he put his arm around her waist and held her close for just a moment, breathing a prayer that all would go well.

Sue bore down with each contraction and, like a cheerleader, Jill kept saying, "It's coming…it's coming."

Hal took Sue's hand firmly in his and murmured encouragement as the miracle of life, with all its mystery, engulfed them.

After what seemed a breathless eternity, the baby slipped into Jill's hands. Tears flowed down her cheeks, and it was a moment before she could say, "It's a boy."

Hal left Sue's side, washed his hands in a waiting basin and then quickly moved to help Jill. He held the baby steady while she tied and cut the cord.

"Is he all right?" Sue asked anxiously.

Jill took the infant and swatted his bottom. There was no responding cry. She exchanged an anxious glance with Hal. Why wasn't the baby crying? The newborn was moving his arms and legs but did not seem to be breathing.

She didn't know what to do.

"Let me have him." Hal took the baby and turned him upside down. Then he stuck his little finger into the newborn's mouth and cleaned out the mucus. A lusty cry rewarded his efforts. *Just like a newborn calf,* Hal thought with relief, knowing that sometimes mucus clogged the air passages at birth.

The baby's cry had brought Gary barreling up the stairs and into the room. He was in worse shape than his wife. The young father started laughing and crying and blubbering like an idiot. "Oh, my God. I'm a father. I'm a father."

The afterbirth was delivered easily and intact, and when Jill had her hands free, Hal handed her the infant and said with a grin, "I think he needs his first bath."

"Give me a few minutes to clean up your son," Jill told the proud parents with a relieved smile. "Then you can start spoiling him. And, Gary, there's fresh bedding on that chair. While we're gone, see to Sue's needs."

Jill was surprised how professional her voice sounded. She laughed at herself as she took the baby down the hall to the bathroom sink. Hal followed her, watching her handle the tiny body gingerly but firmly as she bathed him in the sink. Earlier in the day, she'd laid out the things she'd needed.

"He's perfect, just perfect," she said, giddy with relief. To Jill's inexperienced eyes he seemed like a full-term baby. Maybe Sue had her dates mixed up. She was amazed at how much she remembered from tending Randy when he was an infant. Maybe bathing a baby was like riding a bicycle, you never really forgot.

She hid a smile as Hal looked over her shoulder. His laugh was almost as giddy as hers. "Wow, isn't he something. Hard to believe a tiny baby like that will grow up into a strapping youngster like Randy."

"I know," Jill said with a catch in her throat. Her newborn son had been the most beautiful baby in the world. How blessed she'd been to have him. More than anything, she'd wanted to have children.

After she'd dressed the infant and wrapped it warmly in a blanket, they silently gazed upon its sweet, round face, tiny puckered mouth and a cap of soft fair hair. The moment was charged with emotion.

"So perfect," she murmured. "And when it's your own, it's unbelievable. There's no feeling like seeing your child for the first time."

"No, I don't suppose there is." The raw longing in his voice was undisguised. The deep sadness was back in his eyes.

She chided herself for being so insensitive. Impulsively, she held the baby out to him. "You hold him while I clean up here," she ordered.

"Are you sure?" He took the bundle gingerly, and a soft smile crossed his face as he looked down at the newborn in his arms. "Welcome to the old homestead, little fellow."

The storm and all its threats were forgotten. In an overflow of happiness, they returned the baby to the arms of his mother. Jill's own eyes filled with tears, and she was pretty sure that Hal's were misty, as well.

"How can we ever thank you, the both of you?" Sue said, her expression tired but glowing.

"All the thanks goes to Jill," Hal said readily. "She had the situation under control the whole time. Just the way I knew she would." He smiled at Jill, giving her shoulders a squeeze. "The only credit I get is for bringing her here."

They took their leave of the new little family a short time later, and Hal slipped his arm around her waist as they walked across the hall to her bedroom. As they paused in the doorway, she turned and earnestly studied his face—the finely drawn skin across his cheeks, the strong firm curve of his mouth and intense blue eyes that could change so quickly from dark to light, like winter skies to summer.

"Why are you looking at me with such earnestness?" he asked with a soft smile.

"I'm not sure. I mean, I don't think I've ever really seen you before, not until now." She put her hands lightly on his chest and lifted her face to his, knowing full well she was inviting his kiss.

His mouth touched hers lightly at first, slowly lingering on her warm lips in a kind of amazement. His hands molded the curves of her waist and hips as the pressure of his kiss deepened, and she felt a powerful response vibrating through his body. When he lifted his mouth from hers, they stared at each other like two strangers drawn into an intimacy that left them both bewildered. A feeble warning that her judgment could not be trusted in the heightened situation went unheeded.

In this quickening moment of physical desire, they were oblivious to the pair of eyes watching them from the shadows of the hall.

What in the hell! The top of his head felt like it was exploding when he saw her in Haverly's arms as they stood in the bedroom doorway. His stomach began to cramp, his eyes narrowed and the uncontrollable slither of a demonic anger twisted his in-

sides like an ugly serpent coiled and ready to spring. He wasn't about to lose her now. Not when he'd been so patient. So careful. He would have her...and soon. Anyone who got in his way would pay the price. His right hand clenched as if his fingers were on the cold metal of a gun.

Chapter Five

Hal couldn't sleep. The ticking of his bedside clock reminded him that it was well past midnight. He thrashed about the bed, fighting a legion of warring emotions. His body remembered every touch of her soft skin, the searing warmth of his lips on hers, and the exploding desire to make love to her. The incredible real-life drama that had played out before them had washed away all strangeness between them. But everything was moving much too fast. He'd always prided himself on his self-control. But what on earth had happened to his usual grasp of common sense? How had Jill gotten so deep under his skin that his whole life suddenly seemed out of focus?

Even as he denied it, he knew the answer. He was afraid of opening himself up to love. He remembered the pain, the devastation. He hadn't thought about his old sweetheart for a long time. They'd just been kids when they became friends in the small country school, and somehow, in the process of growing up, they'd become a couple. Even when he went away to the University of Nebraska, he'd been happy and secure in knowing that he had a sweetheart who would become his wife, the mother of his children and his partner on the ranch. And he'd been happy for Carrie when the chance came for her to take a trip back East to visit a relative in New York. Then the whole fabric of his life unraveled when he got her letter, brief and to the point. She wasn't coming back. She said she was sorry, hoped that he would understand, but she'd found a new life and a new love. She wished him well and was sure he'd find his own happiness. Hurt and anger had stayed with him for a long time, until he'd buried the old dream deep enough to give him peace.

Tonight when he'd held the baby in his arms, the old dream had surfaced, bringing disturbing longings that he'd thought he'd buried forever. Until Jill Gaylor invaded his house, he'd been satisfied with the way things were in his life. It had been a long time since he'd even thought about sharing himself with anyone, let alone a woman who had city roots. A couple of times in recent years, he'd brought some gal he'd met and liked to the ranch, but the relationships never took. A brief vacation was one thing for an attractive young woman, but he'd watched the romantic glow of living on a ranch quickly fade in the reality of the demanding daily workload. How could he expect things to be different with someone as city-bred as Randy's mother? She was an intelligent, competent woman, and he'd be a fool to think that a struggling rancher could hold her affections for long.

JILL SLEPT for a couple of hours and then relieved Gary, sending him into her room to catch some sleep. She curled up in the easy chair beside the sleeping child and mother, but her vigil was uneventful until after midnight, when Sue woke up, glanced around the room and frowned. "Gary?"

"He's sleeping across the hall in my room," said Jill,

quickly getting up from the chair where she'd been curled up under a thick quilt. "Do you want me to get him?"

Sue shook her head. A faint smile crossed her lips. "Let him sleep."

"Are you hungry?"

"Not really."

"Maybe some warm milk and toast? You'll need some nourishment to nurse the baby."

Jill took the baby out of the cradle and handed him to his mother. True to his word, Hal had polished the cherry wood to a glistening shine and had found a firm pillow to put in the bottom. Jill's heart tightened a little when she thought of the robust man who had once been a tiny infant rocked in this very same cradle.

Sue touched the small bundle at her side. "He's so tiny," she murmured in wonderment.

"They don't stay that way." Jill chuckled as she thought about her own strapping son. "It's unbelievable how fast they grow up. Sometimes you wish you could keep them little for a longer time," she added wistfully. Thinking about Randy brought a tender mist to her eyes. She knew he was all right, but they had rarely been separated even for a night, and she felt as if a part of herself was missing. She suffered a moment of regret that she had left him, then she gave herself a mental shake. Her task at the moment was to take the best care she could of Sue and her baby. She'd be back with her son soon enough, and she'd have to tell him he'd been right about Hal Haverly. She'd changed her mind about him, but just how much, she wasn't ready to admit to herself.

"I can't thank you enough, Jill," Sue said. "And Mr. Haverly, too. He really gave me courage when I needed it."

Jill could have echoed the same sentiment. Just the thought of having tried to handle the delivery by herself was overwhelming.

"I can't believe he doesn't have a family of his own. He seems so...so supportive and understanding. Has he ever been married?"

"I don't think so." Jill wasn't about to pass on anything Scotty had told her about Hal's unhappy love affair.

Sue sighed. "What a loss. Maybe he just hasn't met the right woman."

"I don't think he's looking for one," Jill answered evenly. The conversation was heading in a direction that made her uncomfortable. "Why don't I raid the fridge and see what I can find for a snack. Take another little nap while I scoot down to the kitchen."

Sue nodded, closed her eyes, and Jill would have bet the new mother was asleep even before she left the room. All of the bedroom doors were closed as she went down the hall. Earlier, Hal had poked his head into Sue's room to say good-night. "Don't be afraid to call me if you need anything."

"I won't," she'd promised.

As she passed his door, she visualized him in tumbled sleep, shocks of wayward hair drifting forward on his face, his wonderful full lips relaxed and supple. The memory of his kisses shot a jolt of warmth through her. She bet he slept in the nude. Somehow, pajamas didn't fit with the image of his strong, muscular virility. She remembered the tantalizing length of his hips and legs pressed against her body and the sweet promise of his mouth tugging at her lips. What would it be like to fall asleep with his naked body cupping hers? To turn over in his arms as demanding desire arched between them? Stop it, she chided herself. Don't be an adolescent fool. An emotional situation had created the intimacy they'd shared. Once reality settled in, they'd both have the good sense not to blow the momentary attraction out of proportion. She wasn't looking to complicate her life any more than he was. Sadly enough, both of them had lost loved ones, her husband by death, and his Carrie by rejection. She was no more willing than he was to open herself up to that kind of heartache again.

A hushed somnolence lay on the house. The stairs were illuminated by a small wall light. Her slippers whispered on the carpet and her elongated shadow played ahead of her as she descended to the floor below. She paused near the front door to listen to the assaulting wind and seemingly endless snow. No sign that the storm had grown weary of its rampaging and was losing energy. How long would they be snowbound? Surely they would be able to dig out before another twenty-four hours went by. Isolation seemed to be creating a growing claustrophobia. Her own nerves were frayed, and the tension and short tempers rising among the men were nearly unbearable.

The door to the den was slightly ajar as she passed through the hall and she could hear someone snoring loudly. She smiled, wondering whether it was Zack or Kirby who sounded like a bull moose. Since the two men usually shared the bunkhouse, she supposed that such nightly snoring was part of the challenge of rooming together. Maybe one of them wore earplugs.

At the end of the hall, the kitchen was dark except for a small light over the stove. She let her fingers play over the wall and found a light switch just inside the door. The wagon-wheel chandelier that hung by a chain over the long table instantly sent a glow of light below. Kirby had left the kitchen in an orderly state, counters clean and the floor swept.

She started across the room toward the refrigerator, but before she reached it, the kitchen was suddenly plunged into darkness. For a stunned moment, she froze, blinking against sudden blindness.

Her ears were filled with the fury of the storm battering the house. The wailing wind rose in a threatening crescendo, and in the darkness, the house seemed to vibrate from the onslaught.

What should she do? She swallowed, trying to suppress a rising panic. Would the backup generator automatically kick in with the loss of power? Was there a switch somewhere to turn it on? Would anyone else in the house realize the electricity had gone out? She wasn't sure that she could make her way upstairs to Hal's room in total darkness. As she hesitated, a soft whisper of movement behind her reached her ears. An instinctive awareness alerted her that she wasn't alone in the darkness.

She jerked around. "Hal?"

No answer.

"Who's there?" Even though she couldn't see distinct forms in the enveloping blackness, she knew someone was moving toward her. "I never did like blindman's buff," she said with a false laugh. "Hal, is that you?"

Faint, hushed, quickened breathing was her only answer. Her mouth went dry. No, not Hal. She felt a cold menace in the unseen presence. The insidious miasma in the darkness was almost palpable.

"Who is it?" Recoiling from an undefinable threat, she jerked backwards. In the hasty movement she bumped a kitchen chair so hard that it went crashing to the floor. As the noise reverberated in the room, she sensed the unseen presence retreating. At once, doubts began to assail her. Had the darkness made her paranoid? Was her imagination making a fool out of her? She choked back a scream, and for a long moment just stood there in the dark, afraid to move, but hesitant to raise everyone in the house with frightened cries.

When she heard loud footsteps in the hall, she was thankful that the decision had been taken out of her hands. The beam of a flashlight broke the darkness in the kitchen doorway, and as the circle of light caught her, she heard Hal's surprised, "Jill? I didn't know you were down here. I was trying to read when the lights went out. Stay where you are and I'll go down in the basement and see to the backup generator. It doesn't have an automatic switch."

"No, don't leave me." Her voice was shaky. "I'll go with you."

"There's no need."

"Please, I don't want to stay here...alone."

He moved quickly to her side and was instantly aware that she was trembling. She must have been shaken by the lights going out. He never would have guessed that she would be so terrified of the dark. He took her hand, surprised to find it moist with perspiration.

"You really don't like the dark, do you?" he said lightly. "All right. The basement door is just beyond the pantry. You'll have to be careful. The basement steps are steep."

She clutched his hand so tightly that her nails bit into his flesh as he guided her across the room to the basement door and shone his flashlight down into a pit of blackness.

"Watch your step," he cautioned, carefully guiding her down the narrow staircase. Her breathing was strained and she cowered against him like a child expecting the bogeyman to jump out at any moment.

When they reached the bottom, he let the ray of light play over the musty, low-ceilinged cellar so that she could see her surroundings and be reassured that no one was hiding in the corners. When central heating had been installed, the old coal furnace had been taken out, but the acidic coal smell had lingered in the rock walls and flagstone floor. He'd emptied out most of the accumulation left by his parents. Nothing much remained since he used storage areas in the attic, garage, barn and bunkhouse, rather than this dank, fusty-smelling cellar.

"The generator's over here." He led the way around a central butane furnace. "You hold the flashlight so I can see what I'm doing."

A moment later, Hal let out the breath he'd been holding. Thank heavens, the backup generator was functioning. The lights in the kitchen and the one he'd turned on in the basement came on in all their glory.

"Let there be light," he said with a satisfied smile, but as he looked at Jill, his expression sobered. She was as rigid and taut as a strung bow. Her face was drained of color and anxious lines marred the corners of her eyes. He was startled by the fright in her eyes. "I'm really sorry." Gently he touched her face and smoothed back some tousled strands of hair around her face. "I should have made sure you had a flashlight in case we lost power. If I'd known you were so terrified of the dark—''

"It's not that," she answered curtly, trying to organize her thoughts so they made sense. "I'm not afraid of being in the dark."

"Then what?" he prodded gently. He put his arm around her waist, and she kept close to his side as they walked back upstairs. "Please, tell me what's the matter."

She hesitated. Would he think her more of a fool if she tried to explain? She wasn't sure herself what had happened. As lingering quivers trailed up her spine, she decided to go with her gut feeling. "Someone frightened me."

"Frightened you?" He looked steadily into her anxious eyes. "I don't understand. Who? When?"

"I don't know who." Her voice gathered momentum. "But when the lights went out, I sensed someone in the kitchen with me."

"And he touched you?"

"No, but I knew someone was there. I could hear the whisper of his breathing." She shivered again, remembering.

"It could have been the wind outside. In the dark, sounds are often indistinguishable."

"It wasn't the wind. It was someone's breath."

"What did he do?"

"Nothing."

"What did he say?" He put his hands on her shoulders, holding her as firmly as he would a child.

"Nothing."

"Maybe you just got rattled because it was dark. You could have simply imagined that somebody was there."

"I could have, but I didn't." She lifted her head and

met his eyes squarely. "Believe what you want. Someone scared me spitless, and I knocked over a kitchen chair trying to back away. The sound of the crash must have scared off whoever it was. Didn't you hear the noise?"

"Yes, but I thought it was outside. I didn't know it came from the kitchen. Why would anyone want to frighten you?"

"You tell me." Even though she was tempted to lean into his strong embrace, she turned around and sat down in a chair. "Did you run into anyone in the hall?"

"No. But I didn't pay much attention. I suppose I could have passed someone in the dark. I thought the whole house was asleep and was startled to find you standing in the dark kitchen." He didn't doubt for a minute that she'd been truly frightened, but he was just as certain that her imagination was responsible for it. From the set of her chin, he knew better than to challenge her. "Well, the lights are on now. And I'm here to make sure that you're safe and sound." His warm eyes bathed her face.

"You don't believe me. Do you? Just like you didn't believe me about the bookmark." She couldn't let it go. She needed to be convinced of her own rationality.

"I know something frightened you," he said softly.

"Not something—someone!" she protested.

"Jill, you've been under a lot of stress the last twenty-four hours. I think it's time you let Gary tend to his wife while you get some sleep," he said, frowning with concern. "You've held up beautifully. It's no wonder your nerves are a little frayed."

She could tell he was patronizing her. He didn't believe her. Not for one minute. And how could she blame him? Now that she stood in the well-lighted kitchen, she was beginning to have doubts herself. Only the over-turned chair seemed to be valid evidence of the unseen stalker's presence. Stalker? Why had she used that term?

"What is it?" His eyes swept over her face. "You've suddenly gone as white as a bleached bone. What's going on? There's something more, isn't there?"

She searched his face and felt a rush of gratitude for the sincere concern she saw there. "Yes, there's more."

"Would you like to tell me about it?" He drew up a chair beside her. He took her hand and waited. "I'm listening."

She hesitated, then drew in a deep breath and took the plunge. What did she have to lose? He probably already thought her some kind of neurotic female. This was the second time she'd unloaded on him, first in the attic, and now in the middle of the night.

In crisp, succinct sentences, she told about the silent phone calls, the book, the notes, the pink scarf and the doctored photo. She watched his face, trying to decide what he was making of all of it. "The whole thing has put me on edge, made me feel vulnerable all the time."

"Good heavens, Jill," he said, frowning with concern. "Now I understand why you reacted the way you did, plunged into the dark like that. And you've no idea who the bastard is?"

"None."

"And what have you done about this harassment?"

"Nothing, yet."

"What are you waiting for?" he asked, exasperated. "Some nut's running around stalking you, and you don't even go to the authorities?"

"Until I received the doctored photo I didn't realize this person had been close enough to take my picture without me even knowing it. Even if he used a telephoto lens, he was too darn close.'' Her voice broke. "I wasn't really frightened until then.'' She turned quickly away from him so he wouldn't see a sudden fullness flooding her eyes. "I'm sorry,'' she choked.

"Sorry for what?'' He gently pulled her to her feet and once again cradled her in his arms. Tears eased out from the fringe of her eyelashes and slowly trickled down the sweet curve of her cheeks. Fury that someone could put her through this kind of hell mingled with a tumultuous swell of protective tenderness. "After what you've told me, it's no wonder you reacted the way you did when the lights went out.''

"But you still don't believe me. You still think I was imagining the whole thing.''

"The mind can play all kinds of tricks, especially under stress,'' he said softly. "And you've had plenty of that in the last twenty-four hours. I honestly think that your recent anxieties about a stalker must have triggered the impression that someone was closing in on you. But you're safe here. Absolutely safe. I guarantee it.'' He brushed back a wisp of a curl on her cheek. "And I'll talk to the sheriff myself. I'll make damn sure he listens to me. You'll get the protection you need against any nut out there.''

Instead of protesting with her usual independence that she could take care of the matter herself, she simply nodded. His strength and confidence neutralized any argument. She willingly drew on his assurance. When he let his hands slip down to the rigid cords of her neck and shoulders and began to knead them gently, she didn't protest, either. He had good hands. Strong. Firm. And wonderfully gentle. She knew that she was dangerously vulnerable. It had been a long time since she'd been cosseted by such a tender loving touch. She relaxed against him, and to her astonishment, he lightly swung her up in his arms and carried her out of the kitchen.

"Put me down," she gasped, instantly wary. She wasn't sure whether to be angry, indignant, or amused at the manhandling. "What do you think you're doing?"

"Putting you to bed."

"I've...I've got to get some milk and toast for Sue," she stammered.

"I'll see to it," he said briskly as he carried her upstairs.

"Gary's sleeping in my room," she protested.

"No matter," he said as he purposefully carried her into his room. The bed was still made up and a light shone over a chair where he had thrown down the book he'd been reading.

"No," she protested as he set her down on the bed.

"No, what?" He raised an innocent eyebrow.

"You know what!" Had she given him the impression that she was the kind of woman who didn't care whose bed she slept in? The fact that they had shared a few explosive kisses was not enough for her. Even though he'd ignited desires that fired her passionate nature, she wanted more than a few scattered hours of ecstasy. She searched for the right words to tell him so. She couldn't sleep in his bed. She couldn't. And did he imagine that she'd have no objection to sharing it with him? She was disappointed in him and in herself, too—the thought of lying in his warm arms was much too inviting. "I prefer my own bedroom, thank you."

"What's the matter with mine? Doesn't the decor suit your fancy?"

She gave a hasty glance around the large combination bedroom and sitting room. The furnishings were a mas-

culine tan and brown but with a surprising touch of jon-
quil yellow in the drapes and bedspread. Even in the
dim light of the one lamp, she could see that there was
a harmonious blend of new and old furniture. "It's a
nice room but—"

"I'm glad you approve," he said as he opened a bu-
reau drawer, took out a blue-striped pajama top and
tossed it to her. "Put that on."

She knew her mouth had dropped open. Before she
could get to her feet in indignation and throw the top
back at him, he turned his back on her and walked away
from the bed.

"Better lock the door after me," he said, giving her
a departing grin, so knowing and so amused that she
wanted to throw something at him. "And don't show
yourself until you've gotten some sleep," he ordered,
closing the door with a punctuating click.

She felt more than slightly foolish. He'd known darn
well that she was all fired up to ward off his romantic
advances. He must have been chuckling to himself as
she prepared to defend her honor. The truth of the matter
was that she wasn't at all certain she would have resisted
his persuasive advances. And even though she bristled
at his heavy-handed orders, she knew he was right about
her need to get some sleep. Her nerves were frayed. The
long day with Sue during labor and the emotional drain
of delivering the baby had taken their toll. She'd been
on the edge of hysteria when Hal had found her. In ret-
rospect, it could have been paranoia that made her think
someone was with her in the dark. That business with
the stalker had set her on edge. Anxiety had been building with every frightening contact made by the stalker.
The horrible photo had finally broken her nerve. No
wonder she let her imagination fill her with terror. Thank

heavens Hal had found her before she made a fool of herself by waking everyone up with her hysterical screaming.

The pajama top fell below her knees like a nightshirt as she crawled under the heavy weight of thick blankets and discovered that one side of the mattress was bumpy with dents that must have been made by Hal's body weight. Obviously he slept on the left side of the bed, she thought as she scooted to the other side and laid her head on one of the pillows.

She knew it was adolescent foolishness, but she felt self-conscious sleeping in his bed. His presence in the room and in the bed was undeniable. A disturbing sensual awareness teased her with a vision of his warm body stretched out beside her. What kind of a lover would he be? She'd glimpsed a deep core of sensitivity that he kept hidden under an outwardly confident manner. If he ever gave himself to a woman, it would not be a shallow gesture. He wasn't that kind of man. She wondered what dreams filled his head when he laid it upon this very pillow? Did he think about Carrie? Did he feel a deepseated loneliness when he awoke in the morning, the way she did?

She sighed and closed her eyes. As she drifted off to sleep, she wondered at the strangeness of life that had brought her into this house and filled her mind and body with reawakened desires she had thought long buried.

HAL PEEKED IN on her mid-morning and saw that she was still asleep. She was curled up on the far side of the bed, hugging a pillow like a slumbering child. Her hair had come loose from its usual long braid, and her long lashes lay like dark fringes upon her fair cheeks. Her lips were soft and relaxed, her breath even as she sighed deeply.

His pulse quickened as he looked at her and stilled an absurd impulse to lay a kiss upon her forehead. This surge of protective tenderness and desire took him by surprise. The firm grip he'd always maintained on his emotions wavered. Seeing her in his bed was like a fulfilled promise that he hadn't even known lay close to his heart. After Carrie, he'd never felt this way about the few women who had briefly entered his life, and he'd watched them move on without any regrets. The feeling he had for this woman curled up in his bed frightened him. He wanted to throw back the covers and climb in beside her. He'd glimpsed the passion in her seductive body when he'd held her close and kissed her. He knew she would be a woman who would hold nothing back from a man she loved. He didn't know what kind of a man her husband had been, but one thing was for sure, the guy had been damn lucky to have a wife like Jill and a son like Randy. Was she content to live with her memories?

She stirred. For a moment he was afraid she was going to open her eyes and demand to know what he was doing standing there, staring at her like some lovesick fool. He quickly retreated and quietly closed the door. *It's the damn storm!* he silently swore. All ranchers knew that animals reacted to increased atmospheric pressures. Sometimes they acted plain crazy. *Like me,* he muttered to himself.

THE DAY HAD DAWNED cold and gray. Even though heavy clouds hung low, there was no sign of fresh snow. Hal knew the drifts must be nearly six feet, because early that morning the barn cat had peered in the top ten inches of a kitchen window. She'd walked around on top of the snowdrift, meowing loudly, wanting her morning ration of milk.

"Couldn't wait for me to bring you some breakfast, huh?" He chuckled as he forced the back door open enough to let her in. He picked her up and stroked her cinnamon-colored fur. She'd left a litter of kittens in the barn and he scolded her for venturing out in the storm. "You should be keeping your babies warm."

All of the men except Gary straggled into the kitchen for breakfast. Kirby set out his usual breakfast feed, and when they were finished eating and enjoying coffee refills, Hal announced cheerfully, "Time to start digging out."

"Now?" Neither Zack, Kirby, Scotty nor Larry looked happy about the pronouncement. Obviously, his ranch hands and house guests would prefer to hole up in the den and indulge in a game of poker, but Hal ignored their lack of enthusiasm.

"Time to make sure the livestock in the barn and corral have feed and water."

"Still looks bad out there to me," Larry said, and the other men nodded in agreement.

"No use doing the job twice," Kirby grumbled.

"Makes more sense to wait until it clears," Scotty agreed.

"I put out plenty of feed," Zack said. "Stacked up a half dozen bales in the corral under the shed so it wouldn't get buried in snow. The horses in the barn should be all right for another day."

Hal slapped the young man on the back. "There's only one way to know for sure, isn't there? We'll have to take turns with the shovels and follow the rope guide to the barn. Zack, why don't you and Kirby get started? Scotty and Larry can take the second shift. We might get the garage shoveled out and make it to the bunk-house if we don't get any more snow today. We're lucky to have so much manpower, aren't we?'' he said, grinning.

"It's colder than a well-digger's butt out there,'' Kirby muttered as he pulled his coat off the antler rack. Zack's reply was inaudible, but he flashed Hal a look that clearly expressed his disgust with the boss's orders.

BY THE TIME JILL came down to the kitchen later that morning, Kirby was the only one in the kitchen. "Where is everybody?''

He told her that the others were taking shifts shoveling a narrow path through snow banked as high as their heads. "I just came in to fix lunch.''

Jill was startled when she looked out the back door and saw that the blizzard winds had swept across the open ground between the house and the barn and piled up snow against both buildings. "It looks like a fairy-land,'' she said to Kirby.

He groaned something that she suspected was not meant for a lady's ears. His face was ruddy from the cold, and his hands seemed stiff as he chopped vegetables and meat for the stew pot. He swore at the tabby cat threading his legs, and Jill quickly picked it up to get it away from his threatening feet.

"Is she hungry?'' Jill asked as she shifted the cat in her arms.

"She's always hungry. Especially since she's got five kittens nursing. I try to keep her bowl full, but it's always empty. Some mother! Leaving her babies to freeze. Someone needs to take her back to the barn.''

The cat began to purr as Jill cuddled her close against

her chest and stroked her soft fur. "She's a sweetheart. What's her name?"

"I call her cat."

"She deserves better than that."

Kirby shrugged. "The boss calls her Gypsy. Fancy name for a stray cat, if you ask me. Damned if I'm going to carry her back to the barn."

Jill thought for a moment. "I'll do it. I'd like to get a little fresh air. Besides, I'm a softy when it comes to kittens."

"But you don't have a cat," he said in an accusing tone. "How come, if you're so crazy about them? You don't have any pets."

She stared at him. "How do you know that?"

"Guess."

Her throat tightened. "I can't."

The cook gave her a crooked smile as if enjoying a private joke. "Easy. Your son was making a fuss over a lamb when he was here with the 4-H kids one day. I thought the boy was going to talk the boss into letting him have the lamb for a pet, but then he said his mother wouldn't let him have any."

"We've always lived in apartments," she said defensively. She knew well enough how much Randy loved animals, but someone had to be realistic about keeping animals in such small quarters. Had part of Hal's initial frosty manner toward her been caused by Randy's longing for a pet? She bristled to think how unfair his judgment about her had been. He'd been prejudiced before he'd even met her. *Just like you were about him,* a mocking voice reminded her.

She slipped into her coat and hat, and clutched Gypsy against her breast. The glass in the back door was completely frosted over, and she wasn't prepared for the blast of razor-sharp wind that tossed snow into her eyes and nose. She swiped at her face with one gloved hand, ducked her head and headed down a shoveled path, which was more like a narrow trench.

When she reached the barn, she quickly darted through a small door that had been shoveled free of snow. Large double hay doors were still banked high with drifts. After the enveloping whiteness outside, she was momentarily blinded in the dim interior of the long barn.

"Hey, what are you doing here?" Hal's surprised voice echoed from the depths of the barn.

"I brought Gypsy back," she said, walking forward, peering ahead, trying to see where his voice was coming from.

He stepped out of a stall, a pitchfork in his hand. "You have no business out in weather like this," he scolded in a rough voice that hid his delight. She hadn't been out of his thoughts for a moment this morning as he carried out his chores. The memory of her sleeping in his bed mocked his attempt to put her soft, luscious body out of his mind. It was a good thing he had a lot of hard work to keep him occupied.

"Kirby said Gypsy needed to get back to her kittens," she said, stroking the cat in her arms. The barn was chilly. Animal heat from the horses and several tons of hay stacked overhead provided roof insulation, but it was a good thing all the horses had thick coats of hair, she thought.

"And so you decided she wouldn't be able to find her way and brought her back. The fact that the drifts are six feet high didn't bother you?" he teased.

"I just followed the shoveled path and the rope. Are the kittens all right?"

With a smile of amusement, he propped the pitchfork against a stall gate and jerked his head toward an open stall where a wooden box was almost buried in straw. When the cat struggled to get out of Jill's arms, she quickly put her down. A welcoming sound of meowing greeted the mother cat as she bounded into the box and settled down in the midst of five hungry kittens.

"Oh, they're darling." Jill knelt down and watched the tiny bundles of fur work their little paws against their mother's tummy as they spilled warm milk into their puckered mouths. "I'm glad they're all right."

"Which one do you want?" He hunkered down beside her, and laughed at her surprised expression. "Take your pick. I kind of like this little white and black one, myself." He picked up one of the tiny soft kittens and placed it in her hands.

She held it gingerly. "I wouldn't know how to take care of something so tiny."

"By the time she's weaned, she'll be a nice size, probably not as big as the others, but the runt is sometimes the best of a litter. They have lots of spunk, and won't let anyone push them around." His eyes crinkled in a smile. "Kind of like you."

She blushed. "Maybe one hard-headed female in a family is enough."

"It's not polite to refuse a present," he chided. "Besides, Randy would love a kitten."

"I know, but I'll have to think about it," she said as she put the kitten back in the box. *And about a lot of other things too,* she admitted silently. It was impossible to think rationally about anything when he was so close. She couldn't forget the way his kisses had sent her reeling with unexpected desire. The kitten would be just one more reminder of emotions that had gotten out of hand.

Several horses hung their heads over the half gate and were snorting and stomping restlessly. "Are the horses okay? They seem agitated," she said as she stood up and looked down the row of stalls.

"Just impatient for their bucket of oats. I decided to muck out the stalls before I feed them." He surveyed her with a quizzical lift of an eyebrow and a teasing glint in his eyes. "Since you're here, you might as well help."

Cleaning out stalls wasn't exactly her choice of occupations, but she supposed that it was something one could get used to. There was an amused challenge in his eyes that she couldn't ignore. She'd show him that she wasn't any shrinking violet. "Sure," she said, expecting him to hand her the rake.

He laughed at her stoic expression. "Well, you're in luck. That's the last stall."

She didn't try to hide her relief. "Good."

"I tell you what, you feed the horses while I get more hay down from the loft."

She looked down the row of snorting horses bobbing their heads and turning wild eyes in her direction. "Me?"

"Yes, you. What's the matter?"

She knew he was silently laughing at her. Might as well be honest, she thought. "I'm a city girl, remember, and the only horses I've been around were on a carousel. But I'm a fast learner," she said bravely. "Just point me in the right direction."

"All right. You'll stay warmer if you keep moving. Besides, I never refuse the offer of help. You'll find the oats in the tack room."

"In the what?"

"Maybe I better *lead* you in the right direction," he said, sighing in feigned exasperation. "Come on."

They walked down the length of the barn to a square room filled with bridles hanging on the wall, saddles resting on wooden horses, and a variety of currying brushes and horse-shoeing tools laid out on a worktable. "This is called a tack room, where we keep all the horse paraphernalia and feed," he explained and pointed out gunnysacks filled with grain stacked at one end of the room. A couple of the sacks were already open and he quickly showed her how to fill up a bucket with oats using a bent coffee can.

"All right, now what do I do with it?" she asked as she stood with the full bucket in her hands.

"Find a horse, reach over the gate and set the bucket inside the stall. Start with Calico. She's in the first stall."

Jill was well aware of the quirking smile at the corner of his mouth as she carried the pail out of the tack room. A spotted mare hung over the stall gate and stretched out her neck in anticipation of the oats. Pausing in front of the stall, holding on to the pail with both hands, Jill had no idea how to get the bucket past the mare and into the stall.

As she hesitated, Hal came up and put a firm hand on the mare's neck and pushed. "Back, girl. Back."

Quickly, Jill lifted the bucket and almost had it over the gate, when a beautiful tiny foal that had been resting in a mound of straw rose up on wobbly legs. Jill was so startled that she dropped the bucket, spilling feed all over the stall. "Oh, I'm sorry, I—"

Hal laughed. "No problem. Calico would just as soon eat off the ground. That's her brand-new filly. Only a couple of weeks old."

Jill marveled at the long-legged foal with its roan coat

splattered with black spots on its hindquarters. The same spotted coloring, only in a different pattern, marked Calico's smooth coat, and her hooves were striped in black and white. "She's a little princess," Jill breathed in awe. Her chest tightened with a strange emotion. She had never seen anything more beautiful. It was one of those times when her spirit seemed to expand beyond her mere senses.

As they stood together in silence, watching the beautiful young foal nurse while its mother buried her mouth in the half-filled bucket of oats, Jill had never felt such completeness, such harmony as she did that moment. Suddenly she wanted to share everything about her life with him. Gazing over at him, she sensed that he felt the same.

"Beautiful horses, aren't they?" he said with obvious pride. "I suspect you've seen a lot of Appaloosa horses in western pictures. Sometimes they're called Indian ponies."

She nodded, remembering how proudly he'd showed off the horse photographs to the Millers. She smiled inwardly at his burst of enthusiasm as she began to ask him more about them.

"The Haverly Ranch has a reputation for breeding these western horses," he told her. "There's always a market for good riding stock. Appaloosas make excellent pleasure mounts and hold their own in competitions, too. They're versatile and easy to train. Every year some of our horses take prizes in the more than seven hundred horse shows across fifteen states," he told her proudly. "There's nothing like the excitement of seeing a colt you've raised beat the competition. I don't suppose you've ever been to the Denver Stock Show or Frontier Days in Cheyenne, Wyoming?"

She shook her head.

"Ever seen a rodeo?"

"On television."

He scoffed. "You have to be one of the crowd. You have to wave your hat, stomp and cheer, and breathe the dust of the arena. There's no art more beautiful than lariat ropes whirling and spinning, and no sight more breathtaking than beautiful horses conquering an obstacle course."

Jill delighted in his sketch of a world she never knew existed, and his enthusiasm grew with every story and description that he shared with her. He told her about his grandfather and father, who had seen the Haverly homestead through both good and hard times. "I'm trying to hold on to the ranch and keep the tradition going, but the land is worth a lot now, and I'm under plenty of pressure to sell. The whole valley is filling up with condos and ski resorts. Greedy vultures are everywhere, destroying a way of life that allows a man to follow his own heart." The lines in his face deepened and the blue of his eyes took on an iced chill. "No one is taking this ranch from me. No one. And anyone who thinks he can will wish to heaven he'd never tried."

Jill didn't know what to say. Her easy companion of the moment before had disappeared. Obviously something ugly and destructive was eating at him. Any platitudes about progress forcing change seemed hollow. To him, the ranch was almost a living, breathing soul, and she knew from the fierce determination in his eyes that he would never willingly let it slip out of his hands.

He broke the tense moment with an abrupt wave. "We'll never get the chores done this way." He led the way back to the tack room.

As they worked together to feed the rest of the horses, she asked him about his work with the 4-H kids and thanked him for spending time with Randy. "He really loves coming here."

"I'm glad you let him. You should have stuck around some after you dropped him off. You could have seen him in action."

"Well," she began hesitantly, "you have to admit, you weren't exactly Mr. Congeniality the couple of times I came here with the kids."

"Wcll, I've had to fight shy of a few overbearing mothers from time to time. I made a mistake including you with the rest of the mothers. I had blinders on. Or maybe I was afraid."

"Afraid? Of what?"

How could he admit that she'd sent his pulse racing the first time she'd smiled and held out her hand for a shake. Her high spirits, easy laughter, and friendly openness had jolted him, as if he was a maverick hitting a wired fence. Back then he'd thought there was only one thing to do: keep his distance. He'd tried, but fate had taken matters out of his hands. "Let's just say a pretty woman with gorgeous honey-brown eyes can unsettle a man." He gave her a quick smile as he took a deep breath and picked up a water bucket. "I'm curious to know how a nice gal like yourself ended up in a place like Rampart," hc said as he carried water to a nearby stall.

"Not much of a mystery. I was office manager at a small airport in southern California and became acquainted with Jack Slade when he passed through the airport a few times. Whcn he offered me an office job at Slade's Adventures, I grabbed at the chance to move to Colorado. I was looking for a better place than a big city to raise my son, and I needed a change of scenery for myself. There was nothing to keep me in California. My parents died when I was eighteen and that's the year

I married, probably too young, but I desperately needed to belong to someone. After my husband passed on, I still had Randy, thank God.''

"How long have you been a widow?"

"Almost eight years now. Doesn't seem possible. Funny, how the past fades. Seems as if Randy and I have always been on our own. He was only six when my husband died of a heart attack."

"And you never remarried?"

"No."

"Why not?"

"Probably for the same reason that you're single. I'm guessing that you never found anyone you liked enough to share your toothbrush." She laughed at his expression. "Sorry, that's an inside joke. Somehow Randy got the idea that marrying someone meant you had to share everything—including your toothbrush."

He chuckled. "I'm thinking that there might be a lot of sharing that wouldn't come easy—not to someone who's always guarded his or her own independence. What do you think?"

She met his eyes squarely. "I don't know. I guess it would depend on the person and what was important." Then, like a coward, she turned away, deliberately cutting off any more speculative conversation. She wasn't ready to face her own confused feelings, let alone deal with the sexual awareness that had exploded between them.

Gypsy had abandoned her kittens and was brushing against Jill's legs trying to get attention, so she reached down, and picked her up. She cuddled the warm body and buried her cheek against the soft fur. The cat began to purr, and Jill closed her eyes for a brief, contented moment. When she opened them, she saw that Hal was watching her with a heated, sensuous and compelling expression.

He moved closer so that there was only the cat in her arms between them. As his caressing fingers plied Gypsy's soft fur, her own skin began to tingle. A muscle flicked in the line of his cheekbone, and the intensity of his blue eyes pulled her into their depths. She wanted to throw down the cat and let his hands caress her in that way. She wanted to lift her lips to that arresting touch and feel the heat of his body invading hers. She wanted—

"Meow!" Gypsy protested. Jill set her down, and neither of them paid any attention to the cat as she scampered off.

Hal's arms went around Jill and his mouth descended on hers, pulling, tugging and tasting her lips with an urgency that drove all thought from her mind. She clung to him, returning his kisses with an abandonment that made her a stranger to the sudden wild hunger invading her body. When he breathlessly lifted his mouth from hers, he buried his lips against the warm pulse in her neck, and she felt the delicious flicking of his tongue against her soft skin. If he had lifted her up in his arms and carried her up to the soft bed of hay in the loft, she would not have resisted. But as desire danced with tantalizing heat through her body, he slowly and deliberately drew back.

"Whoa," he said hoarsely. "Time to pull on the reins."

"Yes. Too fast." She gave him a wavering smile.

He kept his hands on her until she caught her breath. "Feelings under stress are not always reliable," he warned as he continued to make love to her with his eyes.

"One has to be careful." She broke the heightened moment with a soft laugh. "Shall we agree to a cold shower or a snowball fight?"

He grinned. "You're on. Let me finish up here and I'll show you what a champion snowball looks like." Reluctantly, he picked up the empty buckets and disappeared into the tack room.

The mother cat had not gone back to her box but had headed toward the back of the barn where Jill could make out a door that looked slightly ajar. "Gypsy, come here. No, don't go outside."

Jill ran after her, but before she reached the back of the barn, the cat slipped out through the open door. Powdery snow had blown in through the crack but not enough to cover the threshold. When she reached the door, Jill opened her mouth to call the cat again, but the words never left her mouth.

Her eyes froze on a splintered bullet hole in the door frame above her head. Then, slowly, she lowered her eyes to a patch of dark dried blood just inside the door.

She stood there, stunned, with a terrible image running through her head—the dead man in the car!

He saw her rush out of the barn as he shoveled snow near the corral. He caught his breath and almost called her name, but something held him back. There was a frantic movement about her scrambling down the shoveled path and the bang of the back door as she went inside. What had happened? A warning alarm went off in his head. Had he lost control of the situation? Had something put her guard up? Hell! He'd waited too long for an opportunity like this to let it slip away. Time was running out. He'd have to seize the right moment to act—and soon.

Chapter Six

Jill fled upstairs to the hall bathroom, closed the door, leaned back against it and shut her eyes. Breathing heavily, she struggled to get control of herself. She wanted to deny the reality of what she'd seen, but she couldn't. Even as she searched for some other explanation, the vision of the ugly bloodstain and the splintered bullet hole in the door frame changed like a horrible kaleidoscope into the dead man in the car drenched in his own blood. There couldn't be any connection between the two, could there? But even as she grasped at a thin thread of disbelief, her intellect scoffed at such a coincidence. There had been a shooting in the barn—the physical evidence was there. And she'd seen with her own eyes a man dead from a bullet wound, sitting in a car parked at the edge of Haverly Ranch property. Now she realized that there would have been more blood splattered all over the front seat and some sign of a weapon if the man had shot himself. Her stomach turned over, remembering Hal's lack of urgency about notifying the sheriff.

There has to be a different explanation.

Maybe someone else had shot the man. Zack? Kirby? They could have been in the barn. But Hal must have noticed the bullet hole and the blood, which could very well mean that he condoned the killing. Maybe one of them had carried the man to his car. *Stop it!* All this speculation wasn't going to solve anything.

She splashed cold water on her face as if the chilled washing would take away the nausea churning her stomach. She had no idea what she should do. How could she pretend ignorance of what she'd seen? Was she snowbound with a killer? She buried her face in a towel to muffle a sob.

When she heard a knock at the bathroom door, she stiffened. Hal must have come after her. What should she do? Pretend ignorance? Or demand an explanation? How would he react if she came right out and accused him of shooting someone? As long as they were snowbound, she was trapped inside the house and there was nothing she could do about it.

"Jill! Are you in there?"

It was Gary's voice and not Hal's. Thank heavens! She needed more time to marshal her thoughts. She brushed at her eyes and smoothed her hair. Then she crossed the room and opened the door. When she saw the young father's worried face, she asked quickly, "What is it, Gary?"

"It's Sue. I think she's running a temperature."

Jill silently groaned. What would they do if she had a fever and needed medication?

"I feel hot and weak," Sue admitted as Jill took out the small first-aid kit she'd brought and prepared to take her temperature. The young woman's face was flushed and her eyes were heavy.

Gary watched anxiously as they waited for three minutes and Jill withdrew the thermometer, then he tried to read it over her shoulder. "What is it? Is she running a fever?"

Jill nodded. The mercury band indicated a temperature of a hundred and three. "A slight one," she lied. She knew it was well above normal.

"I'm sorry to be such a bother," Sue murmured.

"What's the matter with her?" Gary asked anxiously.

"Could be just a reaction from the delivery, and a couple of aspirins will put her right," Jill said, not believing the optimistic words for a minute. The most logical diagnosis—and the one that sent a chill through Jill—was that the new mother was fighting an infection. The fever could be a warning that Sue needed to be on antibiotics—and soon.

"But what if it isn't?" Gary's voice rose and his eyes reflected new fear. "We've got to do something!"

Jill fervently agreed. "It's stopped snowing. Maybe there's a chance we can move Sue and the baby once the roads are cleared."

"How soon will that be?"

"Maybe this afternoon," she said with more hope than conviction. She handed Sue two aspirin from a bottle she always carried in her bag. "How's the little one doing?" Jill peeked at the bundled baby and saw with relief that he was sleeping peacefully. The newborn's tiny nose wiggled in contentment and his little lips curved in a cupid's bow. She'd never seen anything more precious. New determination gave her strength. She straightened and said briskly, "Let me go downstairs and talk with the men. We'll decide the best thing to do. Both of you try to get some rest while you have the chance."

She was halfway down the stairs when she stopped abruptly. Hal stood at the bottom waiting for her. She could tell from his glower that he was bewildered by her sudden departure from the barn without so much as a mumbled goodbye. Bracing herself, she went down the remaining stairs.

He searched her face, his eyes anxious. "What happened? Why did you run out of the barn like that?"

Her mind whirled with indecision. What did she know about this man? Nothing except that being in his arms had triggered a tornado of emotions and desires. She felt totally confused and off balance. Should she come right out and tell him what she'd seen? Was there danger in being honest?

"I came out of the tack room just in time to see you running out the door," he said. He reached out a hand to her but she ignored it. "What is it, Jill?"

Her emotions were too much in a whirl to make any rational decision about what she should or should not say. She took a deep breath and sidestepped his question. This wasn't the time to voice her fears about being under the roof with a killer, or to challenge his knowledge of the bloodstains and bullet hole. "I don't want to talk about it now. We've got trouble. It's Sue. She's running a temperature of a hundred and three. I'm afraid she may be fighting an infection. We have to get her medical attention."

"Oh, no." He ran an agitated hand through his hair. "There's no way the road crews are going to make it as far as the ranch today, or even tomorrow." His mind raced, trying to find an answer. "Someone would have to plow the highway from Rampart all the way to the house for us to get out. The way the drifts have blown in, we couldn't even dig our way to the main road."

"There has to be a way." She fought to stem a rising panic. "Maybe they'll have the telephone lines repaired soon. We have to get the word out that we have a potential emergency.''

The lines around his eyes deepened. "Maybe we can get to Scotty's cellular phone now."

"I forgot all about Scotty's phone! How soon can you have it here?"

"I'm afraid it's one of those cellular phones that's powered by a car battery, which is why even if we could have gotten to it yesterday, we couldn't have been in constant contact throughout the birth.'' His expression lightened. "But it's stopped snowing and even if the wind is still kicking up, we might be able to dig our way to the stalled truck. And if the damn phone's still working, we can call 911."

A spurt of relief went through her. Making contact with the outside world would solve a lot of things. Her mind raced ahead. The first priority was getting medical attention for Sue. But there were other calls that should be made, like to the sheriff. And she intended to make use of the phone herself. "How long will it take to get to the phone?"

"Depends on how much digging we have to do. Scotty abandoned the truck somewhere on the drive up to the house. The pickup is probably buried up to the roof. We'll have to dig it out before we can get to the phone."

"I'm going with you."

"No, you're not," he said flatly. "I told you, I don't know what the situation is with the truck. There's no way to tell how long it will take to get to it."

"I don't care. I want to make the call for medical assistance."

"Why? Don't you trust me to make it?"

She bit back a sharp retort. This was no time to challenge his honesty about making calls. "I know how these things work," she said evenly. "I can speak to the guy who makes the decisions. They have to know that it's crucial that Sue gets proper medication—and soon. And if there's a phone that's working, I'm going to call Randy." He opened his mouth to protest, but she snapped, "We don't have time to argue."

"All right. I'll round up the men. If we get a path open to the truck, you can come along." He paused for a moment and, ignoring her stiff posture, laid a brief kiss on her cheek. "It's going to be all right, you'll see."

She went with him as he headed for the kitchen to explain the situation to the men.

"The wind's come up again, boss," Zack said when Hal told them what he wanted to do. "Half the shoveling we did this morning is already filled in."

"What good will it do to call out?" Scotty frowned. "Everything's socked in. There's no way any ambo is going to make it here."

Hal ignored their protests. "We'll do the shoveling job two by two. Zack, you and Larry take the first shift. From what Scotty says, the truck stalled at the edge of the clearing in front of the house. When you get halfway there, come back, and Scotty and I will handle the rest."

"Better you guys than me," Kirby said as he dumped chopped vegetables into a pot of beef stock. "I gave up this morning before I got halfway to the bunkhouse, and I'm not hankering to do any more shoveling till I see some blue sky."

Hal turned to Jill. "No need for you to venture out until we have passage all the way to the truck. Then I'll come and get you and you can make the calls."

"Are you sure? I'm willing to help."

"You can take my shift, Jill," Larry said as he slipped into his coat. "Or come along to keep us company."

"Those narrow snow tunnels would be a lot cozier with you along," Zack added, winking at her.

"Down, boys." Scotty laughed. "You heard the boss. She's staying with us. We'll keep the lady warm."

"Let's get on it, guys," Hal said, putting an end to the banter, not liking them flirting with Jill. He realized then how possessive he'd become about her.

Jill ran upstairs, told Sue and Gary what was happening, settled both her and the baby for a nap, and then came back downstairs, just as Zack and Larry were ready to leave.

The most direct route to the stalled truck was from the front door of the house. A narrow road that ran to the property from a county road widened into a broad clearing as it reached the front of the house. They would have to dig across the open space and far down the driveway to reach the stalled truck. Zack and Larry plunged outside into the whirling wind and snow, and Hal quickly shut the front door behind them.

"Looks like the storm is settling in again," he said, frowning as he looked out of the narrow windows flanking the front door. He could barely see the two dark figures tossing shovelfuls of snow in the air. "Can't tell whether new snow is coming down or the wind's just blowing what's on the ground around."

"I'm not sure the old truck will start after sitting out this long." Scotty frowned. "And the phone won't work without power from the car battery."

"That's just what we need to hear," Hal said with a sigh of resignation.

"I'm sorry I didn't get the truck closer," Scotty said

regretfully. "I just didn't think about something like this happening."

"None of us did," Jill assured him and he sent her a grateful look. No use putting a guilt trip on Scotty. If his phone worked, they'd all be in debt to him.

"We might as well wait in the den," Hal said, turning away from the front window. "Maybe there's an updated forecast on the radio."

There was, but the news wasn't what they'd hoped to hear. The forecaster warned that a new cold front had descended upon the region. No new snow was expected, but blizzard conditions would continue as high winds whipped existing snow into a blinding frenzy.

"Old man winter's really laying it on," Scotty said with a shake of his sandy-colored head. "Kinda makes me wonder if we all shouldn't sell out and head south."

Hal moved restlessly around the room, and when Kirby brought in coffee, Jill gratefully accepted a cup. It seemed like an eternity had passed since breakfast. She cupped the warm mug in her hands, trying to appear calm and confident, while her body tensed with waiting.

NEARLY AN HOUR PASSED before Zack and Larry returned to the house, looking like walking snowmen. Larry's ski mask was totally white except for the dark circles of his eyes, and Zack's hat brim and hair were crusted with snow.

"It's a losing battle," Zack told them. "The path was filling in behind us almost as fast as we shoveled the snow. And if the blasted truck isn't parked exactly where Scotty says, you'll have a hell of a time even finding it."

Larry nodded. "You could dig right past it, thinking it's just another rounded snowdrift. You can't make out anything out there." He sighed. "I bet there's a great powder base on the slopes. Lucky skiers! This is a dream storm for the resorts.''

Hal ignored him. "How far did you get, Zack?"

His ranch hand shrugged. "Maybe halfway…maybe not. Until the wind dies down, it's plain stupid to be out there throwing more snow in the air."

"Seems like the sensible thing to do is wait," Scotty agreed. "And we're not even sure the truck will start when we get there."

"There's only one way to find out," Hal answered shortly. "Come on, fishermen. Let's go." He turned to Jill. "Sorry, but you'll have to stay here."

"I—"

"Forget it. *If* we find the truck, *if* it starts, and *if* the phone is working, I'll make the 911 call."

If there'd been any way she could have reached the phone on her own, she would have defied him. Without his willing consent, she was stymied. "But I wanted to call Randy," she protested as if this might have some influence on him.

"I'll check on him. Make sure he's okay. Anything you want me to tell him?" he asked gently, wanting to take her in his arms again. If the other men hadn't been there, he'd have ignored the stiffness in her manner and pulled her close.

Jill bit her lip. She wanted to hear her son's voice. It seemed ages since she'd hurriedly kissed him goodbye. So many things had happened that she felt they'd been separated for weeks instead of just three days. Relaying messages wasn't the same thing as talking to him. "Just tell him that I'll be home soon…that I miss him…and love him…and…" Her voice trailed off as a swell of emotion choked her.

"I'll give him the message." One of his hands cupped her chin as he looked down into her eyes. "I promise."

She forgot about the horrible discovery in the barn, as the warmth of his eyes seeped through her. For a moment, there was nothing ugly between them. Then she heard herself say, "And make that call to the sheriff."

"Sheriff?" Zack echoed. Larry and Scotty looked puzzled, and Kirby frowned as the three men exchanged quick looks.

"Why tie up the phone lines with something that can wait?" Hal asked in a dismissive tone.

"Because he needs to know." Jill knew with sickening certainty that he wasn't going to make the call. He'd had time to call the sheriff before the phones went out, and he hadn't done it. Now, more than ever, she wanted to get to the cellular phone, but she couldn't see any way to defy Hal's orders to stay in the house.

"What's she talking about, boss?" Zack asked.

"Some guy got stranded in his car. He must have thought he was going to freeze to death and decided to take a quicker way out. He shot himself."

A flicker of caution kept her silent. Until she could tell someone else about her discovery, she'd better play along.

"I think we ought to take care of first things first," Hal said briskly. "Come on, Scotty."

"Keep your fingers crossed," the Scotsman told Jill. "Could be we're making all this effort for nothing."

"Happy shoveling," Zack told them with a grin as the two men left the den.

Jill walked with them to the front door. She was secretly hoping that conditions might have changed enough so that she could insist on going with them, but as the door swung open, a blast of snow poured through the opening, and the wind howled like a wounded beast. She knew there was no chance of Hal changing his mind.

"Holy cow!" cried Scotty.

Suddenly Jill was fearful that even strong men like Hal and Scotty would be at risk trying to make their way through the quickening blizzard. She remembered Hal telling her about people losing their way and freezing to death before finding their way back to the house. "Be careful! Don't get lost. I don't want to have to come after you two," she yelled.

She thought Hal laughed but couldn't be sure. As the two men put their heads down and pushed outside, she wanted to call them back. One minute they were in the doorway, and the next they had disappeared into a curtain of whipping snow. Jill had to put all her weight behind the door to close it.

She turned around just as Larry came down the hall from the den. "Come on, Jill. Kirby's spreading out lunch."

"Thank you, but I'm not hungry."

"Sure you are. Food and drink are the antidotes for any trouble." Strands of his blond hair waved wetly around his tanned face. "I've been trying to get Zack to tune up his guitar. Nothing like music to set the world right. All we need is the company of a pretty gal," he coaxed as he smiled down at her. "You have to do your bit to keep our spirits up. No telling what Hal will send us out to do next. Besides, we're having the cook's specialty—cold beef sandwiches. Again."

Maybe waiting for Hal and Scotty to come back would be less stressful if she had lunch with the others. Gary would come and get her if Sue or the baby needed her. She sincerely appreciated what the skier and Zack had done to help out, and she didn't want to appear rude or standoffish. "All right, I'll join you for a little bit."

HAL COULDN'T HEAR anything but the driving wind as they pushed ahead through the narrow passage that Zack and Larry had dug. Just as Zack had predicted, the wind was busily filling up the shoveled path with blowing snow. Already the depth in the passage was back up to Hal's knees. Fortunately, the powdered snow was soft and light, and they made pretty good time until they came to the high drift where Zack and Larry had stopped shoveling. Blocked by the bank of snow, Hal couldn't see anything ahead. He hoped the blockage wasn't a solid drift. As wind swept across the open ground, it made irregular mounds of snow, some shallow, some deep.

Side by side, like a pair of automatic shovels, Hal and Scotty dug their way forward. As the wind whipped around them, flying snow filled their eyes, ears and mouths. The only directional reference they had was a tall light pole that stood at the end of the drive, where Scotty said he'd left the truck.

Hal had to keep stopping to clear his vision and to make sure that they hadn't been wandering off course. He hoped to heaven Scotty was clear about where he'd abandoned his truck. Their laborious efforts seemed to go on forever. Hal fretted at the snail's pace. The clearing in front of the house seemed to stretch a mile even though he knew it was far less. Despite the fact that he was in good physical condition, his muscles were beginning to protest at the brutal exercise. If they didn't reach the truck soon—

Scotty let out a yell. "Yahoo! Here she be!"

They might have missed the vehicle buried in the high

drift if they'd been shoveling farther to the left. Just the black roof of the camper bed on the back of the pickup was visible in the mound of white snow.

With renewed energy, they dug away the snow until they could open the passenger-side front door. Scotty slipped in behind the steering wheel and Hal beside him. Once inside, the two men just sat in the front seat for a few minutes, breathing heavily, savoring victory over the forces of cold, snow, wind, and their own muscles.

Hal looked at the rectangular cellular phone mounted on the dash and his chilled body was suffused with new apprehension. What if the damn thing didn't work? He turned to Scotty sitting behind the wheel. "Well, give the engine a try. See if she'll start."

Scotty fumbled in his pants pockets with his thickly gloved fingers. When his hands came up empty from one pocket and he shifted in the seat to try the other one, Hal choked back a spurt of exasperation. "You didn't forget the keys, did you?"

Scotty frowned. "They're here somewhere." He finally jerked off his right glove and searched his pockets again. This time his round face broke into a grin as he pulled the keys from an inside jacket pocket. Finally locating the right key, he inserted it in the ignition. Hal's chest tightened as Scotty turned the key.

A responding sputter from the engine was at once promising and threatening. There was still power in the battery, but only a few tries could wear it down.

"Start, damn you, start," Scotty mumbled. As if his cursing had some effect, a few grinding sounds later, the engine sputtered, coughed and caught. "Good girl." Scotty laughed and patted the steering wheel. "Hasn't let me down yet. We've been through a lot together. I don't call her Queenie for nothing."

To Hal's relief, the cellular phone made a beeping sound and responded with a lighted face and a flash of its cellular number.

"There you go." Scotty handed the phone to Hal. "Make your calls. Dial the number and push the 'Send' button."

The emergency 911 number was answered immediately. As succinctly as he could, Hal identified himself and explained the situation. "We have to have medical assistance for the mother and baby immediately."

The dispatcher's response was evasive and Hal's voice rose. "Don't tell me there's no way to get anyone here. Find a way! I'm staying on the line until you make the arrangements."

Scotty chuckled. "That's telling them."

There was a muffled exchange on the other end. Then a man came on the line and identified himself as a paramedic with the county hospital. "The only option we have is to try to bring the mother and infant in by helicopter. Is there a clear spot near your house where it would be feasible to land? No trees, cliffs, or canyons."

Hal's mind quickly ran through the possibilities. "There's a pasture on the west side of the house. The wind always whips across it and piles up the snow around the bordering fences. If you land there, we can shovel out a gate and you'll be able to bring a stretcher to the back of house and pick up the patient."

"All right. But we won't be able to make the lift until tomorrow. Wind is supposed to die down by then. If it doesn't, we won't be able to put a whirlybird in the air."

Hal wanted to argue that tomorrow was too long to wait, but common sense told him they'd be lucky if the weather settled down enough by then to land a copter.

"I understand," said Hal with a prayerful breath that for once the forecasters would be right.

"Shall we say high noon? We'll fly over the locale and check it out. If we can land, we will. If not, you'll have to wait until ground rescue can make it."

"I hope to hell that's not the case," Hal answered.

"We'll do our best."

There was nothing more Hal could do but assure the man that he'd have the mother and baby ready for transport once the copter landed. Before he hung up, he asked if there was anything they could do for their patient in the meantime.

"Give her aspirin and keep her comfortable."

And call me in the morning, Hal silently finished with a sour curve to his lips.

Scotty had been listening to the one-sided conversation with undisguised curiosity. "They're going to send a whirlybird?"

Hal nodded.

"When?"

"Tomorrow. They'll land in the west pasture. We'll have to dig out the gate so they can bring a stretcher to the back door. Of course, everything depends upon the wind dying down. If it's safe to land, they'll set down about noon. I hope to heaven Sue isn't any worse by then."

"There's not much we can do about it if she is," Scotty said philosophically.

Hal dialed the Rampart Mountain Rescue office and recognized Randy's eager voice, "Mountain Search and Rescue."

"Hi, Randy. It's Hal Haverly. Your mom asked me to call and check up on you."

"Is she all right?"

"Fine. She sends her love. How are things going? You doing okay?"

"Wow, you wouldn't believe this place." His boyish voice vibrated with excitement. "What a bummer of a storm. All kinds of calls coming in. I keep telling 'em to call the sheriff or 911." With a tinge of bragging, Randy told him about all the emergency calls that had come in and how he and Zeb were completely on top of the situation.

"Good job. I'll tell her that she left good men in charge. You'll have some stories to tell when this is over. Your mom's mighty proud of you."

"We tried to call the ranch but couldn't get through."

"Our telephone lines are down. I'm using a cellular phone in a friend's truck."

"Zeb and I have been worried. We were thinking that maybe Mom shouldn't have gone." There was a slight hint of blame in his boyish tone. "She's never gone out on a call before."

"We couldn't have managed without her, Randy," Hal said sincerely. "She's a special lady." He could have added that she was an intelligent and strong-willed woman, utterly feminine and provocative. He settled for a contrite admission. "I never realized what a remarkable mother you have. I can see why you're proud of her. Anyway, she wanted me to call and see how things were going."

"When do you think she'll be coming home?" There was less bravado in the question and more of a little boy wanting his mother.

"Maybe as early as tomorrow. If the wind dies down, they'll start clearing the roads."

"Did Calico have her foal?" Randy asked eagerly.

Hal smiled, remembering how wide-eyed the boy had

been when Hal had explained to the 4-H youths how mares were mated with certain stallions to keep a line going. "Sure did. A beautiful spotted filly."

"Awesome."

"Haven't named her yet. You'll have to come out and give me some ideas. Your mother calls her Princess."

"Ugh!"

Hal chuckled. "Maybe we can outvote her."

"Did Mom say she wanted to learn to ride?" Randy asked hopefully.

"No. But you should have seen her help feed and water the horses."

"My mom?"

Hal laughed at his astonishment. "For a city gal, she didn't do half bad."

"Maybe she'll bring me out to the ranch lots now," he said wistfully.

"Maybe," Hal answered, but there wasn't much conviction in his tone. He didn't know what had happened, but he sensed a gulch a mile wide between them. He must have come on too strong, frightened her with the exploding desire that made him want her more than he'd ever wanted any woman.

"I was kinda hoping that you two might be friends now," Randy said with touching honesty.

"To tell the truth, I was kinda hoping the same thing," Hal admitted.

After he said goodbye and hung up the phone, he didn't say anything until Scotty made a noise that might have been a snicker. Hal glared at him. "What was that for?"

"Nothing. Nothing at all."

"All right, out with it."

Scotty chuckled again. "It's just that I never thought

I'd see the day. That pretty gal's about to get you hog-tied. My, my, when the tough ones fall, they fall hard.''

"Mind your own business, Scotty."

"Sure...sure. Just making a harmless observation."

Hal dialed another number.

"Who you calling now?"

"Jerry's garage." Hal was relieved when a gravelly voice on the other end answered on the third ring.

"Hi, Jerry. This is Hal. I'm at the ranch. Our phone lines are down, but I'm using Scotty McClure's cellular truck phone."

"This modern stuff beats all, don't it? What can I do you for?"

"I need to have you send me out a battery as soon as the roads are open. Maybe even one of the fellows headed this way with a snowplow could drop it by."

"Sure thing, but it ain't going to be today. The way this thing is settling in, it may have to be tomorrow or the next."

"Make it as soon as you can. I've got some important things to do and I'm stuck without my Bronco."

Jerry just snorted, and Hal knew he was rightly disgusted with people like himself who waited until an emergency arose before taking care of things like a worn-out battery.

"Are you through with all your calls?" Scotty asked when Hal hung up. "What about the sheriff? Jill wanted you to call him. Remember?"

"I remember."

"And?"

"And what?"

"Well, are you going to do it? What's this all about, Hal? Is there something going on that I don't know about?" Scotty looked puzzled.

"I've had a call in to Sheriff Perkins's office for a week."

His closed expression stopped Scotty from asking any more questions. "Well, then, I guess we can get back to the house," the Scotsman said.

"Is there anyone you want to call, Scotty?" Hal asked. "Might as well take care of everything while we're here."

The Scotsman shook his head. "There's nobody at my place. Everything's shut down for the winter. That's why I headed this way when my power went out. By the way, I've got some foodstuff in the truck's camper that we could take back with us. Kirby said he was running short on flour, beans and a few other things I've got stashed away. Feeding eight people, three times a day, takes a lot of grub. You're darn lucky to have a cook like Kirby."

Hal had to agree. The truth was, he'd gotten so used to Kirby's cooking that good meals were something he took for granted. He didn't know what he would have done if Kirby hadn't been around to cook for the stranded guests. The fare would have been a darn sight skimpier, he knew that.

"Okay, but we'd better make it back before Jill panics and sends someone out to rescue us. Or comes herself," he added with a wry smile.

AS JILL AND LARRY entered the den, she looked around in surprise. From what Larry had said about food, drink and music, she had expected that Kirby and Zack were waiting there for lunch. "Where is everyone?"

"Oh, they'll be along. Let's sit over here by the bar." He motioned to a corner sofa on the far side of the room.

"Kirby put out these sandwiches and coffee. How about a beer or something stronger to whet your appetite?"

"No, thanks. Coffee is fine." She sank down wearily on the couch. Her emotions had been on a roller coaster since she woke up that morning in Hal's bed. She was already regretting her decision to stay downstairs and make conversation. She only took half a sandwich from the tray Larry offered.

"Sorry you've had such a rough go of it," he said as he sat down on the leather couch beside her. "Beats me how you did it, delivering that baby all by yourself."

"I didn't do it all by myself."

"Hal said you did."

"He's just being kind—and modest." She remembered how the two of them had shared those long anxious hours and the strange bonding that developed between them. The explosive sexual attraction that had ignited when he drew her into his arms and kissed her had leveled all her defenses. She didn't understand why she'd been drawn into such an emotional whirlwind. How had it happened? Had she completely taken leave of her senses? She couldn't be in love, not when every strand of common sense denied it. Falling in love was for dewy-eyed romantics. She was a sensible woman with a son to raise. She lowered her eyes so Larry wouldn't see the emotions warring within her.

"We should be getting out of here by tomorrow," Larry said as if trying to cheer her up. "Guess you'll be glad?"

She nodded. These few days of bewildering emotions had made her a stranger to herself. "I'll be happy to have things back to normal."

"Getting snowbound like this has been the pits. Cost me money."

"There's no need for resort shuttle service in this weather," she said puzzled, remembering that he'd told her that was one of his jobs.

"Oh, I'm not talking about that. What do you think of my belt?" he asked "And my hair tie?"

She hadn't even noticed the intricately woven leather belt or hair tie before. The Indian design was quite detailed. "They're very nice," she murmured, wondering why he was beaming at her with such pride.

"I made them. And my brother and I have leased a shop at the resort to sell them. He's the businessman but I'm the creative one. We've been working our butts off trying to make enough money to get started. Sometimes he pushes me a little too hard, you know what I mean?"

Jill wasn't sure she did but she nodded sympathetically. "Well, I wish you luck with your venture."

"Thanks." He launched into a detailed account of the problems of a little guy trying to get into business.

More than ever, she wished she'd avoided this kind of one-on-one chitchat. She wasn't up to it, but he didn't seem to notice. At the first opportunity, she put down her half-finished sandwich and murmured her apology. "I really should go upstairs now."

"But you haven't eaten anything," he protested, as Zack came into the den. "Here's the troubadour now. Glad you showed up, cowboy. I'm sure Jill was thinking I'd lied to her. Where's your guitar?"

"I left it in the bunkhouse. I reckon I'll choose my own time to play it."

"Oh, don't be such a poor sport. Go get it. I promised Jill you'd play us some of them corny country songs. You know the tear-jerking kind I mean. Love gone wrong. Some good old boy's horse up and dying." He laughed. ''Jill would get a kick out of hearing a cowboy strumming away and yodeling to the moon.''

One look at Zack's thunderous expression, and Jill stood up quickly. ''I don't think this is the time for any entertainment. You'll really have to excuse me.''

''See what you've done,'' Larry lashed out at Zack.

Without looking at either of the men, she abruptly left the room. She wasn't going to stay and be a witness to any confrontation that put Hal's den in shambles.

IT SEEMED TO JILL that Hal and Scotty had been gone for hours, when she finally heard them returning to the house. A few minutes earlier she had sent Gary down to be with the other men. His anxious worrying only added to his wife's stress, and Jill had better luck keeping Sue's spirits up without him.

The slam of the front door vibrated up the stairs, and then Hal's booming voice floated up from the hall below. A poignant stab of relief shot through Jill. She knew then how worried she'd been that they would lose their way and get lost in the storm. Every minute they'd been gone had been an agonizing eternity.

For a brief moment, her mind wouldn't handle anything else. Then a legion of anxious questions whipped through her mind like frantic birds. Had they reached the truck? Was the telephone working? Had they been able to make the calls? Was help on the way?

She wanted to rush downstairs without a second's delay, but she was in the process of helping Sue get the baby to take a bottle of water. Since Sue was taking aspirin and there was a chance she had an infection, it seemed wise not to let the baby try to nurse. Jill felt that she couldn't leave until the infant was satisfied and she'd made Sue as comfortable as possible. She tried to be patient until the sleeping baby was tucked in the crib and she was free to leave.

"I'll be back in a few minutes," she promised and hurried out of the room. She'd only taken a few steps down the hall when she heard her name called.

"Jill, wait up."

She jerked around just as Hal came out of his bedroom, obviously having changed into dry clothes. She rushed at him. "What happened? Did you make the call? What did they say?"

"Easy...easy, relax," he soothed and then lowered his voice. "Yes, we got through. The weather's supposed to clear by morning, and the pickup is set for noon," he assured her. "A helicopter will set down just west of the house. The attendants will load her and the baby and have them to the county hospital in a few minutes."

"You're sure they're coming?"

"Trust me, we've got everything under control."

Trust him! She wanted to laugh hysterically. She was racked with feelings of doubt and suspicions about him to the point that she didn't know what to believe. This man was at the center of a disaster that was tearing her apart.

"Jill, what is it? Talk to me!" He looked and sounded genuinely concerned.

Raising her eyes to his, she knew that she couldn't pretend ignorance any longer. She had to know. This horrible thing between them was tearing her apart. She moistened her dry lips and took the plunge. "I think you know more than you're telling me about the man in the car. I saw blood and a bullet hole in the barn."

He dropped his hands from her shoulders as if an electrical shock had gone through him. The genuine bewilderment in his expression sent a rush of relief through her. *He didn't know!* She was sure of it! Why had she been so stupid not to tell him about the discovery when she made it?

He pulled her back into his bedroom. "You saw what? Tell me! Now."

She bit her lip and tried to steady her voice. "At the back of the barn. There's blood on the ground. And a splintered bullet hole in the door frame. When I saw it, I thought...I thought..." she stammered.

She didn't know whether his expression was one of utter disbelief or horrified acceptance. Before he could say anything, heavy steps sounded on the stairs.

"Sorry to interrupt, boss." Kirby drawled an apology as he looked around the half-opened door. His narrowed eyes swept over Jill's flushed face and Hal's head bent close to hers. "I didn't know you were...er... er...busy."

Jill stiffened with the cook's suggestive hesitation that he'd intruded upon some compromising situation. The crackling tension between her and Hal was not at all the kind that Kirby's leer implied.

"Well, what is it?" snapped Hal.

"I was just thinking you might want to get out to the barn. It's Calico's foal. She's down."

"No! What in the hell happened?"

Kirby shrugged. "Zack just said you'd better take a look."

Jill didn't know what to do or say in this new crisis. She had seen the love and tenderness in Hal's eyes as he'd stroked the foal. She winced just thinking about what the loss would mean to him.

"Could be she's been hit like the others," Kirby stated matter-of-factly.

Hal's expression changed to one of black rage. "The bastards!"

"What is it?" Jill asked, her heart tightening. She didn't understand the unspoken communication between the two men.

"I'll explain later."

She nodded. He looked torn between her and the crisis in the barn, so she gave him a slight push toward the door. "See to the foal."

Kirby lingered in the doorway as Hal bounded down the stairs. His watchful eyes took in Jill's slumped shoulders and lowered head. "You want me to tell the boss to lay off?"

"What do you mean?"

"Easy to see, he's putting his spurs to you. I've seen it happen before. Some gal comes around and before you know it, Hal's got a hackamore on her. You know what a hackamore is, don't you?"

"No, and I really don't care," she answered tersely.

The cook just gave her one of his thin smiles. "Don't say I didn't warn you."

Jill moved past him out into the hall. She wasn't about to discuss her tangled emotions with Hal's cook. It wasn't any of his business. "I'm sorry about the foal."

"There'll be hell to pay if he loses her," Kirby said, then added, "Hal doesn't take kindly to disappointments, especially where horses and women are concerned."

She decided to ignore his pointed warning.

HAL BENT HIS HEAD against the blowing snow and biting cold and slammed his way to the barn. Zack swung around at Hal's entrance, stepping back from Calico's stall and pointing to the foal lying listlessly on the straw. "Doesn't look good, boss."

Hal unlatched the stall gate and stepped in. "Easy, girl," he soothed as he let his hand run down the mare's neck. Then he knelt down beside the foal. "What's the matter, baby?" he asked gently.

The filly raised her head but didn't try to get up. Her dark brown eyes were clear and he was relieved that there was no distortion of the belly. That was a good sign. He let his hands move over her neck and withers, stroke her back, and then slip on down her long legs. She didn't seem sensitive to his touch and there was no indication of pain.

"What do you think, boss?"

Hal sighed heavily. "Maybe she's not getting enough nourishment. Our best bet is to give her the stuff the vet left the last time a mare had a foal. Fix a bottle."

"Won't do any good if she's been poisoned," Zack said flatly.

Poisoned. The word was like a dagger in his side. He clenched his fists as he stood up. His face a dark glower, he pushed by Zack and strode the length of the barn.

Then he stopped. For a long moment, he couldn't get his breath. He just stood there, frozen. The evidence was all there, just as she had said.

Zack came up behind him. "What's the matter, boss? You—" he broke off as his eyes fell on the splattered blood and bullet hole. "Well, I'll be! Would you look at that?"

Hal drew in a long breath. "I should have figured it all out before now."

"What you going to do now, boss?"

Hal straightened up. "I guess I'll have to admit I shot the bastard."

A sudden intake of breath warned Hal too late that, completely unnoticed, Jill had come into the barn and stood, appalled, a few feet behind them.

Chapter Seven

The expression on Jill's face told Hal that she'd heard everything. The truth lay between them like odorous carrion. He would have done anything to spare her this moment. But it was too late. Everything he didn't want to see was in her face. Horror. Repugnance. And fear.

"Uh-oh!" Zack said, hastily making a retreat from an atmosphere that was charged like a threatening hurricane.

"You don't understand." As he took a step toward her, she stepped back, defensive and guarded.

"Why did you kill him?" Her voice was thin and strangled, and he winced inwardly at her tone.

"I didn't. I mean, I didn't know I had."

Disbelief was etched in every taut facial muscle as she stared at him. He hadn't expected her to believe him. Even now he had a hard time believing it himself. He cursed himself for not having checked out the barn before. Not that it would have made a damn bit of difference. It had all happened too fast. Even now he had trouble putting everything into the right sequence. He could see her shock giving way to fiery emotion.

"You didn't know that you shot a man?" she flared.

"I'll try to explain."

"Please do." Her voice was as cold as the breath that formed clouds in front of her lips.

"Someone's been poisoning my stock. Just this month I've lost a dozen head of cattle and a valuable Appaloosa stallion I had in the corral. We've been trying to catch whoever was doctoring the feed. I've kept a sharp eye out when I did my chores or rode out to check on the cattle, watching for anybody sneaking around the place. No sign of the sneaking bastards until the other morning. I came in to feed the horses and saw a shadowy figure hiding behind some bales at the back of the barn. I called out, but he didn't show himself. I always keep a rifle in the tack room for predators—until that moment, the animal kind.

"When I came out with the gun, he took off, running toward the back door. I fired a couple of warning shots and you have to believe me, I didn't know I'd wounded him. I fired two warnings shots, one over his head and one to the side. Neither bullet came anywhere close to hitting him. I didn't intend to shoot him, and I wasn't off on my aim." He dropped his eyes to the bloodstains, his expression one of disbelief.

"Then how did the blood get there?"

For a moment he didn't answer. He bent his head back and looked up at the bullet hole in the door frame, then turned his searching gaze to the side of the door where some metal feed troughs were stacked up on end. Slowly he reached out his hand and fingered an indentation in one of them. Then he let out a slow whistle. "So that explains it. I'll be damned."

"What? Tell me!" She couldn't make any sense out of the attention he was giving to the feed trough.

His expression was grim. "See this indentation. The bullet must have ricocheted off this metal trough and hit him. And I didn't know it. He didn't stumble at all, just bounded out the door.''

"But you must have run after him.''

"Hell, yes, but I went out the side door because I saw him veer to the right when he fled the barn. I thought I'd intercept him as he came around the corner, but he must have fled into a thick stand of trees behind the building. Blowing snow was already falling fast, covering up his tracks. I ran back and forth and around the building, but he was gone. I didn't see any sign of him. Now I realize he must have parked his car in a rutted road in the trees behind the barn and managed to drive as far as the highway—where you found him.'' He took another step toward her, but she backed up farther.

"Why didn't you tell me all of this when I told you about finding the dead man?''

"I didn't see the connection between the two. Don't you see? The man I'd caught sneaking around my barn hightailed it out of here. Until you told me about the blood at the back door, I didn't know I'd hit him. Damn it, I wanted to catch him. Find out who in the hell he was and if he'd been hired to poison my stock.''

"But why would anyone do such a horrible thing?''

"Isn't it plain enough? I told you before that more than one land grabber has been pressuring me to sell the ranch. My property is sitting in the right spot for development, and it's no secret that if I keep the ranch, my profit margin is very thin. I can't keep taking losses. Someone knows that. And killing off my animals is about as low as greed can get.'' His jaw hardened. "If I hadn't come to the barn when I did, every one of the horses could have been fed poisoned feed...including Calico and her foal.''

Jill's stomach took a sickening plunge. She could only

imagine the devastation of losing the mare and her beautiful foal, as well as the other horses, to the agonizing death of poison. "How could anyone be so heartless?" She couldn't believe human selfishness could sink so low.

"Greed," he muttered. "I was just trying to save my animals. I put in a call about the poisonings to Sheriff Perkins a week ago, but he never called back. I'll confess everything if he ever shows up. That ought to make you happy."

Nothing about the ugly situation made her happy. She reached a hand out to him, but he stiffly ignored the gesture. His rejection was deserved, she thought helplessly. She'd hurt him. Believing the worst, she'd given him no quarter. How readily she had judged him. Even if the situation had been beyond her understanding, she should have had some faith in his integrity. The distrust she'd shown so pointedly was like barbed wire stretched between them, cutting them both, and she didn't know how to remove it. Hal had every right to protect his livestock from such deliberate cruelty, but suddenly another fear stabbed at her. Would there be retaliation? Could Hal have put his own life in danger over the shooting? Afraid for his safety, she asked in a strained voice, "Where will it all end?"

"I don't know, but I'll tell you one thing. It'll be over my dead body before anyone gets his greedy hands on my ranch."

Over my dead body. His words sent a chill of fear quivering up her spine. She wanted to plead with him not to jeopardize his own life in this situation, but she knew such pleas would be useless. He would never give in to harassment and threats.

"Because I had more immediate problems on my

mind, I brushed aside a dead man in a car without giving the matter much thought,'' he admitted.

She drew in a shaky breath. ''Now that I know the whole story, I understand how the tragedy could have happened. A real fluke. You had every right to fire the warning shots. I'm sorry that I jumped to the wrong conclusion. But now I understand. Really I do.'' The load he'd been carrying on his shoulders touched her heart and conscience.

He was staring at her, stiff and rigid, as if he couldn't believe that she'd thought even for a moment that he was a killer. She wanted to slip her arms around his neck and draw his face down to hers, but she knew he would reject her feeble attempt to make things right. She had hurt him deeply and ruined the beginning of something tender and beautiful by her unfounded suspicions and quick judgment.

Zack broke the tense moment, calling from Calico's stall, ''Boss, you'd better give me a hand. I can't get the filly to take the bottle.''

''Coming,'' he said, his face set in rigid lines and the shadowed sadness back in his eyes.

They were strangers again, she thought helplessly. His pointed rebuff hurt more than she would have thought possible. The warm glow of affection between them had faded as if it had never been. She determined that she would do what she must to make up for hurt she'd seen in his eyes.

She followed him to Calico's stall and watched as he knelt down beside the filly, tenderly stroking the foal and coaxing her to take the bottle. She knew from the hours they had worked together during the birth of Sue's child that Hal Haverly was a man of caring patience and tenderness. His brisk, tough exterior was a cover-up.

Clearly, he would be devastated if he lost the foal. The loss of his other animals must have torn him apart.

"Come on, sweetheart. You can do it." Patiently he urged the delicate little mouth to nurse the nipple.

"What do you think, boss? Is she sick or just weak?"

"I don't know."

After several frustrating minutes, the tiny foal began to suck the bottle, and the men looked at each other in relief. "If Calico's milk is the problem, we'll have to make sure we keep her on the bottle."

"Why would Calico dry up? If someone got to the mare's feed, she'd be the one down," Zack speculated.

"I checked all the feed. Threw out all the opened sacks in case the dirty work had been done before I came into the barn. I have enough evidence from the first round of poisonings to show the sheriff, if he ever gets his butt here." He brushed his eyes with his hand. "If I'd been a few minutes later with the chores, I'd have never known."

Zack nodded. "I'd say it's a good thing you keep a rifle handy."

"I hope I never have to use it again," Hal said grimly. "Get one of the horse blankets and cover up the foal."

As he closed the half-gate of the stall, Jill said, "I know you have a lot on your mind, Hal, but can we talk later?"

"I don't think talking ever changes very much," he said wearily. "And I don't think there's much more to say. What happened, happened. There's nothing to be done about it now. The man's dead. Besides, the way things are going, I think it would be better for you to keep clear of my problems."

"It's a little late for that," she countered. "And I disagree that we have nothing to say to each other.

There's no way we can just ignore the way we feel about each other, is there?''

He silently groaned at the soft, guileless beauty of her eyes as they searched his face. All of this was his fault. He never should have drawn her into his life. She didn't belong in the middle of this kind of turmoil. What did she know about the struggles for survival against men, beasts, and weather? She was meant for a better life than that. He'd lost his head and now it was time to get it back on straight.

At that moment Zack returned with the horse blanket. As Hal took the blanket from him, he nodded at Jill. ''I think you'd better get back to the house. Zack, go with her. See that she doesn't get lost.''

''I can find my way,'' she answered, frustrated. Why couldn't she say something that would put things right between them?

''Better let me walk you back,'' Zack readily insisted. ''Still nasty out there. We don't want you wandering off into some snowdrift, do we, boss?''

''There's no need—'' she began.

''Please, Jill, don't argue. I've got enough on my mind without worrying about whether you made it safely back to the house or not.''

His strained look made her swallow her protests. She turned without another word and headed toward the door.

''Wait up,'' Zack ordered as she plunged out into the storm before he could catch up.

Lowering her head against the biting wind and snow, she spurted forward for a few feet along the shoveled path. Frustration and anger fueled her steps. *Stubborn, hard-headed, infuriating man!*

Snowflakes collected on her eyelashes and biting cold

air seared her lungs. Her feet seemed shackled with weights as she lifted them through the snow. And then it happened. Her legs went out from under her.

She pitched forward, facedown on the path. Pain exploded behind one ear, and she gave a muffled cry as the side of her head hit something hard, just under the surface of the snow. As suddenly as she had fallen, she was pulled to her feet.

"Did you hurt yourself?" Zack's rough gloves cleared her face, brushing snow from her eyelids.

A ball of pain throbbed above her ear, and her legs seemed to be floating away as her knees suddenly turned to mush. She tried to put some rigidity into them, but couldn't.

"Steady now." His arms went around her in a possessive grip and as she wavered unsteadily, he swung her up into his sturdy arms. She could feel his strong legs thrusting through the snow as he carried her.

She wanted to protest that she was perfectly capable of walking, but instead she closed her eyes. As she pressed her chilled cheek against his leather jacket, the distance to the house seemed like an eternity. She was chilled and shivering by the time he threw open a door and brought her inside.

When he didn't readily put her down, she lifted her throbbing head and squinted at a shadowy interior. A blurred impression came to her of bunk beds along one wall, two chairs and an ugly brown sofa in front of a Franklin stove, which had a black stovepipe snaking up one wall to the ceiling. A bookcase made of boards and bricks held a lot of books and magazines. An open door showed a small bathroom at one end of the long room. She looked around in bewilderment. She'd never seen the place before.

"Where..." she managed to croak.

"The bunkhouse," he answered with an amused chuckle. "I was thinkin' I'd bring you the rest of the way, being as how you were heading this direction."

"I was not." She started to shake her head in denial but stopped when the pain rolled like a demolition construction ball from one side of her skull to the other. "I know my way back to the house."

"Most likely you got yerself turned around." He smiled at her as if he was content to stand there holding her in his thick arms. "As soon as you get your feet under you, I'll take you back to the house."

"Put me down."

He smiled at her agreeably but didn't slacken the firm circle of his arms. "That big old sofa is the only halfway comfortable sitting place we've got. Reckon you wouldn't mind resting there a bit. Me and Kirby don't have many lady visitors."

She grimaced as he plopped her down on a bumpy couch. She wondered if she looked as green as she felt. Snow coated her from head to foot and he fussed over her, removing her wraps and brushing layers of snow from her hair.

"There now. That's better. That fall shook you up a bit. Better lie down a spell."

"No, I'll sit up." She resisted the pressure of his hands as he tried to ease her on her back.

"You're sure? You look a little peaked to me."

"I hit my head," she told him. "That's why I was wobbly on my feet."

"Let me see." He gently took her head in his hands. "Don't see any blood, but I reckon you might have a goose egg, sure enough."

She was slightly dizzy as if the blow above her ear

had brought on a hint of vertigo. "I'll rest for just a minute and then I'll go."

"No hurry. Sorry the place isn't spruced up more," he apologized, sitting down beside her. "A couple of cowhands don't spend much time worrying about the way things look. Not a bad place to hang your hat, though. We spend most of our time in the big house. I don't reckon any gal would think this was much."

The bunkhouse looked liveable for sleeping and loafing, she thought, not really caring one way or the other. She glanced at a book left on a side table, surprised that either Kirby or Zack was a reader. She was uncomfortable in the situation. In fact, she was ill at ease with Zack's whole manner. A spicy scent of men's cologne touched her nostrils, and his dark hair looked newly trimmed. He was more than just friendly, and as soon as her legs regained some rigidity, she'd better get the heck out of there.

"Me and Kirby don't have many gals paying us a visit," he repeated. "Good thing we dug our way out here this morning and built a fire in the old stove. Feels good, don't it?"

When she inadvertently shivered instead of answering, he got up, grabbed an army blanket off a nearby bunk and carefully tucked the blanket around her. He smiled in satisfaction. "There you be. All cozylike. I'm a-thinkin' it was a good thing I was right behind you to pick you up."

Maybe I wouldn't have fallen if you hadn't been right behind me, she thought with a flicker of unbidden suspicion. Why had her legs gone out from under her? She hadn't tripped over anything, had she? How close behind her had Zack been before she fell?

She raised a hand to the side of her head and winced

against the light touch of her fingers against a swelling. She was going to have a bump for sure. As soon as she could navigate, she'd better get back to the house and put some ice on it. She certainly wasn't going to ask Zack to play nursemaid. She was out of there the minute she was sure she wouldn't fall on her face when she stood up. The whole situation was too weird.

"I've been hankering for the chance for us to have a little private talk," he said, as if reading her thoughts. "I know the boss is coming on to you pretty hard. And you must be scared, knowing he killed that man and all."

"He didn't mean to shoot him. Didn't you hear him explain what happened? It was a fluke accident."

"So he says."

If Jill's head hadn't been breaking up into aching, fragmented pieces, she might have been able to respond in some intelligent manner, but she wasn't up to any coherent arguments at the moment. He sat down, crowding closely against her on the couch.

"I reckon I should have warned you earlier." His mouth moved, but only fragments of what he was saying registered above a roaring in her ears. "Hal's a dangerous man...don't let him fool you. I can tell he has his branding iron out. Really a shame. You come here to help and all. And then he puts his spurs to you." His expression hardened. "You get my meaning?"

She knew that what he was saying tied together in some way, but his words were like a gnarled knot in her aching head. She managed a hoarse laugh. "Clearly. You're bad-mouthing your boss, and I'd really rather not hear it."

"Hey, I'm trying to offer my help."

"Thank you, but I don't need it."

He gave a short laugh. "Just like Betty May, another gal I knew. Got herself in more than one mess, she did. Always figuring a man's worth in dollars and cents. But she learned the hard way. I don't want that happening to you."

She didn't want to hear about Betty May or anyone else. Zack's face was only inches from hers, and she was trapped by the prison of one of his arms around her shoulder. *I can't cope with this, not now.* Her head was a throbbing locomotive threatening to derail. She moistened her dry tongue. "Zack, could...could I have a drink of water? Please?"

He hesitated a moment before he stood up and said, "Sure. Sure. And I've got a surprise for you, too."

That's what I need, more surprises, Jill thought grimly as he went into a small utility kitchen. She was preparing to try out her rubbery legs when he returned with a glass of water in one hand and his guitar in the other. *Oh no,* she silently groaned. A thumping guitar was the last thing she wanted to hear.

After handing her the water, he placed a stool in front of her and sat down. With all the determination of a Nashville hopeful, he stroked the instrument's gut strings and turned knobs to get it in tune. "I guess that birdbrain Larry gave you the wrong idea. He made it sound like I didn't want to play my guitar for you, but I've been waiting for the right moment. I wanted to get you alone. This song is for you, Jill. It's a love song." His eyes glazed over, as if drawing on some sensual fantasy.

Her head vibrated with an onslaught of wild chords as he began to play. *I've got to get out of here.* Even without a headache, the frenzied music would have been hard to take. She wanted to cover her ears and plead with him to stop the torture. This wasn't happening. The knock on her head must have sent her into some weird hallucination. *It's a nightmare. Dear God, let me wake up.*

The song he'd composed wasn't a sentimental love ballad, but an explosive, almost satanic offering about being consumed by a fire in his heart. Her name was scattered all through the horrible rendition. Every time she heard, ''Jill, Jill,'' she felt as if she was being hit on the head with a baseball bat. When he stopped playing, relief was an instant shock to her whole system.

He fixed intense eyes on her and her stomach turned over. How could she respond? What did he expect from her?

''Did you like it?'' he demanded, when she didn't say anything.

Taking a deep breath, she choked something about the piece being forceful. That was the best she could do.

She didn't like the set of his mouth and the look in his eyes as he put aside his guitar. He wanted more from her than lukewarm praise. A lot more.

Summoning strength against the vertigo swirling in her head, she threw off the blanket. ''I'd better get back to the house now.''

When she stood up, the floor swayed like the deck of a ship, and she might have fallen if he hadn't leaped off the stool and grabbed her. As Zack steadied her, holding her firmly in his arms, she nearly fainted as she looked over his shoulder and saw Hal standing inside the door, his face as black as a storm cloud.

''What in the hell is going on here?'' Hal couldn't believe what he was seeing. The two of them cozying up in the bunkhouse. The sound of Zack's guitar had reached him as he left the barn, and he'd expected to find his ranch hand goofing off as usual. But not holding

Jill Gaylor in his arms! He felt like an utter fool. And he'd been feeling like garbage because of her lack of trust in him. She was holding on to Zack as if even the embarrassment of being caught with him was of little importance.

"Excuse the interruption," he lashed out. "I thought Zack had seen you back to the house. I didn't know the two of you had sneaked away for some privacy."

"Hal, please," she said in wavering voice. "You don't understand—"

"I think I do," he cut her off. She pushed away from Zack and staggered toward him. If he hadn't reached out to grab her, she would have fallen at his feet. He was so startled that he gasped, "Jill, what's the matter?"

"She fell," Zack answered bluntly. "Hit her head. I carried her in here."

"Why in the hell didn't you come after me? You kept her here, listening to your caterwauling—"

"I was taking care of her. We were having a nice little visit while she got her feet under her again."

"Just a little dizzy," Jill mumbled as the angry voices ricocheted through her head. "Got a bump on my head. I need to lie down with some ice."

"Give me that blanket," Hal ordered. Zack handed it to him and he bundled her up like a child, pulling her coat around her as well. Then he lifted her in his arms, gave some curt orders to Zack about checking on the foal, then carried her through the snow, back to the house.

Enveloped in the warmth of the blanket and his arms, she closed her eyes and drew upon the strong rhythm of his body. As she rested her head against his chest, she closed off all thoughts but an invading momentary peace that even her aching head could not destroy.

Hal flung open the back door and bellowed at Kirby to bring an ice pack. The cook's eyes rounded. "What in—"

"Jill fell. Stop gawking and get the ice bag."

Kirby muttered something inaudible as Hal carried her through the kitchen and into his mother's sitting room just beyond. When he set her gently down on the floral sofa, she winced and touched her head. "Could I have some aspirin?"

"I'll get it. Don't try to get up."

"You have my promise," she said dryly, closing her eyes against the bongo drums in her head. Only once in her life had she had a migraine headache, but she remembered it well enough to concede that the present pain in her head was a close cousin.

He returned with a glass of water and the requested tablets. After she had taken them, he pulled up a chair beside the sofa. "Let me see."

Gently, he turned her head to one side. An ugly bump showed through her tumbled hair just above her right ear. Ouch, he thought. She'd hit something hard, all right. He cursed himself for being so caught up in anger and disappointment over her lack of trust that he hadn't walked her back to the house himself. But he'd sent Zack with her. A question hit him. *Why didn't Zack keep her from falling?* And why had he taken her to the bunkhouse instead of telling somebody what had happened and getting help? Hal's mouth tightened. *How long would Zack have kept her there if I hadn't heard his guitar?*

"I...I didn't mean to cause trouble," Jill apologized. Hal's glower seemed to be directed at her. "Don't be mad."

His frown dissolved and his eyes softened with concern as he gently touched a hand to her cheek. "I'm mad at myself. Not you. This is my fault. I should have taken better care of you."

Her usual retort, that she could take care of herself, seemed inappropriate. Why not be honest? She wanted nothing more in the world than to be cosseted and foolishly indulged. Yes, even spoiled.

"I never expected something like this to happen." He cursed himself for being so abrupt about sending her back to the house. When he'd come in the bunkhouse, and had seen Zack's arms around her and her head resting on his shoulder, he'd felt like someone had hit him with a two-by-four. Now he asked Jill quickly, "Zack didn't hurt you...or anything?"

"No," she said, and then added, "but his behavior was strange."

"What do you mean?"

"I'm not sure." She needed time to sort things out and get some perspective on what had happened. Maybe it was her imagination that suddenly made him seem a little frightening. Sighing, she said, "Don't ask him to play his latest composition—not without earplugs."

At that moment, Kirby came in with an ice bag that must have been ten years old. "Sorry it took me so long. I couldn't find the thing. I remembered Zack used it for one of his hangovers and had been lying down in the den with it. There it was, on a shelf behind the bar. Hope it doesn't leak." The cook squinted down at Jill as he handed Hal the bag and a small towel. "You don't look so good, gal. Knocked yourself out, did you?"

"No. Nothing like that. My legs got watery and my head started spinning."

"The ice should keep the swelling down," Hal said as he rested the ice bag on the side of her head.

"Brr, that's cold," she protested. "Feels good, though." The choice between cold and pain was an easy one to make.

"I guess we'll have two patients for the copter tomorrow, eh, boss?" asked Kirby.

"Don't be ridiculous," Jill answered quickly. "I just have a bump on my head. That's all. After a little rest, I'll be up and about, taking care of Sue and the baby."

"Sure you will," Hal agreed, not looking directly at her so she wouldn't see the worry he was trying to hide. "But right now, you're going to stay put."

"Would you like a cup of tea? And a fresh apple turnover?" Kirby asked, obviously dedicated to food as a cure for all ills.

"Maybe later. My stomach's kinda queasy," she said.

"Call me if you change your mind," Kirby said as he left with a shake of his thinning hair.

"I'm feeling a little sleepy."

"That's too bad," Hal said gruffly, "because you're going to stay awake just in case you've cracked your skull hard enough to get a concussion." He was truly worried. Any blow to the head could be dangerous. What if she'd seriously hurt herself? The possibility made his heart grab like an iron vise tightening his chest with every breath. The fear of something happening to her made him realize with shocking force how much she meant to him. He wanted her with him, safe in his house, away from anything and anyone that might harm her.

"I'll get a fire going in here. We keep this room shut off most of the time."

A roaring fire that Hal laid in the small brick fireplace soon dispelled the chill in the attractive sitting room. Floral drapes and slipcovers harmonized with pictures of garden flowers on the ivory wallpaper. An oval braided rug lay on the planked floor, and a bright ruffled pillow accented an antique rocking chair. It was definitely a woman's room, and Jill wasn't surprised when Hal referred to it as his mother's sitting and sewing room.

"Doesn't get much use. I suppose I could redecorate and turn it into an office or something," Hal admitted, but she could tell that there were too many memories connected with the room to make it into something else. Once again the close tie between him and his parents brought a momentary flicker of envy. Even though her adopted parents had been kind and loving, there was always that deep longing to know the two people who had given her life. How wonderful to grow up in a home like this, surrounded by loved ones. Hal was blessed, indeed, to have such a wealth of family ties, giving him an identity and the courage to hold on to his heritage.

There was a steady procession of people in and out of the sitting room. When Larry and Scotty appeared at the doorway, they were still holding a handful of cards from an interrupted poker game.

"We heard you cracked your head open," Scotty said.

"Don't see any blood," Larry said with undisguised curiosity as he looked her over.

"There isn't any," Hal answered curtly. "She's got a bump, that's all. Nothing to worry about. She'll be fine." His tense expression belied his words.

"Kirby said she fell. How'd it happen?"

"I slipped coming back from the barn," Jill answered Larry, a little annoyed that the men were talking over her. "Hurrying too fast, I guess. Wasn't watching my step. Hit my head on something just under the snow. And got a goose egg to show for it," she said, trying to make light of her headache.

"Zack was supposed to make sure she got to the

house safely,'' Hal added shortly. ''And then he carried her to the bunkhouse instead of bringing her here. I don't know what he was thinking.''

Larry gave a dirty chuckle. ''I do.''

As color quickly shot up into Hal's cheeks, Scotty said quickly, ''No harm done, I guess. Anything we can do, Jill?''

She wished there was another woman in the house to take over for her with Sue and the baby. Gary would have his hands full. ''I'm worried about Sue's fever. I'd appreciate it if you'd check on her and the baby. The new father may need some help.''

''I was just up there,'' Scotty said. ''Both mother and baby were sleeping and Gary was thumbing through a magazine. It looked to me like everything was under control.''

''Thank heavens,'' she breathed. Her place was upstairs tending to the new mother, not stretched out on a couch with an ice bag on her head.

''The snowplows may be out by midnight if it starts clearing,'' Scotty said hopefully. ''After they get the main roads open, they'll dig us out.''

Hal nodded. ''Wouldn't be surprised if the county plows don't get to the ranch about the time that copter is supposed to set down at noon tomorrow.''

''But what if the copter doesn't show?'' Scotty asked with infuriating pessimism. ''What then?''

Hal glared at the Scotsman. Leave it to Scotty to plant more worries in Jill's mind. He could see the anxious lines around her mouth deepen. ''Then we'll have to make other plans. If the roads get open, we can drive into Rampart. Take Sue and the baby to the hospital and have a doctor check Jill.'' He was worried about the nut who had been calling her and leaving weird presents on her doorstep. He'd have a few things to say to the sheriff about finding the guy.

Scotty rubbed his chin thoughtfully, "The camper shell I have on the truck would work as a kind of ambulance. There's a good bed and enough room for several people. Of course, the truck won't do us a darn bit of good if the road to the house isn't plowed so we can get out."

"I guess it's a good thing we'll all be clearing out tomorrow," Larry said, going over to a window. "The clouds seem to be lifting," he said peering out. "I bet I can get on my skis first thing in the morning and head out of here. Of course, there's still tonight to have a kind of farewell celebration." As he turned around, his eyes settled on Jill. "Kirby has a gin bottle stashed away in the kitchen. We ought to have a little party."

"Why don't you fellows get back to your card game?" Hal suggested pointedly. He'd had enough of Larry and Scotty's company and he didn't think their chatter was doing Jill any good. He could tell she was worried about Sue and blaming herself for not being upstairs with her.

"I've got some Excedrin, if you need it. And I'll be glad to sit with you if Hal has some chores to do," Scotty said pointedly.

"We both will," Larry countered curtly.

"Shut the door on your way out," Hal said purposefully, effectively shutting off any more offers.

As soon as the two men left, Jill insisted on sitting up.

"Did you need more ice?" Hal asked anxiously.

"No, that's enough." She set the ice pack aside. "My head is feeling better, really it is."

"You're not thinking of going upstairs, are you? You're staying here even if I have to hold you down."

"Is that a promise or a threat?"

Instead of responding to her light suggestive tone, his expression remained solemn. He sat down beside her and eased her head into the cradle of his arm and chest. When she closed her eyes, he ordered, "Don't go to sleep."

"All right, then talk to me."

"I'm not much good at idle conversation, all the stories I know are a little off-color for a lady," he admitted. "So are all my jokes, I'm afraid."

"Tell me about yourself."

"That's even more boring than talking about the weather."

"Not to me. Please?"

Maybe it was the bump on her head that made her reckless, or the intimacy of the situation that clouded her judgment. She couldn't believe it when she heard herself saying, "Tell me about Carrie."

"Who told you about her? I suppose one of the fellows has been talking."

"It doesn't matter," she said quickly. "I shouldn't have asked.'

"Nothing much to tell. Carrie lived up the valley and her folks and mine were good friends. She was a part of my life as long as I can remember. We grew up together. She was born to this kind of life, knew how to ride as well as any fellow, and could handle herself with the roughest of cowhands. We were planning on getting married when I got out of college, but it didn't happen. She turned her back on the life we'd planned, took a trip back East, and found someone else. End of story."

His matter-of-fact tone was at odds with the sadness

she'd seen in him at other times. The tender longing in his eyes when he'd held the baby, and his crispness about not needing the cradle showed that his dreams of having a wife and family had run deep. He fell silent but Jill couldn't let it rest. "And you never found anyone else?"

"No."

"Why not? I'm sure you've had plenty of chances to meet someone else. And don't tell me you've lived like a monk all these years, 'cause I won't believe it."

"Oh, I've had female companionship from time to time, enjoyed some very good times, as a matter of fact, but nothing more. There was never anybody I'd want to build a future with."

"Why not?"

He tightened his arm around her. She filled his senses so completely that he wanted to ignore the whole damn world and think about nothing but keeping her in his arms, but he couldn't do that, not to her. She deserved honesty and integrity. Holding out empty promises would only delay the hurt and unhappiness. "I guess the time has come for that talk you wanted."

His sober tone made her wish she'd kept quiet. She realized too late that she didn't want to hear what he was going to say. On some deep, unspoken level, he had already withdrawn from her. He had made a decision. It was in his voice. She knew before he said anything more that he had decided to end the closeness that had sprung between them.

"I hope you'll understand what I'm going to say, Jill. This whole thing is my fault. I never meant it to go this far. I knew the minute I saw you and listened to Randy talk about you that it would be easy to make the same mistake my brothers made."

"Mistake?"

"They fell in love and married gals who were totally unfit to be ranchers' wives. They weren't willing to accept a hard and demanding life that offered so much less than they were used to having. After a few short months they'd had enough, and in order to save their marriages, my brothers had to pull up their roots and settle their families somewhere else. I'm not willing to do that. This ranch is my life's blood."

He couldn't have been any more direct. She got his message loud and clear. Despite the sexual attraction between them, there was no place in his future for a city gal who barely knew one end of a cow from the other.

His arm tightened slightly around her shoulders. "I want you to understand why I can't commit myself to any relationship, however tempting it may be. God knows, I wish I could, but it wouldn't work."

"How can you be so sure?" she asked skeptically.

"No telling what sacrifices I'll have to make to keep this place. One thing's for sure, I don't want you involved. I didn't really know how ugly things could get until now. The sooner you're back in town, the better."

And out of your life, Jill mentally added.

At that moment, a ruckus like that of a barroom brawl exploded from the direction of the back porch and then reached a crescendo in the kitchen. Swearing and crashing furniture rose above the sound of physical fighting.

Hal leapt to his feet. "What in the devil is going on?"

Jerking open the sitting-room door, he strode into the kitchen, his face like a thundercloud. The antler coatrack was sprawled on the floor, and the kitchen table knocked at a crazy angle as the two men lunged and whirled, fists flying in every direction. Hal had half expected to see the skier and Scotty exchanging blows over a poker hand, but it was his two ranch hands slugging at each other like drunken sailors on leave.

Kirby had the advantage of height but not muscle power. Zack's smaller stature was hard and well-conditioned, and his fury seemed to be greater than that of the lanky ex-sailor. Not that Kirby wasn't equally the aggressor, taking the fight to Zack with every thrust of his long arms and clenched fists. The air was purple with oaths as they lunged at each other.

"That's enough. Break it up!" Hal's shout went unheeded. He barrelled between them, trying to shove them apart. In the melee, he got caught with an uppercut intended for Kirby, Zack's fist landing squarely on Hal's nose.

Larry and Scotty, who'd been watching from the doorway, took a step forward, but Hal waved them back. Zack got to his feet. His face was flushed and his eyes fiery, but the blood pouring down Hal's face seemed to sober him.

Kirby's lean shoulders drooped. "Sorry, boss. Things got a little out of hand." The cook handed Hal a wet cloth for his nose. "I was just telling the truth as I see it."

Zack set his jaw. "I don't take crap from nobody."

"You've had gals out in the bunkhouse," Kirby flashed back. "No need to lie about it. Ain't nothing wrong with my eyes, nor my nose either—cheap perfume lingers, you know. I've put up with a lot having to bunk with you, but you're not taking a gal like Jill down to your level. Not while I'm here to stop it."

"Why not, sailor boy? You got some plans of your own?"

"Is that what this is about?" Hal looked from one

man to the other, a sick feeling developing in his stomach.

"Zack was trying to make out with Jill in the bunkhouse," Kirby said flatly. "He told me he carried her there when she fell. I know how he works. Gets them all softened up with a song or two. A real cowboy Romeo. Makes me sick, it does. I told him so. He'd better be keeping his roving hands off her."

Zack made a threatening movement toward Kirby and Hal stopped him with a glare. "That's enough. You'd better cool it unless you both want to find yourselves out in the snow tonight. I mean it. Kirby, straighten up this mess and get some supper on the table. Zack, see to the evening chores." He started toward the hall bathroom to wash his face. "Show's over," he told Larry and Scotty.

"Is it true?" Larry pried, as they followed him down the hall. "Zack really made out with Jill?"

"You should have punched him in the nose instead of the other way around," Scotty said knowingly.

"Nothing happened," Hal said shortly.

"How do you know?" Larry muttered.

"A gal with a bump on the head could be easy picking," Scotty protested.

"I tell you nothing happened." Hal raised his voice. "Give it a rest!"

"All right. All right." Scotty held out his hands in surrender. "But it seems to me you're in for a mite of trouble with your ranch hands, especially if you plan on keeping company with Jill after this storm is over."

Jill had watched the fight from the sitting-room doorway. Knowing that she would only make matters worse if she tried to interfere, she held back and kept quiet. The taunts Zack and Kirby launched at each other made it clear that she was at the center of the whole sickening episode. And she hadn't known what Zack's intentions had been when he carried her to the bunkhouse. If Hal hadn't interrupted them, the guitar-strumming cowhand might have been more than she could handle, especially with her head feeling like a hatchet was buried in it. But Hal had come and that was that. She didn't need Kirby defending her virtue and picking a fight with Zack over it.

She heard Hal snap at Larry and Scotty as they left the kitchen, something about him having to get rid of Kirby and Zack because of her. She put a hand up to her aching head, wondering where it was all going to end.

Chapter Eight

In the bathroom, Hal splashed water on his face and tried to stanch the bleeding by putting pressure on his nose. His shirt looked as if he'd been butchered, and even his trousers were spotted with blood. Holding a cloth to his face, he went upstairs to change.

Zack slammed out the back door and Kirby quickly put the kitchen to rights again. When he caught sight of Jill leaning up against the door frame, he quickly came over and mumbled an apology. "Sorry about that. I put a burr under Zack's saddle, all right. Just couldn't stand the thought of him treating you like one of his cheap floozies. I look the other way when he wants to shack up with someone but hitting on you is too much! I warned him if he didn't keep his distance from you, he have more than his head in a sling."

Jill didn't have the energy to try to explain that the only thing Zack had done was torture her with a head-bashing, frenzied song. What other intentions he'd had, she wasn't sure. She shivered, remembering the sensuous way he'd close his eyes when he was saying her name over and over during the song.

She walked slowly into the kitchen, sat down at the table and resisted the impulse to rest her head in her hands. "I'll take that tea now," she told Kirby. Her stomach needed settling and a deep weariness made her feel as if she'd aged ten years in the last couple of hours. She knew that she had to pull herself together. Until the copter picked up Sue and the baby tomorrow, she had to keep functioning. One more patient was something none of them needed.

"There you go." Kirby set a porcelain cup and saucer and a small teapot in front of her. "Hal's mom had a nice collection. All shapes and sizes of tea sets. Nobody's used them for a long time."

Jill gave an appreciative murmur and held the cup with both hands as she sipped the hot tea. The brew was stronger than she really liked, but she hoped the stimulant would give her some energy. She finished one cup and poured another before she realized the tea was having the opposite effect. Her eyelids felt weighted, and she was fighting a battle to keep them open.

When she glimpsed Kirby putting a bottle back in the cupboard, she wondered if he'd laced her tea. She tried to say something, but her tongue was thick and her head was suddenly floating away in a kind of revolving motion.

"Feeling better?" he asked, his satisfied face wavering in front of her. Somewhere in her befuddled mind flashed the warning that people who had struck their heads should not go to sleep. Too late...too late....

EVERYTHING WAS QUIET on the second floor. Hal was finally successful in getting the nosebleed stopped, and he stepped out of his bathroom. He discarded his soiled clothes for some clean ones and tossed the bloodsplattered shirt and jeans in the hamper. The stains would probably not come out, but at the moment he had more on his mind than ruined clothes. He was anxious to get back downstairs to Jill. He wondered what she had made of the fight. No way she could have avoided hearing the heated exchange between Kirby and Zack. Damn fool men! He itched to knock their heads together for embarrassing her like that.

Leaving his bedroom, he poked his head into the Millers' room and was relieved to see that Gary had fallen asleep in a chair with the opened magazine on his lap; his wife and child were also sleeping. So far so good, Hal thought, as he quietly turned away.

A muffled sound from the bedroom across the hall stopped him. If he hadn't seen Gary asleep in the chair, he would have assumed that he was resting in Jill's room. Puzzled, he peered in the slightly open door. The soft murmuring came from a man bending over the bed. Hal shoved the door open. "Kirby? What the—"

The cook put his finger up to his lips in a shushing gesture. "She's asleep. I brought her upstairs and put her to bed."

Hal saw then that Jill was lying under the covers on her back. Her mouth was relaxed in a peaceful expression and her deep brown hair lay loose over her shoulders. "Why'd you move her from the sitting room? You could have made her a bed on the couch there."

"She fell asleep at the table. I thought it would be easier to put her in her bed." The cook smoothed the covers under her chin. "She's sleeping like a baby."

"A person who's had a blow to the head shouldn't sleep." He shoved Kirby away and gently tried to wake her. "Jill, Jill, wake up."

There was a slight break in her heavy breathing, but she went on sleeping. What should he do now? Let her sleep? Or try to wake her? Hal cursed the fight and the nosebleed that had taken him away from her. He hadn't finished trying to explain why he couldn't make any promises about their future together.

"I bet she's out till morning," Kirby said. "You want me to stay with her?"

"No, I will," Hal answered shortly.

"Too bad she hurt herself," Kirby said. "I wouldn't be surprised if Zack didn't arrange it all. Her fall and everything. He's been looking for a way to be alone with her. You ought to set him straight about a few things."

"Don't worry, I will," Hal promised curtly. "When he finishes the chores, tell him to come up here and give me a report on the foal."

"What's the matter with the filly?"

"I wish I knew. The vet left some nourishment here the last time one of the mares had a foal. I'm hoping it'll take care of whatever's ailing her." Hal ran an agitated hand across his chin. "We ought to know something by morning. Either she'll be getting her strength back or we'll have lost her."

Kirby shook his head. "Tough luck. All this happening at once. And the storm likely to kick up again. How many more things are going to go wrong?"

"I would appreciate it if you'd keep your pessimistic thoughts to yourself, Kirby. If we make it until tomorrow without anyone else getting hurt, sick, or killed, we'll have a chance to put all this behind us. The copter will take the Millers to a hospital, and I'll take Jill into Rampart." He was trusting Jerry to send a battery for the Bronco with the snowplow driver. Everybody knew everybody else in Rampart, and folks were used to depending on each other to help out when they could. The driver wouldn't mind dropping off the battery when he reached the ranch.

Kirby sighed as he looked at Jill's wan face. "Worn out, she is. Better let her sleep tomorrow as late as she wants. When everyone clears out, this will be the best place for her to rest."

"You could be right," Hal agreed. "But getting Jill to agree to stay another day will be something else. She's anxious to get back to that boy of hers. And I want someone to look at that head, no matter what she says." He sighed. "We'll have to see how she is in the morning."

Kirby gave Jill a lingering look as he started toward the door, then paused in the doorway. "If you have to run out to the barn later, boss, I'll be glad to look in on her."

Hal didn't answer. He pulled up a chair beside the bed. At the moment, trouble in the barn was the farthest thing from his mind.

Jill moved with weightless buoyancy through a gray mist that parted in front of her as she tried to run away from the dark figure behind her. Flinging frantic glances over her shoulder, she glimpsed his shadow through the swaths of thin clouds. Sometimes she could see his arms and torso. Sometimes his hips and legs. But never his whole body. Never his face. She darted this way and that, trying to lose herself in the swirling haze. But she couldn't hide. Every way she turned, the fog would part and he was there. Sometimes behind her. Sometimes in front. Sometimes close enough to brush against her side. She ran and ran until she fell. When he reached down for her, a terrifying scream broke from her throat.

"You're all right. Jill, darling, you're dreaming." Hal's voice broke into the nightmare. "I'm here. I'm here."

His face swam in front of her as if she were looking

at him through moving water. In the dimly lighted bedroom, his dark figure loomed over the bed. When he reached out and caressed her cheek, she drew back. The nightmare was still heavy upon her. Fear screamed silently in her throat. Her heart raced madly. Her chest was so tight, she couldn't breathe. Lingering sensations of the dream fought with reality.

"Don't be frightened. Are you awake?" he asked anxiously.

Am I? Her eyes rounded as she stared at him and then relief rushed through her with the force of a wellspring. She saw his tired face laced with worry and tenderness. "Yes," she whispered. "I'm awake."

He stroked her flushed face. "You must have been having a doozy of a nightmare. Your scream just about jerked me out of my skin."

Only a vague, lingering sense of being chased remained. The dream had already retreated into her subconscious. She was thankful to be fully awake with Hal's strong protective body sitting beside her.

"You slept clear through supper and the night, and now the sun's about ready to come up. How are you feeling?" he asked as he gently brushed back moist hair from her perspiring forehead.

"Kinda washed out."

"How's the head? Does it still hurt?"

She waited a moment before replying. Gently touching the side of her head, she was relieved that the swelling had gone down. "I just have a slight headache."

She'd slept in her clothes. The idea of Hal undressing her without her knowing it would have been embarrassing, or disappointing, she didn't know which.

The hours sitting by her bed had been hard. He blamed himself for not keeping her from harm while she was in his care. He wanted only the best for her, even if it meant sacrificing the deepest longing he'd ever had in his life. She deserved to find happiness with a man who could give all of himself without reservation, without heavy clouds over his future.

"I'd better get up," she said, trying to put her thoughts into some order. "How is Sue?"

"No worse." He'd checked with Gary a couple of times during the night. Her temperature was staying about the same.

"And the baby?"

"He's fine. I think he's off to a good start."

For a moment they looked at each other, remembering the long tense hours of delivery, and the joy of holding the newborn in their arms. Neither spoke until finally Hal cleared his throat and said, as evenly as he could, "I heard the weather report. The wind is down."

"Then this is D-day?"

"D-day?" he echoed.

"Departure day."

"If all goes well, I'll have you back in Rampart later today," he promised.

The thought of Randy sent a wave of energy through her, and she was glad he didn't argue when she insisted on getting up. "I have to check on Sue."

"Take it easy," he cautioned.

"I'm fine," she assured him, but she was grateful for his support as he helped her to her feet, then kept a firm arm around her waist as they walked down the hall to the bathroom. "I'll take it from here," she told him at the door.

"Are you sure? I don't want to scrape you up off the floor."

"I promise to stay upright," she said, shutting the door.

After she'd splashed warm water on her face, then dried it, she looked in the mirror and groaned. Long straight hair, glazed eyes, and wrinkled clothes made her look like a reject from some Mother Earth compound. She never felt so unkempt in her life. And so vulnerable. Vulnerable? She wondered why that thought had crossed her mind. Why did she feel she'd lost something she never had? She knew that Hal had made up his mind that she wasn't wife material, at least for him. A long time ago, a childhood sweetheart had set the standard for the mate he wanted. She doubted that any woman would ever meet that mark. One thing was for sure, she missed it by a mile, Jill admitted to the face in the mirror. City bred, adopted, no family ties, and no traditions to bring with her. No wonder Hal had warned her off.

"Are you all right?" Hal called through the door.

"Fine." She straightened up and gave her reflection one last disparaging look. As soon as she collected some clean clothes from her backpack, she would come back and take a shower.

Opening the door, she saw the relief on his face and quipped, "What's the matter? Did you think I'd fallen in?"

He heard their laughter from the bottom of the stairs. Mocking, taunting laughter! Fury burst like deafening, clanging cymbals inside his head. His heart pounded loudly, and he felt a rush of hot blood sluicing through his veins. He felt control slipping away. He fought an overpowering urge to rush up the stairs and bury his fists in anyone who dared to interfere. Time was getting short. It had

*to happen today. He took his hand out of his pocket
and let his arm drop to his side. Everything would
begin to fall into place when the helicopter came
at high noon. High noon. He liked that. As he
turned away from the stairs, he put his mask in
place.*

Chapter Nine

Kirby passed around a bowl of scrambled eggs to Hal, Scotty, and Larry. Zack had eaten his breakfast earlier, and Kirby had told Hal that the cowhand was apparently packing up and leaving.

All for the best, Hal thought. *Saves me from firing the guy.* No way he was going to keep Zack around after what had happened with Jill.

"How's the foal?" Kirby asked.

"Better." Hal had been relieved to see that the filly was on her feet, nursing, when he checked on her. He'd have the vet take a look at her as soon as possible, but for the moment, a heavy weight had been lifted off his shoulders. "I think she's going to be all right."

"Thank God for that."

"And what about the new mom upstairs?" asked Scotty. "Is she any better?"

"Still running a fever," Hal said. "But the baby's doing fine."

"And Jill?" asked Larry. "Somebody said you were sitting up with her all night?" There was a suggestive lift to his eyebrows. "Did either of you get any sleep?"

"Some." Hal gave a noncommittal shrug.

Scotty scooted back his chair. "Well, then I'd say everybody and everything is on the mend."

"What do you think, boss? Will that copter get here?" Kirby asked, filling the coffee mugs around the table.

"Weather report says it'll be clearing today," offered Scotty before Hal could answer. "I guess those whirly-birds can set down about anywhere they want to. Don't need a big pad to do it either."

"As long as the wind stays down," Larry agreed. "They set 'em down in parking lots and on hospital roofs. Guess they can find a flat place near the house in spite of the snow."

Hal nodded. "Heavy winds swept the ground almost clean in some spots and piled the snow up in drifts against fences and the like. The west meadow should be blown pretty clean with the wind we've been having. Once the copter lands, we can tell if we need to do some shoveling." He ignored the chorus of groans from Larry and Scotty. "They'll use a stretcher to get Sue and the baby from the house to the copter. We'll probably have to make a path for them."

"If they'd land in front of the house, they could use part of the path we dug to the front door," Scotty said hopefully.

"Too many drifts. You know how deep the snow is in some spots."

"Well, I'm glad we got the truck dug out. Shouldn't be any trouble to head it down the road once the plows take a run by. The radio says they've been out all night. Should be coming by here before long."

"Don't count on it. They'll probably do all the main highways first," Larry warned.

Scotty laughed. "Maybe, but I doubt it. One of the county commissioners has a place just down the road from here. Somehow they always manage to get his place dug out real fast-like. I'm betting we'll see a plow heading this way anytime now.''

Scotty was right. Less than an hour later, they heard the snowplow clearing the county road. The Scotsman grunted in satisfaction as it disappeared in the direction of the commissioner's house. "Told you. The driver will turn the plow around and head back this way. You wait and see.''

A young fellow wearing earmuffs, a checkered mackinaw and snow boots was at the wheel of the snowplow. He waved as he tackled the driveway leading up to the ranch house and the nearby garage. When Hal and Scotty went out to speak to him, he opened the door and handed Hal a box.

"Got a battery for you. Jerry sent it out. He said you were lucky he had one more. Guess he's been handing them out like sugar candy.''

"I appreciate it," Hal told him. "We're mighty glad to see you. We've been snowbound long enough.''

"It's been a bear, all right. I've been out nearly fourteen hours and ain't nearly done yet.''

"Did you get to my place?" the Scotsman asked anxiously.

"Sure thing. Went all the way to the river bridge.''

"How are the roads into town?" Hal asked. Even though he'd rather have Jill stay at least one more day, he knew she'd insist on leaving for home as soon as the copter took off.

"The highway's still snow-packed but traffic's beginning to get through. Going to be a while before everything's back to normal.''

UPSTAIRS, JILL GATHERED up the Millers' belongings making ready for Sue and the baby's flight to the hospital. She'd checked her temperature again; it was still high. Thank heavens they'd made arrangements to get her medical attention without any more delay. She glanced at her watch. Would the copter be there at noon as promised? She prayed that nothing had gone wrong. What if the flight had been canceled? What if it didn't come? *Stop it,* she silently rebuked herself. A snowplow was clearing the roads. They'd get Sue and the baby to the hospital somehow. It would just take a little longer.

"I don't like to fly," Sue fretted as her husband helped her into some warm clothes. "Especially not in helicopters."

"You've never been in one," Gary answered patiently, but Jill could tell the young man wasn't all that thrilled about taking a trip in one either.

"It'll only take a few minutes," Jill assured Sue as she diapered the baby and snugly wrapped him in a blanket. "And the paramedics are well trained. You'll be in good hands. When you get to the hospital, a doctor will be ready to tend to you and the baby. And I'll come by later today and see how you're doing. The snowplow is here now. Hal will be able to get his car out and drive me back to Rampart. I'm pretty anxious to see that boy of mine."

Sue smiled gratefully. "You've been an angel."

"That's me," Jill quipped. "Have halo, will travel."

They laughed.

Hal poked his head in the door. "Can I come in, or is this a private party?"

"Sure, come on in," Gary said warmly. "We've been wanting to tell you something, Mr. Haverly."

"Let me," said Sue.

Jill expected her to thank him again for his hospitality,

so she was as surprised as he was when Sue said, "We've decided to name the baby Hal, after you."

Hal's face flushed and he looked totally embarrassed. Jill remembered how his eyes had glowed with tenderness when he held the baby. He seemed too choked up to say anything. Finally, he managed, "I'm really honored."

"And we'll be bringing little Hal back for a visit with his namesake. Since he was born on a ranch, he's bound to like horses," Gary said proudly.

"I bet you're real good with kids," Sue said. "You ought to have some of your own." Her eyes deliberately moved from his face to Jill's. "I know a nice name for a little girl."

Hal laughed. "You're pretty obvious, young lady."

"She can't help herself," Gary apologized. "She gets some idea in her head and won't let go."

"That's right. When I see two stubborn people pulling in opposite directions, I have to say something."

"There it is! Hear it?" Gary shouted as he hurried over to the window, stretching his neck one way and then the other. "Can't see it, but it's coming."

The noise of the whirling blades of the helicopter grew louder and the house seemed to vibrate with the approaching aircraft. For a moment Jill was so weak with relief she couldn't say anything.

"We're in business," Hal said, his expression one of total relief.

"Where's the copter going to set down?" Gary asked, moving away from the window.

"I'm not sure. The west meadow, I think. Once they land, the paramedics will be coming for Sue and the baby as quickly as they can. They'll take her on a stretcher out to the copter. Then it's up, up, and away—'' Hal broke off as the young mother's eyes rounded anxiously. "Hey, don't be frightened, Sue. I used to fly over the ranch once a year, checking things out. It's great. You're going to love it! Besides, what other baby can claim he flew like a bird when he was two days old?''

Sue gave him a weak smile.

"Come on, Gary.'' Hal motioned for the young father to follow him. "We've got some digging to do. Have to make sure they can get to the house.''

"How long will it be?'' asked Jill.

"Fifteen or twenty minutes.'' He surprised her by planting a quick kiss on her cheek. "Be back in a jiffy.''

Jill couldn't tell whether the sweat beading on the young mother's forehead was from nervousness or a rising fever. She quickly took Sue's temperature again. Still the same. Thank goodness the medics would check her vital signs in flight and have a chart ready for the doctor.

"Why don't you come with us?'' Sue begged, reaching out for Jill's hand.

"There won't be room. And I'd just be in the way. It's going to be fine. Try to relax.'' She squeezed Sue's hand as the roar of the aircraft over the house grew almost deafening, and for a minute she thought they were going to land on the roof. Then she realized that it had set down somewhere beyond the house, probably in the open pasture on the west side of the house, as Hal had predicted.

"Won't be long now,'' she reassured Sue, wondering why her own mouth was slightly dry. In a few hours everything would be back to normal, and these last few days would belong to the past.

HAL THOUGHT the blue helicopter looked like a bird ruffling its feathers as it fluttered down into its white nest on the windswept meadow. He motioned for Gary, Scotty and Larry to follow him to a wide lodgepole-pine gate that was nearly buried in a mound of snow. "We'll have to free the gate to let them through."

Zack had made himself scarce since early-morning chores. I'll have to deal with him later, Hal thought on some detached level. First things first. The whirling propellers had come to a stop, and Hal could see the helicopter door opening and two attendants bringing out a stretcher.

Shoveling as fast as they could, two men on each side, they cleared the gate until they could push it open wide enough to allow two attendants and the stretcher to pass through.

"Thank God, you got here. The baby's fine, but the young mother's still running a fever," Hal told them. "This is her husband. He'll be going with you."

The male paramedic and hefty female nurse were all business as Hal directed them to the front door of the house. "First bedroom upstairs on your left."

"We've got three more pickups waiting," the nurse told Hal and Gary briskly as they climbed the stairs. "There's emergencies all over the place. We'll get this patient to the hospital and then take off again."

Jill heard them coming and met them at the bedroom door, open relief on her face. Hal could almost see the heavy responsibility rolling off her shoulders as she stepped back and let the medics do their job. Gary chattered nervously, trying to bolster his wife's courage and his own.

With remarkable speed, the nurse made sure that Sue and the baby were enveloped in a cocoon of blankets, and then she and the paramedic deftly lifted them both onto the stretcher. Jill hung back as they carried her out of the room and down the stairs with efficient smoothness.

The pilot, a youthful, short man was waiting for them at the open door of the helicopter. As they approached the craft, he stepped out and walked toward them. While the others disappeared into the belly of the aircraft, he came over to speak to Hal.

"You own this spread?" he asked with a wave of his arm.

Hal nodded. "I'm Hal Haverly." He shook hands with the pilot. "Sure appreciate your coming. We've got a sick gal who needs some attention."

"That's my job." Then he frowned. "As we were coming in, I could see about a dozen cattle stranded down in the riverbed. They were pinned in by drifts and broken tree branches." He pointed to a jutting rock formation that bordered the river about a quarter of a mile upstream. "Looked like they'd been trampling each other trying to get out. Wouldn't be surprised if you've lost a few head."

Hal silently groaned. That's all he needed, spending the rest of the day digging out a bunch of steers. If the animals were trapped in pockets of snowdrifts and debris, they'd never get free by themselves. "Thanks for the tip. I'll get my ranch hand and see if we can herd them to safer ground."

"Good luck." The pilot turned quickly back to the copter and disappeared inside. Almost immediately the blue craft was in the air again. As it disappeared over the ridge of the cupping mountains, Hal experienced both relief and a strange feeling he couldn't quite identify. He wouldn't have chosen to help deliver the newborn, but he was damn glad he had not been cheated of such a wondrous experience. Holding the baby in his arms had ignited a yearning that he'd buried deep, along with his other dreams.

As he walked back to the house, his thoughts swung to this new crisis. The trapped cattle. He'd have to see if he could get the trapped steers out of the riverbed and back up on solid ground as quickly as possible.

They'd have to saddle up a couple of horses and make their way through the snow-laden fields to the curve in the river where the cattle were stranded. Kirby wasn't as good a cowhand as Zack. He'd have to take Zack with him to free the cattle and drive them back to the corral.

Hal went directly to the bunkhouse and discovered that Zack had pretty much emptied out his stuff. Cursing under his breath, he went quickly to the garage and found him loading a couple of duffel bags on the back of his old motorcycle.

"What in the blazes do you think you're doing?" Hal demanded.

"I'm leaving, that's what. You pay me what you owe me and I'm out of here."

"Not today, you're not. You're not leaving here without some notice!"

"And who's going to stop me?"

"I don't think you mean that, Zack," Hal answered in a tone as hard as steel. "As you well know, I don't take challenges lightly."

They locked eyes. Zack lowered his first as he intoned, "I don't get pushed around by nobody."

"We both need a little cooling-off time and something's come up to give it to us."

"What's the matter now?" Zack's tone indicated he

didn't give a damn. He plainly had other things on his mind.

"We've got to saddle up and rescue some cattle trapped in the riverbed. The copter pilot saw them as he came in and said the steers were trampling all over each other. I can't get them out of there by myself."

"What about Kirby and them other two?"

"You know Kirby doesn't sit a horse like you do. As for Scotty and the skier, don't be ridiculous. They'd be as much help as my 4-H kids, probably less. We're wasting time. Saddle up a couple of horses and bring them to the house."

Zack continued to glare at him without moving.

"Give me the keys to your bike," Hal ordered.

"No." Zack rammed his hand into his pocket.

In one quick movement, Hal grabbed Zack's wrist and jerked his hand out of his pocket. The cowboy's fingers were fastened around the keys. Hal held out his other hand. "Give 'em to me."

Zack hesitated as if measuring his lesser height and muscle strength against his boss's. He swore under his breath as he handed them over.

"Get the horses. I'll tell the others where we're going."

"You can't keep me here," Zack lashed out. "I've got plans."

"I've always been fair with you, Zack. I've ignored the stuff you've done behind my back and the hell you raised in town that almost got you locked up. I've shut my eyes to a lot of things. You owe me this much. Now, let's don't argue. Get saddled up!"

Without waiting for an agreeing nod, Hal headed back to the house. He tried not to think about what he'd do if Zack set his jaw like a stubborn mule and refused to do as he was told.

Both Larry and Scotty were sitting at the kitchen table enjoying the last lunch Kirby had set out for the stranded travelers.

"Why you looking so glum, boss?" Kirby asked. "The copter got off all right, didn't it?"

Curtly, Hal told them about the stranded cattle. "Zack's saddling up some horses—*I hope*—and we'll have to take a ride out and see what the situation is. The steers must have tried to get out of the wind against that wall of rocks along the river and got trapped when heavy snow broke some of the trees and pinned them in."

"You think you can get them out?" Scotty asked. "Sounds to me like you're going to have to shovel a heck of a lot of snow."

Kirby eyed Larry. "Why don't you get on them skis of yours and head out that way? You could give us a hand getting rid of some of the fallen branches and stuff."

"Sorry. I've got other pressing plans," Larry said flatly. "Seems to me, you ought to let the stupid animals look after themselves."

Hal didn't bother to answer. He'd put up with the skier's self-centered presence long enough. His departure would be good riddance.

"I was thinking I might hang around until tomorrow morning, though," Larry conceded.

"Think again," Hal said firmly.

Larry's tanned face reddened. "If that's the way you feel, I'll be on my way."

"That's goes for me, too," Scotty said. "It's time we all got back to our own places."

Hal went upstairs to find Jill. She was in the Millers'

bedroom, stripping the bed and trying to put things to right. "Back already? When can we leave for Rampart?"

"I've got some stranded cattle that I've got to rescue." He told her what the pilot had seen. "I've got to ride out with Zack and get them back in the pasture."

"But how long will that take?"

"I don't know, depends how quickly we can get rid of the drifts and fallen trees. I'll hurry," he promised. "Why don't you try to get some rest. You still look a little peaked to me." Sharp concern shot through him.

"I'm fine." She met his eyes, and with a firm lift to her chin said, "Finish your business so you can take me home. I've been gone long enough."

Her curt words cut into him, but he knew she was better off away from him and this place. He paused at the bedroom doorway and for some unbidden reason looked back. "You'll be all right until I get back, won't you?"

She gave him a wave of her hand, and he dismissed an uneasy feeling creeping through him.

Chapter Ten

When Jill came down to the kitchen for lunch, Kirby and Scotty were still sitting at the table drinking coffee. Both men were solicitous, and helped her to a chair.

"Well, I guess this is it," Scotty said. "Last day with a pretty lass sitting across the table from me."

"Lucky for her, she won't be seeing your ugly mug to start the day," the cook quipped.

"Or yours," Scotty countered.

"Oh, I don't know. From the looks of things around here, she might just be around longer than you think. Isn't that right, Jill?"

Kirby's smile didn't reach his eyes and both he and Scotty waited pointedly for her to answer. She knew what they were asking and she wasn't about to satisfy their curiosity. "It's tempting to stick around. I've never had anyone cook for me before," she said lightly. "Your biscuits are the best, Kirby."

"Don't make his head any bigger than it is," chided Scotty. "It grows two sizes anytime a pretty gal is willing to eat his food."

"I don't see you in any hurry to get back to your own miserable cooking. I bet you've put on five pounds since you've been here," Kirby said with a sneer.

Scotty patted his stomach. "Nothing like shoveling and eating to put a man right with the world. I'm sure glad I wasn't stuck at my place by myself. Things were pretty lively around here with that skier fellow throwing his weight around."

"I wasn't sorry to see him go," Kirby admitted. "The world would be a better place if some idiot hadn't invented skis, if you ask me. Don't think much of the sport, myself."

"Can't compare with throwing your line into some deep pool and pulling out a fighting rainbow trout," Scotty agreed. "Well, I best go upstairs, collect my things and get going. No telling when Hal and Zack will get back." He stood up. "I guess you two can get along all right by yourselves. I could stick around if you want me to, Jill."

"Thanks, but I think Kirby and I can manage to hold things together." She offered him her hand. "It's been nice meeting you."

"You'll have to come and see my place sometime. I'll show you how to cast halfway across a roaring stream."

She laughed. "You'd have to be a miracle worker. I've never held a fishing pole in my life."

"All the more reason to pay me a visit. I promise you a good time."

"My son would love to come."

"Better take along a dozen chaperons," Kirby warned. "More than fishing goes on at Scotty's lodge, I'm guessing."

The Scotsman just laughed. "Wouldn't you like to know." He waved his hand and disappeared down the hall.

Kirby finished cleaning the kitchen while Jill had a

second cup of coffee. She kept glancing at the wall clock as the minutes ticked slowly by.

"They'll get back when the job's done," Kirby told her as she glanced at the clock for the fifteenth time. "Better take a nap or find something to do." Kirby walked over to the coatrack and started putting on his hat and jacket.

"Where you going?"

"Out to the bunkhouse. Hal told me that Zack's moving out. I've got to check, make sure he's not taking any of my stuff. That yahoo has treated everything of mine as communal property since he got here. If he'd ever been in the navy and tried that kind of stuff, he'd have had his rear end kicked."

"I guess he was raised in a large family that didn't have much."

"That's a pretty tired excuse." He paused at the kitchen door. "You'll be all right alone in the house for a spell, won't you?"

"Of course. I think I'll take your suggestion about a nap."

He gave her an approving nod and left. After a moment, she stood up, walked over to the telephone and, with prayerful breath, lifted the receiver. Dead silence. The phone was still out. The longing to hear Randy's voice was so strong that a growing ache brought sudden tears to her eyes. Sometimes her son was too impulsive, doing things without thinking them through, and she worried that he might have taken too much on himself. There were times in the past when he'd been right in the middle of things better left to an adult. Had Zeb been able to keep a tight rein on him? Was he all right? He was an unpredictable teenager, after all.

"Would you like to call your son on my car phone?"

Scotty stood in the doorway, wearing a ranch coat and hat, his arms through the straps of his backpack. "I could walk you to the truck and back."

"Would you? That would be wonderful." She didn't hesitate even a moment to accept the offer. "Wait a minute and I'll get my things."

They left by the front door, and Jill blinked against a sudden brightness as Scotty guided her along a shoveled path to the snowplowed driveway. Sunlight shining through rents in thinning gray clouds laid blue shadows on glistening white snow. Now that the danger was past, she could enjoy the dramatic panorama of snow-covered hills and jagged peaks. She knew the view from her little house would be equally fantastic. An eagerness to get home and see her son quickened her steps. Why hadn't she thought of the mobile phone before? Thank goodness Scotty had offered to let her make a call to Randy before he left.

When they reached the truck, Jill was surprised to see a small camper shell on the pickup bed. He pointed it out with satisfaction. "Nice little setup. Ever seen one of these?"

She shook her head. "Is it like a regular camper? It looks so small."

"Has everything you need. All the comforts of home. Want to take a peek?"

She hesitated, anxious to make her call, but Scotty was obviously proud of his camper and wanted to show it off. "The telephone?"

"I'll show you that in a minute." He guided her around to the narrow back door. Icicles were hanging down from the roof from snow that had thawed and then frozen. "I left the oil heater on low when Hal and I were here yesterday. You won't believe how cozy it is."

Scotty broke off the icicles, swung the camper door open and waved her inside. "Go on in." His tone was perceptibly less an invitation than an order.

At that moment a warning bell vibrated.

Jill instinctively pulled back, but too late.

His strong hands fastened on her and before she even realized what was happening, he'd thrown her into the camper. "I've been waiting a long time to show it to you."

She fell forward on her hands and knees. Packed snow from her boots and pant legs dropped off on the linoleum floor and made it slippery. Before she could right herself, he picked her up and threw her down on a long bench.

"At last, we meet," he said as he stood over her. "No more telephone calls. No more games. How'd you like the book and the pretty scarf?"

Her voice cracked with disbelief. "You!"

"You, me." Scotty gave her a slow, chilling smile. "I've been waiting a long time for you to notice. And now the time has come. Everything worked out nicely, didn't it?"

THE HORSEBACK RIDE across the snow-covered ranch was slow going for Hal and Zack. They tried to avoid the deepest drifts, but both horses were often belly-deep in snow as they headed toward the frozen riverbed snaking along the bottom of a rocky draw. The wind had fashioned snow sculptures out of every fence post, rock, tree and boulder. Hal squinted against the brightness of sun breaking through the clouds. In every direction the landscape glistened with specks of diamond brightness. Beautiful, he thought, and misleading. Snow like confectioner's frosting lent a deceptive softness to the rough ground and craggy hills.

Hal gave a wave of his gloved hand to Zack, motioning him toward the outcropping of rock where the pilot had said the cattle were trapped in the riverbed.

Zack nodded. The frown on his face made it plain that he resented being forced to come along.

Tough, thought Hal. Zack could damn well do his job one more time before taking off. Then he could be on his way. Hal was surprised it hadn't happened before now. He'd never expected the young cowboy to settle down for long. In a way, he was sorry. There was a lot he liked about the young man. Oh, he knew Zack did some carousing in town and had girls out in the bunkhouse, but as long as he did his work, Hal wasn't going to play the father figure. If Zack hadn't pushed himself on Jill and gotten crosswise of Kirby, things could have been smoothed over. But not now. Once they got back to the house, he'd hand over Zack's motorcycle keys. Hal was sure now that Zack had been the one who had gone through Jill's things, and spooked her the night the lights went off. He cursed himself for not seeing it earlier. He was glad he had not left Zack at the house with Jill. He'd send him on his way fast enough when they got back.

Which wasn't going to be very soon, Hal thought wearily when they got to an elevated ridge just above the riverbed. Looking down, he saw that the situation was as dire as the pilot had said. About a dozen steers had crowded together against a wall of rock, trying to get out of the wind and blowing snow. Unfortunately, a wide fault in the hillside had allowed the blizzard winds to sweep downward and make a wall of snow on one side of the rock outcropping. High drifts and brittle trees weighted with snow had broken and fallen across the riverbed around the cattle, adding to the barricade that trapped the animals.

Hal silently groaned when he saw a couple of dead steers in the snow. Probably trampled underfoot when the helicopter went over, he thought. He'd lose even more if he didn't get them free and back in the pasture as soon as possible.

Zack reined his horse beside Hal's. "Looks bad. No way just two men are going to dig 'em out," he said flatly. "Better leave them there."

"Leave them there? For how long? Till it thaws?" Hal asked sarcastically.

"Digging through all that snow will take hours."

"Then we'd better get started." He motioned for Zack to follow him down the hill to the frozen river.

JILL SAT UP on the bench and drew back against the wall of the campor. Her mind refused to believe what was happening. Her thoughts whirled in every direction like dried leaves in a violent wind. On some detached level she noticed the row of Stephen King books on a nearby shelf. But Scotty couldn't be the stalker. Not Hal's friendly neighbor. Not the congenial fisherman. There had to be some mistake.

But as the Scotsman stood over her, a satisfied hardness in his eyes, she knew there was no mistake. None at all. He'd only been a heavy breather on the phone until this moment. Now she had a face to put on the nameless stalker—a sandy-haired, blue-eyed, middle-aged fisherman, who had been only inches away from her for four days. She shivered.

"Cold?" he asked solicitously.

"No." She forced her stiff lips to answer, eying the door. He had shut it but not locked it...yet. There was still a chance she could bolt for it if he turned his back on her.

"Let's get those wet things off," he said as if speaking to a child. He sat down on the edge of the bench beside her. His movements were calm, unhurried, and his large hands were deceptively gentle. Her skin prickled as he purposefully removed her scarf and took off her jacket.

"It's nice and warm in here, don't you think?" he asked in the conversational tone she knew so well. What a perfect mask he wore— congenial, helpful, and ever so considerate. There had been nothing to give him away. Nothing. Bitter bile seeped up into her throat.

She wanted to fight off his touch, but some flicker of caution made her resist the panicked impulse. Better to wait, she told herself. Make any physical resistance count. Better to try to defuse the situation with talk. She moistened her dry lips. "I don't understand, Scotty. You made those calls? Sent me those things? Took my picture? Why?"

He reached under the bench and pulled out a wooden box with brass hinges. In spite of herself, she was caught by a bizarre interest in whatever was in that box.

He opened the lid, then thumbed through papers and photos of various sizes until he found a small snapshot of two people. He held it out to her.

Jill blinked. For a moment she thought she was looking at herself. A young woman stood with her hands on the shoulders of a young boy as they smiled at the camera. She was a brunette with a long braid falling over one shoulder, slender build, and wearing jeans, a white blouse and a pink scarf. A cold chill snaked up Jill's back.

"You see the resemblance, don't you?" Scotty's eyes

fastened on Jill's face. "The first time I saw you walking down the street, I couldn't believe my eyes. And when I followed you home and saw Billy come out of the house—"

"Randy," she automatically corrected. The boy in the photo didn't look anything like her son, but there was a hint of a resemblance between herself and the woman in the picture, the same build, the same braided dark brown hair. "Who is she?"

The freckles on his face darkened like black pox. "My wife, Angie...and that's my son."

Jill scrambled mentally to remember what Hal had said about his neighbor. Lived alone. Moved here from Texas a few years ago. Something about a wife and son. "Where are they now?"

His face hardened. "Dead."

She recoiled from his expression but couldn't keep from asking, "What happened?"

"She left me. Took the boy and ran out. Said I wasn't a good father. Too much a loner." He gave a short laugh. "She said I never followed through on anything, but I showed her. In the end, she knew different. I saw it in her face just before my truck sent her car off the road." His eyes narrowed. "I didn't know Billy was lying down in the back seat till later. I might have chosen a different way if I'd known."

Dear God, he killed them. She must have made a breathless gasp, because he glared at her. In the depths of his eyes was unresolved guilt and lingering hatred. As if the past had somehow been superimposed upon the present, he looked at her with hatred. "I thought I could make things up when I found you. But you're just like her. I could tell my little gifts meant nothing. I was in town when you left in the Jeep. I finished up as quickly as I could and tried to catch up with you. It was difficult to see—what with visibility down to practically zero—but I managed to make out your Jeep, that other car, and Hal taking you horseback to the ranch. I decided then to pretend my electricity went out so I could show up at the ranch and be with you. I drove around to the front of the house, parked halfway down Hal's driveway, and waited until the snow thickened. Then I called the house on my cell phone, pretending I was at my place. I knew Hal would invite me over.''

"You were the one who went through my things. And scared me the night the lights went out. And I bet you cut the telephone line, too.''

He nodded. "All the time I was trying to be nice, you ignored me. You gave more attention to those other fellows than you gave to me. But all that's going to change.'' He reached out and stroked her hair. "It's going to be just you and me. Nobody else.''

She stiffened inwardly against his touch but tried not to let him see her repulsion. Her only chance of handling him was to try to play along as best she could. "I'm sorry, Scotty. I didn't realize that I was hurting your feelings. There were so many things going on. I had my hands full with Sue and the baby, and then I bumped my head.'' She knew she was babbling, but she didn't know what else to do. "You understand, don't you? Let's go back to the house and—''

"No! Don't try to sweet-talk me. I know what's going on with you and Hal. I've got eyes in my head. Well, it's not going to happen. I've got one of my cabins all ready for you. Nobody'll think of looking for you there. My place is shut up for the winter. Nobody around. Eventually they'll find you buried in a snowdrift, but not until we've had a little time together. You and I have some unfinished business." He glared at the photo in his hand as if speaking to the woman there.

"I'm not Angie!" Jill's voice broke.

"I know that," he said calmly. "You're Jill Gaylor, a city lass who thinks she can make a fool of a good-old Texas boy and get away with it."

AFTER A FEW MINUTES of fruitless effort to make any kind of progress through the high snowbanks, Hal knew that Zack was right. There was no way two men were going to lift that much snow with the small shovels they had brought along. A fallen tree blocked the only span of snow that was less than five feet high. Its branches were half buried in the snow and reached several feet across the riverbed.

"Hopeless," Hal muttered and motioned to Zack. He led the way up again up a snowy slope above the river-bed where they reined in their horses at a spot over-looking the stranded cattle. Once again, Hal tried to ex-amine the situation from every direction. There was only one low spot in the snow pocket and that was where the tree had fallen.

"Ready to give it up and go back to the house?" Zack asked in an I-told-you-so tone.

Hal narrowed his eyes as he continued to survey the scene below. "No, I have another idea. Come on." He kicked his horse and led the way again down the bank to the riverbed.

IN A SURGE OF PANIC, Jill tried to get up but Scotty shoved her back down. "You had all of them fighting over you, when it was plain as day you had your sights set on Hal. I tried to warn you. I told you to back off and leave him alone. Gave you every chance to see he wasn't the one for you. But you hooked him anyway. I can't stand by and watch you treat him the way Angie treated me.''

''No, you have it all wrong.'' Jill grasped at anything that might keep Scotty's truck parked where it was as long as possible. She prayed that Hal had gotten back to the house and was looking for her. ''I wouldn't do anything to hurt Hal.''

''Lies. Lies. I've heard 'em all before. You can save your breath. Hal's been a good friend to me, the only one I have. But he's plain dumb when it comes to women. It made me sick to see the way he was taken in by you. I was glad that I'd already decided what had to be done.''

''If you care about Hal's friendship, you won't do this. Stop this now. I promise I won't say anything. He'll never know that this has happened. I'll keep quiet about everything. I was going to go to the sheriff and report the calls, but I won't.''

''I know you won't, 'cause you're not going to be doing any talking to anybody. I'll keep you hidden as long as it suits me, and then you'll have an unfortunate accident. Too bad, a city girl like you wandering off by yourself.''

''No one will believe it!''

''Yes, they will.'' Scotty grunted in satisfaction. ''Don't you see that bump on your head made you go a little crazy? You must have decided to go outside while Hal was gone. I have an idea that they'll have to dig through a hundred snowbanks before they find you. Such a shame. I'll be the first one to console Hal. He won't know about the hours I had you in my cabin. It wouldn't be right to taunt him about the pleasures meant just for me.''

Jill was stunned. Her mind couldn't handle his twisted reasoning. Sexually enamored, intending to enjoy himself with her while at the same time filled with diabolical vengeance to end her life.

"Time to get rolling," Scotty said as he put the photo back in the box and was about to close the lid.

In desperation, Jill stayed his hand. "I bet there's some pictures of you in there. Let me see." She reached for the box.

"No." He slammed down the lid. "I'll get you tied up and we'll head out." He bent over slightly to return the box under the bench.

Wild panic shot through her like a prairie fire. She shifted positions, raised a booted foot, and kicked him in the side of the head as hard as she could. He was looking down and didn't see it coming. Miraculously, the blow knocked him off his seat on the edge of the bench and sent the box flying.

She was up in a split second.

He reached for her legs and missed.

Bounding to the door, she flung it open.

"You bitch!" He would have caught her in the doorway if his feet hadn't slipped on the tracked-in snow melting all over the slick linoleum.

She was down the steps and around the corner of the truck before he was on his feet again and out the door after her.

As HAL AND ZACK herded the cattle toward the home pasture, Hal was damn pleased with himself. His idea born of desperation had proved successful. The snow-buried tree lying across the frozen riverbed had provided the answer for freeing the cattle. Hal had grabbed at the idea that it wouldn't take much of an opening to get the cattle through if they could pull the tree back a few feet. Viewing the fallen tree from above, he visualized it as a gate swinging open and its branches sweeping the snow aside as it moved to one side.

"Get your rope," Hal had ordered. "Lasso that top branch and I'll get the limb below it."

"You aiming to drag the damn tree down the river?" Zack's disgusted look had told him what he thought of the idea.

"No. We're going to make a gate out it. If we pull on the end of it in a fanlike motion, the trunk and branches should sweep enough snow aside to make the drift low enough to get a horse in the pocket and drive the cattle out."

A reluctant smile had broken through Zack's frown. "Pretty smart, boss, if it works."

They looped the desired tree branches with one end of their ropes and wrapped the other end around their saddle horns. Backing up their horses, it took the strength of both mounts to move the tree and make a wide-enough sweep of trunk, branches and snow to create an opening to free the animals.

"Yahoo!" shouted Zack.

Hal laughed loudly. "We did it!"

Savoring the success of their efforts, for a moment all friction between them was forgotten. They were two men who had won over nature. In a matter of minutes they had the steers moving across the snow-covered ground toward the corrals.

"Pretty sad-looking," Zack commented as they drove them toward the house.

Hal nodded in agreement. The animals were in bad shape. The mouths of several steers were frozen shut. Four days out in the storm had taken its toll, and they'd left three carcasses in the riverbed. It could have been worse, he told himself. With the storm over, all's well that end's well, he thought as he rode behind the slow-moving cattle.

JILL SPRINTED toward the house. Terror sent adrenaline rushing through her body as gasps of cold air burned her lungs. Could she outrun him? Her arms and legs moved frantically as she ran as fast as she could toward the front door of the house. The snow still held the footsteps she and Scotty had made earlier, but now the shoveled path stretched before her in a seemingly unending line. The house seemed miles away instead of a few hundred yards.

Dear God, don't let me fall. She knew how quickly her feet could go out from under her. One false stumble and all would be lost. She could hear Scotty's faint heavy breathing behind her, but she didn't dare turn around to see how close he was. She wanted to cry out for help, but the frigid air forced every breath back down her throat. She had no heavy coat to weigh her down, but only a few minutes in the freezing temperature could be disastrous.

With gasping breath she reached the front door, grabbed the knob, flung the door open and bolted inside. Slamming the door behind her, she raced down the hall to the kitchen, shouting, "Kirby! Kirby! Help!"

Only silence greeted her frantic cries.

The kitchen was empty. No sounds from upstairs.

As the front door slammed open, she realized too late that she should have bolted the front door.

Kirby. Where was Kirby? He must still be out at the bunkhouse. She heard Scotty's heavy steps in the hall.

Run. Run.

She was out the back door before he reached the kitchen. As she ran down the snow path, she knew that she'd never make it to the bunkhouse before he caught up with her. Her only chance was to hide, and the barn was the only place that offered any chance of concealment. She tried to scream, but the cold air drove the sounds back into her throat.

Frantically, she jerked open the small door and darted inside. After the pristine white outside, the sudden darkness momentarily blinded her. Horses stomped restlessly, and she heard Gypsy's welcoming meow as she fled past the stalls.

Where to hide? In one of the empty stalls. The loft? Should she run out the back door and try to get away like the man Hal had shot? From nowhere came the memory of Hal saying he kept a rifle the tack room to stop would-be predators.

Maybe the gun was still there. The fact that she'd had next to no experience firing a gun was lost in the moment of desperation.

She darted into the tack room, slamming the door behind her. Quickly her eyes swept the small cluttered room. Saddles, bridles, grain sacks, and watering buckets stacked everywhere. She despaired of finding the rifle when, at the last minute, her eyes lit on it propped up in the corner.

She grabbed, swung around, and clumsily pointed it at the door. She didn't even know if it was loaded. She waited. Every second, the rifle grew heavier and heavier in her hands. No sound of muffled footsteps. Maybe he hadn't seen her come in the barn? Or maybe he was looking in the stalls, trying to discover her hiding place?

Then she heard a noise outside the door. A loud meowing, followed by impatient scratching. Her heart plunged. Gypsy had fingered her presence like a red tag.

"So this is where she's hiding." Scotty's amused voice floated through the door as he talked to the cat. "Well, now, I guess I'd better take a look."

As the door swung open, Jill screeched, "Don't move or I'll shoot." The rifle wobbled in her hands. "I mean it."

Standing in the open doorway, Scotty held out his hands in a mock gesture of surrender. "I never argue with a lass with a gun in her hand. At least not one that's loaded." Then he smiled patiently. "You're sure you've got a bullet in the chamber? I'm betting Hal doesn't keep his rifle loaded."

"Stay back. We'll find out if I pull the trigger."

He shrugged and leaned back against a table where feed cans were stacked. "If you want to take a chance on splattering my guts all over the place, go ahead and shoot."

"I want you to leave now!"

"I'm afraid I can't do that. Not unless you're willing to come with me. You see, I'm never one to give up easily. Watch this!" With one hand, he grabbed a half-full gallon feed can off the table and threw it straight at her face. The grain flew like dust pellets into her eyes. She cried out and her finger tightened in a reflex action on the trigger.

The gun went off.

The kick of the rifle sent her backwards. She never saw where the shot went, but when Scotty jerked the rifle out of her hand, she knew that the bullet had missed him.

Chapter Eleven

"What the—" Hal shouted. Sounded like someone was shooting in the barn. He heard the gunshot just as the first steer was herded into the corral. Maybe Kirby had caught someone else trying to do their dirty work. If the poisoners had gotten to Calico and her foal, he'd kill them with his bare hands.

Hal yelled at Zack. "See to the cattle. Pen them in and get them some feed."

"What's going on?"

"Sounded like a shot." Hal kicked his horse in the direction of the barn. As he reined to an abrupt stop outside the door, he heard Jill's frightened scream. He swung out of the saddle with the speed of a calf roper and hit the ground running. He was prepared for almost anything, except what greeted him as he burst through the door. Jill was screaming and clawing Scotty as he tried to subdue her.

Hal let out a yell and ran toward them. "What in the devil?"

Jill gave a strangled cry when she heard his voice. She stopped fighting and Scotty let her go. "Hal, Hal," she sobbed and slumped to the ground before he reached her.

"She's gone crazy," he told Hal. "Tried to shoot me with your rifle. Must have been that bump on the head that got to her. She's been talking funny. Lucky for me she's a bad shot."

Hal took one look at her crumpled body and his heart plummeted. Her eyes were red and watery, an anguished sobbing came from her throat. As he drew her to her feet and supported her in his arms, he tried to soothe her. "It's all right, darling. It's all right."

She grabbed the lapels of his coat, a wild frantic look on her face. "He's...he's...he's the one."

Hal couldn't make any sense out of her hysterical stammering. "Take it easy," he soothed. Her whole body was shaking. "What are you doing out in the cold without—"

"Listen to me!" her voice rose to a frenzied shrill. "He's the one. He's the stalker."

"See what I mean?" Scotty shook his head. "I was just trying to be nice to her and she went haywire. Accuses me of all kind of weird things. When I tried to reason with her, she ran out of the house and hid in the tack room. Then when I came after her, she tried to shoot me."

"No. No." Jill's fingers dug into Hal's arms. "He's lying. That's not the way it happened!"

"Something set her off, Hal. She went nuts. Maybe you can reason with her," Scotty said impatiently.

"Take it easy, honey. Get hold of yourself. Scotty's not going to harm you."

Shock like a live wire surged through Jill. *He believed Scotty, not her.* The past relationship between the two men put her in peril. She felt like someone drowning and reaching for a life preserver that wasn't there. Hal's friendly neighbor was playing his innocent part well. No hint that he'd run his ex-wife off the road and killed their son in the process. Nothing in the past had made Hal think that his good buddy fisherman could be anything but what he pretended to be. On the surface, the Scotsman was congenial and uncomplicated, his true dark nature hidden.

Jill's voice rose to a shrill pitch. "You have to believe me. He was going to take me to one of his cabins."

Scotty gave a disgusted snort. "I'm telling you, she's gone berserk."

"It's true. It's true. His wife…her hair…my hair…" she stammered incoherently. "And after he killed me, he was going to leave my body in a snowdrift."

"I've never heard such ravings in my life," Scotty said disgustedly. "I tell you, the storm's gotten to her. Poor thing. You can see she's having a breakdown."

"I better get her into town and have a doctor look at her." She could tell from Hal's wary expression and the way they were talking over her head that he thought she'd gone over the edge. He tightened his embrace. "It's all right, darling, it's all right. There's nothing to be afraid of."

"No, you have to believe me," she sobbed. "It's true!" She began beating on his chest. "Listen to me. Listen to me!"

"Jill!" He grabbed her by the shoulders and shook gently. "Get hold of yourself. We'll leave right now. Scotty, will you tell Zack to put up my horse and see to the chores?"

"Sure thing. Then I'll head back home," Scotty said. "I'm sure sorry things had to end this way."

The Scotsman reached to pat Jill's arm, and she drew back as he'd been a snake about to strike. "You can't get away with this!" she screamed.

"Easy, honey, easy." Hal stroked her trembling body as if he were soothing a high-strung colt. "Here, you can have my coat."

He had one arm out of a sleeve just as the barn door opened. At first Hal didn't register who was silhouetted against the bright whiteness.

"Well, look who's here. The great skier himself," Scotty said in a chiding tone. "You get lost again, Larry?"

"No," he growled. "I know exactly where I am."

Hal's arm tightened around Jill's shoulders as he laid the coat over her; she felt his whole body go rigid. Then she saw why. She gasped in disbelief.

Larry had a revolver in his hand and was pointing it directly at them.

"Hey, no sweat, fellow," Scotty said quickly. "Just doing a little joshing, that's all."

"Shut up!"

Hal slowly took his arm from Jill's shoulders and moved in front of her. Planting his legs firmly and looking straight at the gunman, he demanded, "What's this all about, Larry?"

"You killed my brother."

For a moment his words didn't register. Then Hal felt a corkscrew twisting his inside. "The man in the car? The bastard who was poisoning my stock?"

"My brother was just doing a job."

"A job? Is that what you call it? Viciously killing good horses and cattle?" Fury erupted like a volcano in Hal's head. "Only the scum of the earth would take a job like that."

"Shut up! He was doing it for me. Trying to get enough money so I could start my shop. I didn't know my brother was dead, or I'd have taken care of you before this. He told me to meet him here, but I thought the storm had changed his plans. Then when I hit the highway today, I found him in his car, shot to death. You did it, didn't you?''

''I caught him in the barn and fired a couple of warning shots. One of the bullets ricocheted off a metal trough and hit him. The devils who hired him are the ones who should be looking down the barrel of your gun.''

''You're the one who pulled the trigger.'' Larry's expression betrayed his anguish and desperation.

Jill's threadbare emotions were on overload. Somewhere in the shadows of her mind was the conversation she'd had with Larry about his brother and the exciting marketing plans they had as soon as they had enough money. *Money earned by killing Hal's animals. Paid by unscrupulous developers.* She recoiled with horror. All the time Larry had known about the poisoning, and he'd been under the same roof with them for four days.

The threat to Hal's life brought an unbelievable resiliency surging through Jill. Her own emotional upheaval was shoved into the background. She forgot about everything else. Ignoring Hal's warning gesture, she boldly faced Larry's gun. ''Your brother wanted you to make something of your talent. He wouldn't want you to do something stupid like this.''

''She's right,'' Scotty said. ''Listen to Jill.'' The stalker's breath was hot on her neck as he moved up behind her. She felt his hand on her back and she lost control of her overwrought emotions. She jerked forward.

''Don't try and take his gun,'' Scotty shouted.

Larry instantly reacted by aiming his gun straight at Jill. Hal's body went past her in a low flying football tackle. Larry fired. The bullet went over Hal's head and the gun flew out of Larry's hand, landing almost at Jill's feet as Hal hit the gunman with a force that sent both men crashing to the ground.

Jill grabbed up the gun, spun around, ready to face Scotty with it...but there was no need. Larry's bullet had gone over Jill's shoulder and struck Scotty as he stood behind her. The Scotsman slumped to the ground, clutching his chest and gasping.

She couldn't tell if Scotty was dying or just wounded. At the moment she didn't care. Her concern for Hal was uppermost as the two men rolled on the dirt floor, swinging and pounding the other with hard fists.

"Stop it. Stop it," Jill cried, holding the gun helplessly in her hand as they fought.

The skier's athletic build was a match for Hal's body, conditioned by hard work. Neither had the advantage physically, but Hal's fury over what had been done to his animals gave him an emotional advantage. With every swing of his fist he made payment for the horses and cattle that had been destroyed.

Larry tried to get away. He tore himself free and stumbled toward the door, but Hal was on him in an instant, jerking him around and landing a blow that sent him crumpling to the floor. When he didn't get up, Hal wiped his bloody face with satisfaction. Then he turned around and saw Scotty on the ground.

"Oh, no," Hal croaked. "Scotty. Scotty."

As he bent over his friend, the wounded Scotsman's eyes went past him to fasten on Jill. As he looked up at her, Scotty's eyes were startlingly clear. "Too bad. I almost had you, lass." Then his mouth twisted in an ugly smile. "I guess you hold the winning hand, *Angie*."

Chapter Twelve

A laggard sun finally dispersed all the lingering clouds and heralded the return of clear blue skies. Jill didn't notice. Hal had carried her into the sitting room and laid her on the couch. Her thoughts were like fragmented pieces buried in layers of cotton. She couldn't put them together in any comprehensible way. A deep weariness coated her mind. She had no energy left. Too much, too fast had left her emotionally depleted and physically exhausted. Her will was not strong enough to throw off the warm comforter that Hal had placed over her.

"You stay here," he had ordered, gently wiping away tears trailing down her chilled cheeks. "I'll see to everything. Just rest. It's going to be all right, sweetheart."

He'd left Zack and Kirby in the barn while he brought her to the house. There had been no time for her to explain to Hal what had happened, but she knew that he no longer doubted her. Scotty's bitter words had taken care of that. Later she'd tell Hal about the horrible scene in the camper, and he could see for himself the photo of Angie and Billy, verifying Scotty's obsession with her and Randy. When the police looked into his wife and son's death, she knew what they would find.

Hal had handled the immediate situation on a calm

detached level that seemed to belong to someone else. When Zack had rushed in to see what was going on, he'd sent the cowboy to the bunkhouse to get Kirby.

The cook had been sleeping too soundly to hear the commotion and admitted he'd been swigging gin pretty heavily, privately celebrating having his kitchen all to himself again. Zack gave him a tongue-lashing as they hurried back to the barn.

"Well, I'll be," Kirby kept saying, rubbing his thin chin as if unable to believe any of the things that were going on. Larry tied up and out cold. Scotty unconscious with Hal trying to stanch the flow of blood from a bullet wound.

"Zack, get to Scotty's phone and call an ambulance," Hal ordered. *Why, Scotty? Why?* he had silently asked as he knelt over the unconscious man. And why was I so dense? Hal blamed himself for his blind acceptance of his neighbor that had put Jill in his hands. If only I'd been more perceptive, all of this might have been avoided. Why didn't I take her uneasiness seriously? Damn it. He'd gone off and left her alone, unprotected, with the very one who meant her harm. What if I hadn't come back in time? What if Scotty had taken her away? He jerked his thoughts away from the unspeakable tragedy that had so narrowly been avoided.

When an ambulance arrived in less than an hour and departed with Scotty, he told Zack and Kirby, "Take my Bronco. And deliver this piece of garbage to the sheriff."

"Sure thing," Zack said with obvious pleasure, glaring at the skier. "What are the charges?"

"Bodily assault or manslaughter, depending upon whether Scotty lives or dies," Hal said. "And tell Sheriff Perkins to find out who hired his brother to poison my stock." He wondered if Larry had been on the same payroll. At the very least, the skier was an accessory in the dirty business.

Hal went back inside the house, and Jill was curled up, hugging herself and still trembling. He gathered her into his arms, and pressed his lips against her wet cheek. "You're safe, love. It's all over," he whispered as he soothed her quivering body with his caressing hands.

"Scotty?" she croaked.

"I don't know." He sighed. "An ambulance took him to Rampart. I guess we'll know soon enough, but whatever happens, you're safe now."

She quieted under his touch, and he felt the surrender of her body against his as they clung together for a long time. Her breathing took on an even rhythm, and in the warm security of his arms, her emotionally drained body slipped into sleep. He picked her up and carried her upstairs to his bedroom.

Her eyes fluttered open as he undressed her, but they quickly closed again as he eased her under the warm covers. He'd been a fool to think he could send her away from him and deny all the love that touched the depths of his being. How could he have lived for even another moment if something had happened to her?

Going into the adjoining master bathroom, he turned on the shower, quickly shed his dirty, bloody clothes, then let the blessed warm water flow over him. Every inch of his body felt battered, the way it used to feel after four periods and overtime on the football field. But that was sport, not a life-and-death situation. He'd have some bruises that were beauties, but he was satisfied that he'd given as good as he'd taken.

After a vigorous towel rubbing that brought a rosy tint to his skin, he went back into the bedroom and slipped into bed. Jill was lying on her right side, facing away from him. He put his arms around her and drew her back into the cupping warmth of his naked body. As he lifted one leg over hers, she sighed, settled her rounded fanny in his lap but did not awaken as they lay together. He closed his eyes, awed by this gift of pure awareness of her every breath. In some mysterious way, as his flesh pressed against hers they were like one heart beating in rhythmic union. Desire was there but not wild or demanding. She would be there in his arms when she awoke. With this assuring anticipation, he fell asleep with an angel in his arms.

THEY BOTH SLEPT SOUNDLY until dawn, when she stirred and came awake slowly. She knew where she was without opening her eyes. She sighed contentedly. They lay side by side, with her back against his chest, his arms, body, and legs curled around her like a protective cocoon. She drew in the wondrous sensation of his warm, masculine body. As naturally as if he'd already become a part of herself, she turned over, trailed butterfly kisses across his bare chest, and whispered, "Morning."

His eyelids lifted slowly and for a moment he was startled to see her face poised close to his. Then he smiled. "Morning, love." He cradled her against him as if she were something precious that might crumble if he held her too tightly. They lay quietly together, contented, not speaking until she suddenly gave a muffled sob, and he knew she was remembering.

He tenderly kissed her eyelids and laid kisses at the corners of her mouth. She sighed and he felt her relax. He knew it would take time for her to put the horror behind her. She raised her face to his, slipped her arms around his neck, and suddenly they were like two lovers starved for each other, as he kissed her again and again.

As her body warmed to his touch and her spirits revived, her thoughts cleared, her eyes rounded and she pulled away quickly. "Randy. I have to get home. My son will be wondering what happened to me."

"He knows you're all right." He reassured her. "I told Zack and Kirby to bring Randy back with them his morning. I knew we needed some time to settle things between us."

"I thought they were settled," she said with a flash of her old spirit.

"That was before I came to my senses."

"But you said—"

"God help me, I know what I said." His eyes pleaded with her to understand. "I was afraid to trust you, afraid to trust myself. In my stupidity, I was convinced things wouldn't work out, even before we gave it a try. I shouldn't have judged you by my brothers' wives, or any other woman. You have every reason to think me a coward. And I don't blame you if you never want to set foot on this place again, but I want you to know that I love you as much as any man could, and I'm willing to do anything but give up the ranch to make you happy."

"I'm not Carrie."

"I know." He kissed the tip of her nose. "Thank heavens, for that." Then his lips moved to her mouth and dispelled any doubts she might have had that he might have mistaken her for anyone else. "It's you I love, deeply and completely. Will you marry me, Jill?"

She searched his face and saw only love shining in his eyes. She let the joy of finally coming home flow through her. "Yes, yes, I will," she whispered softly.

"I think I fell in love with you the first time you smiled at me."

As they gazed at each other in a kind of wonderment, she warned him, "This is the only chance you're going to get to change your mind."

"And give all this up?" When his lips touched hers, he kissed her with the passionate demand of a lover. His embrace tightened and the heat of his body spiraled into hers. She responded by giving herself to him, freely, without guile or pretense. As they made love, all loneliness was forgotten. The miracle of finding each other was the only reality. There was no world but theirs, a new beginning to be explored, and a future filled with whispered promises.

Satiated with love, she rested quietly in his arms, enjoying a deep sense of belonging. As languid thoughts of a wedding and honeymoon brought a smile to her lips, she decided that the main room of the house would be perfect for the ceremony. Randy could give her away. "My son will be beside himself when we tell him the news," she said, smiling.

"He's a smart one." Hal chuckled. "Want to bet he's going to demand a horse of his own? I know he's fond of the small dappled roan he's been riding. That's the one he's going to claim, you wait and see."

The pleasure in his voice made Jill smile. "I think Randy wanted to play matchmaker all along. He'll probably say, 'I told you so' when we tell him the news."

"Too bad some of us are slow learners," Hal conceded, grinning.

"But when we get it right, we get it right," she assured him, the rosy flush of lovemaking still on her cheeks.

He laughed and pulled her close. "What do you

think? Shall we get a little better acquainted before *our* boy arrives?''

Soft, supple and waiting lips lifted to his were his only answer.

When little Adam Kingsley was taken from his
nursery in the Kingsley mansion, the Memphis
family used all their power and prestige to
punish the kidnapper. They believed the crime
was solved and the villain condemned…though
the boy was never returned. But now, new
evidence comes to light that may reveal the
truth about…

Amanda Stevens is at her best for this powerful
trilogy of a sensational crime and the three couples
whose love lights the way to the truth. Don't miss:

#453 THE HERO'S SON (February)

#458 THE BROTHER'S WIFE (March)

#462 THE LONG-LOST HEIR (April)

What *really* happened that night in the
Kingsley nursery?

**Look for these titles—
available at your favorite retail outlet!**

January 1998
Renegade Son by Lisa Jackson
Danielle Summers had problems: a rebellious child
and unscrupulous enemies. In addition, her Montana
ranch was slowly being sabotaged. And then there was
Chase McEnroe—who admired her land and desired her
body. But Danielle feared he would invade more than just
her property—he'd trespass on her heart.

February 1998
The Heart's Yearning by Ginna Gray
Fourteen years ago Laura gave her baby up for adoption,
and not one day had passed that she didn't think about
him and agonize over her choice—so she finally followed
her heart to Texas to see her child. But the plan to watch
her son from afar doesn't quite happen that way, once the
boy's sexy—*single*—father takes a decided interest in *her*.

March 1998
First Things Last by Dixie Browning
One look into Chandler Harrington's dark eyes and
Belinda Massey could refuse the Virginia millionaire nothing.
So how could the no-nonsense nanny believe the rumors that
he had kidnapped his nephew—an adorable, healthy little boy
who crawled as easily into her heart as he did into her lap?

**BORN IN THE USA: Love, marriage—
and the pursuit of family!**

 HARLEQUIN®   *Silhouette*®

Available in March 1998
from bestselling author

CATHERINE LANIGAN

Her genius would change the world...

When Karen creates Mastermind, the beautiful computer whiz isn't completely prepared to deal with people's reaction to it. On the one hand, two men have fallen in love with her. On the other, someone wants the program badly enough to threaten her roommate and attack her. Karen doesn't know who to trust—and for all its power, that's the one question her computer isn't programmed to answer....

TENDER MALICE

"Catherine Lanigan is a master storyteller."
—Rave Reviews

Coming to your favorite retail outlet.

**The Brightest Stars
in Women's Fiction.™**

Look us up on-line at: http://www.romance.net

MCL420